# Reading Late Lawrence

*Also by N. H. Reeve*

HENRY JAMES – THE SHORTER FICTION: Reassessments

NEARLY TOO MUCH: The Poetry of J. H. Prynne
(*with Richard Kerridge*)

THE FICTION OF THE 1940s: Stories of Survival
(*co-editor with Rod Mengham*)

THE NOVELS OF REX WARNER

# Reading Late Lawrence

*N. H. Reeve*

© N. H. Reeve 2003

All rights reserved. No reproduction, copy or transmission of this publication may be made without written permission.

No paragraph of this publication may be reproduced, copied or transmitted save with written permission or in accordance with the provisions of the Copyright, Designs and Patents Act 1988, or under the terms of any licence permitting limited copying issued by the Copyright Licensing Agency, 90 Tottenham Court Road, London W1T 4LP.

Any person who does any unauthorised act in relation to this publication may be liable to criminal prosecution and civil claims for damages.

The author has asserted his right to be identified as the author of this work in accordance with the Copyright, Designs and Patents Act 1988.

First published 2003 by
PALGRAVE MACMILLAN
Houndmills, Basingstoke, Hampshire RG21 6XS and
175 Fifth Avenue, New York, N.Y. 10010
Companies and representatives throughout the world

PALGRAVE MACMILLAN is the global academic imprint of the Palgrave Macmillan division of St. Martin's Press, LLC and of Palgrave Macmillan Ltd. Macmillan® is a registered trademark in the United States, United Kingdom and other countries. Palgrave is a registered trademark in the European Union and other countries.

ISBN 1–4039–1596–2

This book is printed on paper suitable for recycling and made from fully managed and sustained forest sources.

A catalogue record for this book is available from the British Library.

Library of Congress Cataloging in Publication Data
Reeve, N. H., 1953–
Reading late Lawrence / N. H. Reeve.
    p. cm.
Includes bibliographical references (p. ) and index.
ISBN 1–4039–1596–2
1. Lawrence, D. H. (David Herbert), 1885–1930—Criticism and interpretation.  I. Title.

PR6023.A93Z8524 2003
823'.912—dc21
                                                                2003040528

10  9  8  7  6  5  4  3  2  1
12  11  10  09  08  07  06  05  04  03

Printed and bound in Great Britain by
Antony Rowe Ltd, Chippenham and Eastbourne

# Contents

| | |
|---|---|
| *Acknowledgements* | vi |
| *Preface* | vii |
| *Note on the Texts* | xii |
| 1  'In Love' | 1 |
| 2  At Home, at Peace: 'Glad Ghosts' | 15 |
| 3  'Sun' and *The Virgin and the Gipsy* | 49 |
| 4  Parkin's Wedding Photograph | 83 |
| 5  Strange Women with White Hair: 'The Lovely Lady', 'Mother and Daughter', 'The Blue Moccasins' | 119 |
| *Notes* | 151 |
| *Bibliography of Lawrence's Works* | 168 |
| *Bibliography* | 170 |
| *General Index* | 174 |
| *Index of Lawrence's Works* | 177 |

# Acknowledgements

Early versions of some of these pieces have appeared in *The Cambridge Quarterly*, *English*, and on the website of the D. H. Lawrence Research Centre, University of Nottingham. I am grateful to the editors of these journals for permission to reprint. I am also grateful to Pollinger Limited and the Estate of Frieda Lawrence Ravagli for permission to quote from Lawrence's works. I should like to thank the following for their comments, their advice, and the trouble they have taken on my behalf: David Ellis, Maud Ellmann, Tessa Hadley, Andrew Harrison, Richard Kerridge, Christopher Pollnitz, Peter Preston, the late Tony Tanner, John Turner, Lindeth Vasey, Geoff Ward, and Sue Wilson.

I should especially like to say how grateful I am to John Worthen, for all the generous and indefatigable support, encouragement, inspiration and hospitality which he has provided throughout the progress of this work.

The book itself is for Cheryl, with my love.

# Preface

The chapters that follow result from the combination of a conviction and an opportunity. The conviction is that while much of D. H. Lawrence's later fiction, from the period following his final return to Europe in the autumn of 1925, has received relatively little critical attention, it contains some of the freshest and most stimulating writing he ever produced. Stories such as 'The Lovely Lady', 'Sun', 'The Blue Moccasins', and 'Glad Ghosts', and the first two versions of his last novel, *Lady Chatterley's Lover*, deserve in my view to be much better known than they are. The opportunity was provided by the gradual appearance of the Cambridge Edition of Lawrence's complete works, successive volumes which not only present complete and corrected texts for the first time, but which, by gathering together manuscript and other early or variant versions of the material, enable readers more easily to follow the compositional process by which these texts came into being. Lawrence was an inveterate reviser of his work. His commitment to re-imagining possibilities inside whatever was apparently foreclosed, to allowing himself to be surprised into new activity by his own productions, was an essential element of what he felt himself to be as a writer. Whenever he was engaged with a work, he was aware, as Paul Eggert has put it, 'that if he resumed writing tomorrow, he might well be writing out of a different mood, and that yesterday's problem would be inflected differently';[1] each turn of the road might reveal a new thematic direction, or a prospect to be deferred for now but with a chance of being reconsidered later. This almost wilful open-endedness, this 'process of creative thinking . . . that was only temporarily committed to its conclusions',[2] is potentially indefinite, as Eggert suggests, only stopped in its tracks by the demands of publication and making a living – and sometimes not even then, as in the case of 'Sun', which Lawrence completely revised and offered to the public afresh, two years after it had first been printed. At the same time, however, such restlessness runs alongside a counter-urge on Lawrence's part, to tidy perception up, sometimes to organise it into a system, to find for his texts the inevitable destination that was always somehow implicit through their fits and starts of feeling: a registration in the very manner of his work of the unresolved dispute within him between the traveller and the settler, a dispute which constantly refuelled his imagination and which became if anything more urgent as he grew older.[3]

In addition, the works discussed in this study demonstrate something of the variety of motives Lawrence could have for making his revisions, and the variety of circumstances in which revision could occur. With stories such as 'Glad Ghosts', 'The Blue Moccasins', and 'In Love', the numerous variant and discarded passages allow one to trace Lawrence's 'struggle with his material', as he put it in the poem 'The Work of Creation', as he goes along, sometimes labouring or fidgety, sometimes stirred by sudden inspirations or fortuitous new stimuli.[4] On the other hand, as in the case mentioned above of 'Sun', Lawrence was not averse to making changes to a story after as well as before it had been published. He had done so on several occasions in the past, rethinking and greatly enlarging works such as 'England, My England' (where the original 1915 text was more than doubled in length by the 1921 rewriting), 'The Fox' (a medium-sized story from 1918 which was transformed into a novella of seventy pages in 1921), and 'The Thimble', also of 1915, which he used six years later as the basis for a new work, 'The Ladybird', which as it grew almost completely obscured its origins.[5] Now, in 1928, an offer to purchase the manuscript of 'Sun' gave Lawrence the opportunity to reconsider and, as I shall try to suggest, to alter some of the priorities of a story which had only relatively recently been published in an ostensibly finished form. *Lady Chatterley's Lover* had a little of both elements in its history, although the early forms the novel took had not actually been published. It was written in full in the autumn of 1926 and then almost immediately rewritten, turned into something much longer, in a rapid confrontation with the lines opened up by the first writing; and then entirely rewritten again, the best part of a year later, when a new publishing opportunity unexpectedly arose, and when Lawrence's attitudes both to his subject-matter and to his readers had hardened and coarsened. 'The Lovely Lady', by contrast, was heavily cut and revised at the request of the reader who had commissioned it, Lady Cynthia Asquith, despite the fact that Lawrence himself had evidently been happy with it as it stood; it was unusual for him, by this stage in his career, to be subjected to editorial interference, although something similar had happened in the case of the first, short version of 'The Fox'.[6] (A different circumstance again affected the revision of 'The Border-Line', which I have not included in this study as the original story – from early in 1924 – fell outside the period I wanted to address. When Lawrence read the proofs of the collection Martin Secker was about to publish, *The Woman Who Rode Away and Other Stories*, in January 1928, he realised that the closing pages of 'The Border-Line' were missing, lost somewhere between the typist and the printer, and he was obliged, in considerable haste, to rewrite the ending so that it would fit into the blank space in the proofs, having nothing at hand to remind him how the original story had finished – a story he had so completely forgotten that he thought it belonged to 'the 1921 atmosphere of Germany'[7] rather than to 1924.)

I have attempted to write from a kind of moment-by-moment engagement with the late works of Lawrence that interest me most, trying to follow the little undercurrents and stirrings of implication as they feed in and out of the larger flow. Each of my commentaries has been prompted by a particular piece of revision, one which seems to me to reveal something of the textual impulse both in Lawrence's original conception and in its subsequent development – a development to which, however much the two may differ, only that original conception could have pointed the way. These pieces of revision may affect a paragraph, an entire scene, or a single sentence. I am interested in the phantom imprints, as it were, left by Lawrence's first thoughts upon the thoughts that replace them. I am also interested in watching for signs of this across and between works as well as within the one work, given that virtually everything Lawrence wrote, especially in his later years, was a form of re-engagement with something he had already written – the stories and essays from the period at Spotorno, in the winter of 1925–26, for example, which comprise a series of diverse and experimental approaches to essentially the same set of preoccupations.[8]

Paul Eggert, in the essay mentioned above, was building on the fresh attention to Lawrence's work generated in the 1980s and early 1990s by the burgeoning interest at that time in Bakhtin, in theories of the dialogic and the carnivalesque. Eggert implied that a critical climate was developing in which Lawrence could come to be read more for the processes than for the outcomes or ostensible messages of his writing; in a sense more for the continuous drama of position-taking than for the positions taken. My approach has some affinities with this. But while Eggert concentrated on the comic potential of the provisional, demountable, almost throwaway elements in Lawrence, these elements have interested me rather for the signals they send out of something more vulnerable, less confident, more psychologically defensive; the sense of the unremitting effort required to sustain a freewheeling address to the world, to shed, over and again, the sicknesses that keep creeping back, to face up to the persistent survival in him of feelings that ought, in theory, to have been long superseded. The difference obviously owes much to the stage of Lawrence's career that one looks at; Eggert was discussing the relatively jaunty Australian novels of the earlier 1920s. But by the autumn of 1925, when Lawrence came back from New Mexico to Europe, the idea of death, as Proust's narrator says of himself, had begun to take up permanent residence in him, and it becomes increasingly inextricable from that constant play of continuity and rupture which his work both addresses and enacts. Sometimes, as in an essay such as 'Flowery Tuscany' (1927), the mortality that was the covert subject is finally brought into the open and put on the leash, but elsewhere it can slip in almost unnoticed, as it were eluding the gaze of the sentries, or can have its presence more or less elaborately disguised. The late fictions touch frequently upon issues of inheritance, lineage and legacy, often by way of fairy-tale or even Dickensian comings-to-light of hidden or unsuspected family connections, and as a result the function of the body within the general Lawrentian project of openness and renewal becomes increasingly problematic. On the one hand, from 'Glad Ghosts' of late 1925 onwards, there is an insistent reaffirmation, after several years in which he had written very little about it, of Lawrence's belief in the vital role played by sexual intercourse and the touch of the other in the discarding and reconstituting of the self. On the other hand, there is a newly anxious sense of the kind of leasehold one seems to have on one's identity, once the body has started to show, in feature and gesture, the unmistakable marks of its heredity, and appears in momentary glimpses to be simultaneously one's own and someone else's; or when one's orientation to the world appears to have been effectively determined by the way in which the accumulated, unfulfilled desires of one's ancestors turn out to have set up camp in one's being. Meanwhile, there is an intensified dislike of anything that smacks of the monumental, of the oppressively enduring, whether in the Fascist Italy which Lawrence saw at first hand, or in the democratic England that seemed to him more forlorn with each visit, and there is an eager search for the self-repairing properties of even the most unpromising situations. What the texts are drawn to, sometimes in delight and sometimes in alarm, is whatever seems to have something else still in it, latent and yet to be explored: the yearning for metamorphosis, always implicit in the love of charades and mimicry from which Lawrence developed many of the features of his late style, is a yearning that pervades both the commitment to immediacy in writing, allowing in the full measure of one's sensory reach, and the commitment to revision, re-seeing, feeling that a moment had somehow not been fully lived until writing had gone back and grappled with it again.[9]

My concern here has simply been to investigate what I find these texts can yield to reading. If my doing so could prompt other readers to go back to the texts, that would be justification enough. Reading Lawrence can still matter; it can make one want to try to look at more of the world, and to look indeed at more than one might find quite comfortable.

# Note on the Texts

The majority of the stories discussed in this book – 'In Love', 'Glad Ghosts', 'Smile', 'Sun', 'The Rocking-Horse Winner', and 'The Lovely Lady' – are printed complete with variant readings, explanatory notes, and textual apparatus, in the Cambridge Edition of *The Woman Who Rode Away and Other Stories*, edited by Dieter Mehl and Christa Jansohn (Cambridge University Press, 1995). The editors' introduction to this volume gives a full account of the compositional and publishing history of all these stories. I would add, however, that it is considerably easier for the reader to compare the two versions of 'Sun' in the form in which they are laid out in the Penguin Books reissue of Mehl and Jansohn's edition (Harmondsworth, 1996). I have also used Michael Squires's edition of *Lady Chatterley's Lover and A Propos of Lady Chatterley's Lover*, published by Cambridge in 1993 and reissued with a new introduction by Penguin in 1994, and the edition, again by Dieter Mehl and Christa Jansohn, of *The First and Second Lady Chatterley Novels* (Cambridge, 1999), which has yet to appear in the Penguin series. These two works used to be known respectively as *The First Lady Chatterley* (first published in New York by the Dial Press in 1944, and in London by Heinemann in 1972), and *John Thomas and Lady Jane*, published in Milan by Mondadori in 1954 and in London by Heinemann, again in 1972. The other works I have discussed, *The Virgin and the Gipsy* (written 1925–26), 'Mother and Daughter' (1928), 'The Blue Moccasins' (1928), and, briefly, 'The Escaped Cock' (1927–28), are at the time of writing (2002) not yet available in the Cambridge Edition, although in my comments on 'The Blue Moccasins' I am tentatively anticipating one or two of the forthcoming edition's likely findings. For *The Virgin and the Gipsy* I have used the Heinemann edition (*The Short Novels of D. H. Lawrence*, London, 1956), for 'Mother and Daughter' and 'The Blue Moccasins' the edition prepared for Penguin Books by Keith Sagar (*The Princess and Other Stories*, Harmondsworth, 1971), and for 'The Escaped Cock' the text printed with the title 'The Man Who Died', in *Love Among the Haystacks and Other Stories* (Harmondsworth: Penguin Books, 1979).

# 1
# 'In Love'

In October 1926, when Lawrence was revising the story 'More Modern Love' (eventually published as 'In Love'), he changed this passage about Hester's fiancé Joe:

> He was so clever and on the spot, doing things. But he could never really answer you back. He never really came back at you, as the Americans say. He was one of those awfully nice men, who ought to marry some nice humdrum woman, and who almost always don't. No, they insist on hanging on to some wilful, impetuous woman, whom they proceed at once to ruin, by giving in to her. It is the revenge which the "nice" take on the "nasty". For Hester could be nasty enough.[1]

into this –

> He was extremely competent at motor-cars and farming and all that sort of thing. And surely she, Hester, was as complicated as a motor-car! Surely she had as many subtle little valves and magnetos and accelerators and all the rest of it, to her make-up! If only he would try to handle *her* as carefully as he handled his car! She needed starting, as badly as ever any automobile did. Even if a car had a self-starter, the man had to give it the right twist. Hester felt she would need a lot of cranking up, if ever she was to start off on the matrimonial road with Joe. And he, the fool, just sat in a motionless car and pretended he was making heaven knows how many miles an hour. (140)

In the first passage, there is a fairly clear demarcation between voices: one which could be Hester's, using expressions like 'so clever' and 'awfully nice', and another which could not, the voice of a worldly-wise pedagogue who has seen life and no longer expects to be greatly surprised by it. The rewriting, however, gives us something much more slippery and mercurial. Voices, subject positions and levels of engagement seem to alternate so rapidly as almost to have overlapped before the reader can identify them; a good deal of the passage could just as readily be Joe's self-communing as Hester's, and it all wavers continually between the characters' voices and a narrator's satirical imitation of them. The outbursts and exclamations register at least three things at once – the character's wounded or exasperated feelings, the narrator's guffaws of amusement, and the efforts at rhetorical self-stabilising of those uncertain precisely what their feelings are, and in urgent need of relief from them. Occasionally, at the risk of having his or her leaden-footedness exposed, the reader might try to disentangle what seems sympathetic from what seems mocking. Phrases like 'all that sort of thing', 'all the rest of it', are at one moment poking fun at Hester, making her sound like an empty-headed flapper, and at the next colluding with her disparagement of male pedantry and self-importance (rather as Connie, in *The Second Lady Chatterley*, was 'amused once more by the busy, interested freemasonry of men, as soon as it was a question of machinery');[2] while one is still aware throughout the passage of Hester's intrigued curiosity as to what makes her man tick, as it were, her askance and rapid sizing-up of the rival attraction. Mostly, though, the knot seems too complex to tease apart, even too artfully designed, so that one could come away from this passage with the sense that the young people's emotional agitation, the pre-marital mixture of desire and anxiety that lies at the heart of the story, is both made strikingly vivid and somehow belittled by the very aptness with which the car-imagery seems able to express it.

This new passage is a particularly vigorous example of the later style to which Paul Eggert drew attention; buttonholing, exploratory, indeterminate. Much other recent commentary on Lawrence's work has been concerned to discuss these effects.[3] The writing's characteristic reluctance to settle, its restless uprooting of itself in obedience to sudden inner promptings, makes for a continually resumed attack on staleness and complacency; while the almost imperceptible thresholds and transitions between one state and another have something of the 'wonderfully suggestive *edge*' Lawrence found in his favourite Etruscan tomb paintings, 'the flowing contour where the body suddenly leaves off, upon the atmosphere'.[4] It seems to me that this way of writing could equally often be regarded as a kind of treachery, a duplicitous pretence at a commitment it has no intention of sustaining, with even perhaps a strain in it of envy for the peaceableness it persistently disrupts. It is curious, in any event, how this particular passage can evoke a world held together by just the kind of reliable fellow-feeling which the narrator refuses to supply. If we take these words to be Hester's, they seem to be calling out for another woman to listen to them – a ghostly projection of her sister in the future, wiser and more self-assured than the Henrietta who is Hester's younger sister now: a woman who could tease Hester without damaging the affectionate and sympathetic trustworthiness on which their relationship was grounded. Hester would thereby be able both to complain freely and to see the funny side of doing so, to place herself in the long line of those who complain, with varying degrees of agility, that their menfolk pay more attention to their cars than to them, and to dispel with that wry self-placement much of the bitterness in the complaint, releasing herself from a vulnerable solitude into the embrace of an implicit support group. This world of ordinary solidarities and lowered horizons keeps making these odd, fleeting, stubborn appearances in Lawrence's work, for all his apparent commitment to disowning it. Those who live in that world seek to make the best of what they have, since breaking out to some higher fulfilment does not present itself as a feasible option. Relationships between the sexes are more matters of adroit management and conflict-averting than of passionate ebb and flow, struggle or self-renewal; people discover how very different humouring their partners can be from laughing at them (a distinction that for Lawrence would usually be subject to suspicious resentment).[5] We can see such a world emerging through the words before Hester herself has quite reached it; the passage hints at more realistic acknowledgements than it is able to make in its present, agitated state – for example, that one of the reasons some men seem to prefer cars to women is precisely because cars are *not* complicated, because they respond predictably to techniques that anyone can learn; or, that some men, like Parkin in *The Second Lady Chatterley*, may for various reasons feel that they can only properly value themselves through their work, and that dismissing such men as inadequate or contemptible is usually easier and less costly than coaxing out the mutual adjustments needed to live with them. One can glimpse behind these words a maturer sensibility than the one currently using them. It might even be that the very fluency with which Hester keeps her motoring metaphors going, her resourceful work with a language she doesn't fully command, is giving notice of the skill with which, in her married future, she may make productive use of limited material, and be able to offer her husband the careful 'handling' which at present she merely demands from him.

Of course, at this moment Hester's fluency is driven by the pressure of frustrated, fearful desire – she is 'nearly twenty-five', but seems completely inexperienced sexually – desire stirred up by the same petting and cuddling which makes her so angrily uncomfortable; desire which cannot find a satisfying outlet, nor even name itself properly. It breaks out in weird innuendo at 'even if a car had a self-starter, the man had to give it the right twist', a line which manages, with more sophisticated vulgarity than anything Sir Malcolm Reid in *Lady Chatterley's Lover* could have come up with, to condense the entire gist of Mellors' attack on female masturbation in that novel, and even to hint in passing at another excitingly cross-class liaison, since 'the man' in such instances would normally be one's chauffeur.[6] Unappeased sexuality leaks out of the text all over the place, in the imagery of crank handles, accelerators, steering-gear and fingering; in Hester's spasms of physical exertion, the 'wild surge of her limbs' (141), as she crouches, rushes, shakes her hair, climbs trees, and 'flew along Joe's cinder-drive like a maenad' (143); or in another brilliant stream of free-associating which leads her from wondering what Byron might have whispered to his ladies, via the Tchaikovsky which Joe plays on the piano, to the relief of the outdoors, where 'she tossed her short hair again, and felt like Mazeppa's horse, about to dash away into the infinite' (Tchaikovsky's opera *Mazeppa* was actually based on Pushkin's poem rather than Byron's, but not to worry). Mazeppa's horse, however, was not about to dash away on its own, because it had a naked young man tied on its back with 'many a bloody thong',[7] as if somewhere in Hester's mind were a vision of herself as a bondage dominatrix who has finally succeeded in keeping Joe's fumbling hands well out of the way. It is a striking evolution from what Lawrence had originally written in his manuscript, where Hester identified herself with the rider rather than the ridden: 'Ah! on a night like this, a girl could mount bare-back on a pony and gallop off over the edge of beyond' (309). Virtually all these flights of imagery were added at the revision stage, and since the range of allusion involved belongs much more securely to the author's imagination than to the character's, one can sense the glee with which he went back to the story to intensify Hester's state of arousal.

'In Love' was written from Lawrence's reflections on the forthcoming marriage of his wife Frieda's elder daughter, Elsa, to a young man named Teddy Seaman, whom Frieda, mistakenly as it turned out, thought was 'learning to farm'.[8] I like to see the story as a kind of stepfather's offering, a story which develops a little undercover drama of responses to finding oneself occupying a stepfatherly role (it was only after Frieda's daughters had come of age that they were allowed to visit her and Lawrence whenever they wished, and to establish new relationships with them). All through the writing there is a play of impulses between, on the one hand, a detached, avuncular sententiousness about life and what to expect from it (as in the cancelled passage about Joe), and on the other hand something much more racily insinuating and provocative, something driven by the tensions of a not-quite-parental relationship with a young woman who rather dangerously half-resembles the one you are most attached to. Is there a hidden subtext, for example, to Lawrence's having added, in the course of his revisions, an entirely new sentence to the sequence in which Hester, having run away from Joe's 'spooning', gazes over the moonlit landscape in search of the Beyond? 'There was, however, a bunch of strange horses in this field, so she made her way cautiously back through Joe's fence' (142). For Ursula in the final chapter of *The Rainbow*, the encounter with horses in a field – she climbed a tree as well – marked a confrontation with destiny, an apocalyptic rescue from the disastrous marriage-plans to which she was about to commit herself. The contrast in every respect with Hester hardly needs to be spelt out, and would appear to confirm the older character as the representative of everything positive, vital and courageous in Lawrence's universe – except that the allusion seems so knowingly facetious as to leave it by no means clear which of the two women emerges the stronger from their imaginary meeting. Is Lawrence ridiculing Hester for her inability to rise to the occasion, or is he siding suddenly with her common-sense view of what kind of occasion it is?

Contrary and mischievous impulses are also at work in the text's treatment of Hester's first violent recoil from Joe, from 'a certain pressure of his biceps which she presumed was cuddling' (141). One can see several things mingled in her panic. There is Lawrence's own fascinated, slightly terrified disgust with 'the macaroni slithery-slobbery mess of modern adoration'[9], outlined in particular detail in *Mr Noon* (a disgust not just with 'spooning' itself, but with the tyranny of peer-pressure that made people feel obliged to go along with it); there is Hester's disquieting sense that she might despite herself actually to be starting to enjoy it – 'How ridiculous of him to stroke the back of her neck!' (141); and there is a swathe of feelings which Lawrence regarded as specific to Hester's generation and which he as a result could observe from a safer distance: a baffled, claustrophobic sense of flatness and sameness, where the expectation had been of continually renewed excitement. Hester rushes away not just from Joe but from the terror that this may be all that life holds for her. The timber bungalow with Joe's piano in it seems stretched as taut as her nerves, 'a perfect little drum, re-echoing to her favourite nocturne' (141); and although the smallholding has 'thirty-odd acres' (139) of land, the noise pursues her across them: 'It was just like him, to have such a little place that you couldn't get away from the sound of his piano, without trespassing on somebody else's ground' (142). Everything is suddenly 'little' – little bungalow, hot little wooden kitchen, little jobs, stupid little room – everything that at first had the charm of intimacy now suddenly seems cramped and stifling. Hester had already made it clear that she had no intention of settling for life in the dormitory suburbs which were rapidly expanding in the mid-1920s – 'Ye Gods! not Golders Green, not even Harrow!' (139) – and since Joe had 'got sick and tired of business' (139), his Wiltshire pig-farm, with the house he had built himself, had appeared much more enticingly independent and pioneering.[10] But here it is, fenced round by neighbours exactly like themselves, with Joe's old army-friend Bonamy a mile down the road in another farm bungalow just like this one, as if Wiltshire were turning into a version of the sprawling Australia that Lawrence had puzzled over in *Kangaroo*, standardised and levelled-off; or as if the flight from the metropolitan rat-race to the rural margins had become just as programmed and conventional as the rat-race itself, and the new freedoms that made it all possible, the widespread availability of motor transport, the relaxing of social and moral embargoes, all the wherewithal of 1920s enjoyment, were leading only to endless replication.

Lawrence had suggested in *The Virgin and the Gipsy*, his earlier meditation on the lives of Frieda's daughters, that in addition to this physical circumscription, with no 'Beyond', nowhere else to go, the real problem for the new generation was the boxing-in of the mind, the vague sense of having somehow been deprived of the equipment required to recognise alternatives even if they did exist. 'Their parents let them do almost entirely as they liked. There wasn't really a fetter to break, nor a prison-bar to file through, nor a bolt to shatter'; but 'it is very much easier to shatter prison bars than to open undiscovered doors to life. As the younger generation finds out somewhat to its chagrin.'[11] In his review of the memoirs of the Duc de Lauzun (eventually published as 'The Good Man'), written a few days before he began 'In Love', Lawrence argued that the 'true bondage', 'the agony of our human existence', was that modern people can 'only feel the feelings they know how to feel . . . we can only feel things in conventional feeling-patterns'. Hester was clearly intended to be an illustration of this thesis, her outbursts of capriciousness or irrationality being her versions of the 'strange howlings' and 'low, calling cries' of those who struggle to break from that bondage.[12] Her difficulty is rather cruelly intensified at one point, when, in the course of having second thoughts about what she is doing to Joe, she finds that her brain has been so maddeningly infiltrated by bits and pieces of the culture surrounding her that it is as if she cannot even possess her own compassion:

> Then she had a qualm. 'Really, my girl, it's a bit thick, the way you treat him! Poor old Joe!'
> Immediately something began to hum inside her: 'I hear those tender voices calling, Poor Old Joe! – ' (142)

If the self is glimpsed for a moment as effectively composed of the products of its time, if everything inside it is as stale and mass-produced as everything outside, if whatever it tries to lay claim to has already been occupied, then the terms in which feeling could subsequently be negotiated would need a quite radical overhaul. Some of the story's revisions seem to reflect this. Where originally Hester had irritably and forlornly asked herself, as Joe came out to search for her, 'Where was his male magic?' (310), she now says 'Where was his supposed male magic?' (142), her more explicit scepticism leaving one unsure whether her question now sounds less or more forlorn than it did. In the manuscript version Hester complained that Joe 'never really comes forth to me . . . nothing twinkles and comes forth from him' (311), but Lawrence seems to have realised on re-reading that his personal brand of rhetoric could not sound remotely convincing from her mouth, might indeed be too dangerously at risk for his liking; he also cut Henrietta's remark, 'We're modern! We can't get away from it' (316), which may have been a trenchant summary of his own view, but not really something anyone on the inside of being 'modern' could plausibly say. What is especially interesting about 'In Love' is that it is the only story Lawrence ever wrote which shows members of the generation younger than his tackling their own emotional problems, hesitantly finding a path from resentful frustration towards tenderness and warmth, without any help from anyone older, either as a guide or a spokesperson, or as a more or less clearly marked impediment. All they do have to help them are the elements of modernity with which they are most familiar and comfortable – their cars, and the unruffled, amiable pragmatism of those who take it for granted that they can drive anywhere; and in the revised story the confrontation between the lovers is neatly flanked, horses and moonlight at the back of the house, and a car with glaring headlamps at the front, with Hester's turn from one to the other marking the moment from which progress becomes possible.

   Lawrence appears to have been almost as ambivalent about cars as he was about cinema, loudly decrying the contribution they made to the devitalising of modern existence, but quite keenly interested in their effects and workings. Sometimes he seems to hanker after a little of that 'freemasonry' himself, the allure of technical detail, as in the magazine adventure-stories which he loved reading and admired for the reliably authoritative information they gave about the world (although his own grasp can be a bit unsure, as in *The First Lady Chatterley*, when Duncan Forbes, driving Connie home, 'took off the gear', in order, it would seem, to freewheel downhill).[13] The passage in 'In Love' about valves and magnetos was inspired by Aldous Huxley's arrival at the Lawrences' home outside Florence in a brand-new six-cylinder, two-litre Itala self-starting tourer, offering to sell them his old hand-cranked Citroen – a proposal that Lawrence mulled over for some time before turning down.[14] In some of his earlier writings he seems interested in the ways in which the relative novelty of being in a car appeared to affect people's behaviour – the speed and noise and unusual degree of proximity with fellow-passengers inducing a kind of tense light-headedness in which freer and more direct things can be said than were perhaps quite intended; one can sense this once or twice in *Women in Love*, and with more obviously comic effect at the climax of 'The Captain's Doll', where the argument between Hepburn and Hannele about whether he wants 'love' or not has to be conducted at full volume in order to be audible.[15] Later works tend to be more preoccupied with the idea that the increasingly widespread use of cars has put up an invisible barrier between travellers and whatever they have travelled to see, what Lawrence called in his essay 'New Mexico' (1928) the 'curious film' stretched over the earth's surface, so difficult to penetrate. He suggested in another essay, 'Return to Bestwood' (1926), that the more people drive through the countryside, the more it 'retreats into its own isolation, and becomes more mysteriously inaccessible', strangely protected by the very car-induced assumption that one has grasped it (although the passing landscape is not always inaccessible, or perhaps only to the already insensitive, as the various car journeys Connie Chatterley takes, through Derbyshire and through France, are presented as though they actually made visible to her certain essential truths which would otherwise have been missed).

In 'In Love', however, Joe's brother's car, by bringing Henrietta to Hester's rescue, offers the chance of solving a perceptual impediment; and while Lawrence normally associates headlamps, as Linda Ruth Williams points out, with the predatory and destructive gaze of the wilful woman, in this instance they cast a fundamentally benign brightness over the scene.[16] Moreover, the implied limit to one's patience conveyed by waiting in someone's driveway with one's headlamps on helps to speed the lovers' row to its climax, by reminding them that, should either of them want it, an escape route is available, but may not be available indefinitely. The intermittent toots of the horn and the restarting of the engine provide a deft satirical commentary on what is happening inside, even a kind of conducting, since each successive mechanical noise sets off a new phase of the lovers' argument. Meanwhile, Henrietta's wholly straightforward and unironical concern to help, and the easy sympathy with either sex that she brings with her, go some way towards creating therapeutic conditions for the distressed couple, despite the fact that, as the revised text recognised, she doesn't herself have any especially illuminating advice to offer (though one of her comments suggests that she feels much the same combination of revulsion and sensual relish for 'spooning' as her sister does: 'Yes! . . . As if one were a perfectly priceless meat pie, and the dog licked it tenderly before he gobbled it up' [147–8]). What the reader is mainly alerted to by Henrietta's presence is the difference between having a row privately and having it in front of a witness – an aspect of Lawrence's life with Frieda which Mark Kinkead-Weekes has discussed.[17] A complex set of effects can be released by the presence of a third person; in part reducing the tension by making the warring parties rather deflatingly self-conscious, especially so whenever the witness agrees with them, and in part cranking the tension up by encouraging the parties to dramatise themselves. And in a way, by enabling the lovers to perform their row as well as have it, a sympathetic and earnestly judicious witness like Henrietta can help to accelerate their recognition, not only of the mistakes they have made in their readings of each other, but of the part played by performance in human relations more generally. Is this one of the meanings of Hester's final remark, the last line of the story, after Joe has managed to reassure her that she is truly desired? 'I don't mind what you do, if you love me *really*' (150). It is not just that, having satisfied herself that his motives are genuine, she feels free to admit both to herself and to him that she is in fact quite keen on his sexual advances; it is the sense that, if there is a secure bedrock of love, it is possible to cope with all manner of mysterious performances on its surface ('I don't mind what you do'), since she is able to see beyond the naively absolute distinction between the authentic and the false in human behaviour that she had insisted on earlier.

This last line, 'I don't mind what you do, if you love me *really*', was the final step in the revision of 'In Love', the last of those stepfatherly attempts to sidle up closer to the frissons of being young. But by no means all the changes take the text in this direction. In some places Lawrence seems to want to reintroduce the kinds of didactic pronouncement which he had elsewhere crossed out. The first version's dénouement was a little reminiscent of that of Lawrence's 1918–19 story 'Tickets Please', as the apparently cowed male unexpectedly turned on the females who had taunted him ('Brought properly to bay, the sparks came out of him, too, and the women somehow grew diminished' [316]); then came Henrietta's declaration, 'We're modern!'; and finally the entire contretemps rather fizzled out ('It was all very absurd' [316]), without being openly resolved. All this changes in the rewriting. Instead of sitting in the dark with 'his face averted', waiting for his passion to calm down, Joe now feels the need to apologise:

> He looked her straight in the eye. They knew each other so well. Why had he tried that silly love-making game on her? It was a betrayal of their simple intimacy. He saw it plainly, and repented.(149)

Again, as with the passage I began with, these could be the thoughts either of Joe or of Hester, at least until the last line, where the narrator gathers everything back to himself. But is it an adequate summary of what has happened? Isn't it rather that the 'silly love-making' episode has involved a deepening and testing of that intimacy, something they had to move through, a way of showing glimpses of the murkier undersides, both of their desires and of the brother-and-sister palliness to which their 'intimacy' had previously been restricted? Did they really know each other so well? Hester for one has had to confront things she never previously knew, or only vaguely suspected: Joe's 'nasty little smile', for example (in the cancelled passage about him it was Hester who was supposed to be the 'nasty' one [309]); the disillusioning spectacle of sameness stretching ahead of her; her own secret, buttoned-up capacity for self-abandonment – 'Yes, SPOONING! The word made her lose the last shred of her self-respect, but she said it aloud' (141). 'It was a betrayal' sounds imposed from outside, striking a false note, primarily concerned again to restabilise and protect the speaker, whether it be Joe, or Hester, or the narrator saying it; as if the narrative were still straining after, still reluctant to relinquish altogether the tutelary role which the unfolding of the story has threatened to make redundant. In some ways the first version of the ending, where the row cleared the air slightly but did not lead to any homiletic conclusions, appeared more willing simply to gaze wonderingly at, and leave uninfringed, the strange, almost mechanical serenity with which the younger generation seemed able to accept that they were what they were, and that their dissatisfactions were not finally all that important. Lawrence captured an image for this in those coruscating flights of revision when he suddenly saw new ways of identifying the younger generation with cars, reinvigorating the car–horse oppositions he had used before, throughout *St. Mawr* and briefly at the gipsy camp in *The Virgin and the Gipsy*, and would use again in *Lady Chatterley's Lover*, where Clifford is stimulated by motoring while Mellors enjoys working with horses.[18] But it is in just those places where Lawrence's writing most asserts its command over its subjects (and there is something almost churlish about the precision with which he captures their speech patterns), that the glimpses occur of those extra layers I have tried to intimate, something elusive and unaccountable in the experience of the young which keeps slipping away from the textual grasp. Perhaps this is just a roundabout way of trying to talk about the sense of the valedictory in all Lawrence's work after 1925.

Immediately after finishing 'In Love', perhaps even before it was quite finished, Lawrence took his exercise book into the woods near the Villa Mirenda, a few miles outside Florence, and reflected on what he had done: imagined two people, one a 'young man who has suffered during his youth' (149), facing the future by sharing sexual warmth on a smallholding – a pleasant refuge, but in this instance entirely without the kind of glamour bestowed on a place by prolonged struggles to defend it against hostile surrounding forces; so the first *Lady Chatterley*, the very next thing he began to write, seems to have originated in a pressing need to look again at the same cluster of material. And this includes having Duncan Forbes at one point saying 'Nobody ever *loves* anybody nowadays. They're all too busy being in love.'[19] That was the distinction between true and false feeling which 'In Love' had wanted to establish; but it is now put forward in the course of a speech so full of envious bitterness – about Connie's relationship with the gamekeeper Parkin, about her having asked Duncan to pretend, for Clifford's benefit, to be the father of her coming child, and about how her very asking him demonstrated her indifference or obliviousness to whatever dreams he may still have had about the two of them – that Duncan's comment seems to owe more to his sense of being excluded than to any neutral observation of other people's lives.[20]

When Hester closes the story with 'I don't mind what you do, if you love me *really*', the italics link her remark with another passage newly added at the revision stage. Joe is saying:

> 'What are you to do, when you know a girl's rather strict, and you like her for it – and you're not going to be married for a month – and – and you've got to get over the interval somehow – and what else does Rudolf Valentino do for you? – you like *him* –'
> 'He's dead, poor dear. But I loathed him *really* –' said Hester.
> 'You didn't seem to,' said he.
> 'Well anyhow you aren't Rudolf Valentino, and I loathe *you* in the rôle.'(149)

This echoing *'really'* also seems to remember the two uses of 'really' which were erased with the rest of the passage about Joe being 'so clever and on the spot' ('he could never really answer you back. He never really came back at you' [309]), with the word now given its youthful rather than its middle-aged inflection. How might we read 'I loathed him *really*'? Given Lawrence's comments on Valentino elsewhere in his work, on his 'so-called beauty' which 'satisfies some ready-made notion of handsomeness,'[21] on how the cult surrounding him represented the triumph of fake feelings over true ones, one would suspect that the famous name had only been introduced here to bring Hester clearly into the ranks of the Lawrentian elect, those who, despite appearances to the contrary, consider themselves above mere mass enthusiasm, are never 'really' taken in by it, and who can appreciate instead what little remains of the genuine 'male magic' which most 'modern' women hate and abuse.[22] But of course what Hester says draws many other things towards it: it has a touch of defensive bluster, unwilling to admit too openly to being just like everyone else; there is a hint that the sheer preposterousness of Joe's comparing himself with Valentino in the first place is spurring her affections back in the latter's direction, while at the same time paving the way, by its very absurdity, for a knowing and amused relaxation of her antagonism towards her lover. And in her moment of wistful self-communing, 'He's dead, poor dear', tucked inside the combative repartee, is a sense that the reactions aroused by Rudolf Valentino always ranged over a wide spectrum between 'like' and 'loathe', all the way from the excitements of fantasy, through sentimental or frustrated longing, to an earthy, self-satirising humour – reactions which were never fully coherent, which always overlapped, and which were shared between women who sustained rather than despised one another, the women with whom Hester 'really' belongs.

# 2
# At Home, at Peace: 'Glad Ghosts'

## 1

'Glad Ghosts', a longer-than-average short story, was the first fictional work Lawrence began after what proved to be his final return to Europe, in the autumn of 1925. He made by his standards painfully slow progress with it. It was still occupying him after the best part of seven weeks; the whole of his Australian novel *Kangaroo* had been written in six. By the time he finished, in January 1926, he had already completed two other stories which he had started around the same time, 'Sun' and 'Smile', and had also done the bulk of *The Virgin and the Gipsy*. The manuscripts of 'Glad Ghosts', riddled with crossings-out and alterations, suggest that he made two full attempts at it before settling on what he wanted, and even after Dorothy Brett had typed it for him he rewrote several complete sections yet again. One of the passages that seems to have given him most trouble was the letter that ends the story, a letter from one of the characters, Lord Luke Lathkill, to the narrator, Mark Morier:

> The following autumn, when I was overseas once more, I had a letter from Lord Lathkill. He wrote very rarely.
> 'Carlotta has a son,' he said, 'and I an heir. He has yellow hair, like a little crocus, and one of the young plum-trees in the orchard has come out of all season into blossom. To me he is flesh and blood of our ghost itself. Even Mother doesn't look over the wall, to the other side, any more. It's all this side for her now.

'So our family refuses to die out, by the grace of our Ghost. We are calling him Gabriel.

'Dorothy Hale also is a mother, three days before Carlotta. She has a black lamb of a daughter, called Gabrielle. By the bleat of the little thing, I know its father. Our own is a blue-eyed one, with the dangerous repose of a pugilist. I have no fears of our family misfortune for him, ghost-begotten and ready-fisted.

'The Colonel is very well, quiet and self-possessed. He is farming in Wiltshire, raising pigs. It is a passion with him, the crème de la crème of swine. I admit, he has golden sows as elegant as young Diane de Poietiers, and young hogs like Perseus, in the first red-gold flush of youth. He looks me in the eye, and I look him back, and we understand. He is quiet, and proud now, and very hale and hearty, raising swine *ad maiorem gloriam Dei*. A good sport!

'I am in love with this house and its inmates, including the plum-blossom-scented one, she who visited you, in all the peace. I cannot understand why you wander in uneasy and distant parts of the earth. For me, when I am at home, I am there. I have peace upon my bones, and if the world is going to come to a violent and untimely end, as prophets aver, I feel the house of Lathkill will survive, built upon our ghost. So come back, and you'll find we shall not have gone away ——'[1]

Mark Morier himself is Gabriel's real father; it was he who slept that night with Lathkill's wife, Carlotta, and it is his own child he is reading about, truly one person's 'son' and another's 'heir'. Lathkill obviously knows this, as will everyone else he mentions, except perhaps his mother, and even she may have guessed. In the first draft of the letter Lawrence had Lathkill say of the situation, 'I am perfectly in accord' (352). This would have been reasonable enough, since it was always the likely outcome of Lathkill's having invited Morier to help reinvigorate the ailing family in the first place. But 'I am perfectly in accord' could hardly fail to draw attention to the humiliation it affects not to notice; one can almost hear the clenched tones in which someone like Clifford Chatterley would have pronounced it. In the revised letter, where Lathkill makes no mention of such feelings, the trace of that humiliation emerges instead in the restlessness of his writing, the little signals of a lingering wish to be elsewhere. All the time he is protesting his love of where he is, his imagination seems most stirred by thoughts of imminent motion: the idea of 'dangerous repose', for example, or of Perseus, not noted for staying anywhere long (also of course obliquely alluding to the mystic fatherings Lathkill cannot quite push out of his mind); his Conradian phrase 'uneasy and distant parts of the earth' bestows enough rhetorical glamour on what it describes as to sound almost openly wistful. One's suspicion that an ironic view of the happy events might be lurking inside the straight one is increased by the complicated relationship between this letter and the 'family letters' which Lawrence had made fun of in the essay 'Accumulated Mail', written a few months earlier; letters assembled from lists of delete-as-appropriate items, resembling the official pro-formas given to soldiers to post home from the Front, and engaging with the emotions of sender and recipient just as awkwardly: 'Family letters: *We are so disappointed you are not coming to England. We wanted you to see the baby, he is so bonny: the new house, it is awfully nice: the show of the daffodils and crocuses down the garden*'.[2] But it is hard to say whether Lathkill is being consciously satirical at any given point. It is rather that, in writing to Morier, he begins to sound strangely like him, and the sardonic voice that characterised the other man begins to infiltrate his own – a last flicker of the story's fascination with interchanging and surrogacy, a subject which has suddenly become almost intolerably intimate and painful.

It is a highly charged moment, as Morier reads this; the two men seem curiously blended into a single composite figure, while at the same time a great distance opens between them, as they face each other across the child, and watch each other's lives fading out of reach. Lathkill signs off by inviting Morier to come back and visit, but rarely can an invitation have been so laden with well-bred hints not to take it up; his jocular banter barely muffles the sound of the gates swinging shut. Lawrence clearly had second thoughts about where the closing emphasis should fall, since in the first version of the letter the invitation was slipped barely noticeably into the middle, while the last paragraph was entirely taken up with Colonel Hale's pig farm.[3] And in one particularly intriguing revision, Lathkill's 'I cannot for my life understand why you rove about in uncouth places' (353), became

> I cannot understand why you wander in uneasy and distant parts of the earth. For me, when I am at home, I am there. I have peace upon my bones... (210)

The effect of this is to bring the words 'uneasy', 'at home', and 'peace' back into close connection with each other, as they had been at the very beginning of the story, when Morier said of Carlotta, 'Perhaps I was the only person in the world with whom she felt, in her uneasy self, at home, at peace' (175–6. 'Uneasy' in this sentence was itself originally 'deepest'.) Two rival concepts of 'home' augment all the men's other implicit rivalries. Where would one be most 'at home'? In a secure and familiar place, where one can shelter from uneasiness? Or in a relationship which can accept uneasiness, allow it expression, even cherish it, have no need of shelter from it? Morier's idea is a common one in Lawrence's work, that a woman like Carlotta needs a rebellious male outsider – *'sansculotte'* is Morier's description of himself – a figure defined against the conventional notion of 'home', to provide her with another home, a home for that element in her which cannot be satisfied by the accommodations she has had to make with life. In 'The Ladybird', a work which, like 'Glad Ghosts', was inspired by Lawrence's relationship with Cynthia Asquith and her family, the heroine Lady Daphne found that it was not her peace-seeking husband Basil, but the 'outlaw' Count Dionys with whom she seemed most at home, who 'spoke the deepest soul in her'.[4] Perhaps the nursery rhyme was doing some work in Lawrence's mind:

> Ladybird, ladybird,
> Fly away home,
> Your house is on fire
> And your children are gone.

Is the home the same as the house? Is the ladybird being called back, upbraided with the terrible consequences of neglecting her domestic station; or urged onwards, urged to regard the destruction of the house, and the loosening of the bonds that tied her to it, as the chance at last to find her real 'home', the one from which her domestic station debarred her? The conflict of the two thoughts seems to resonate deeply, not only in 'Glad Ghosts', but in much of the writing Lawrence would go on to produce. Making an appeal to the future, to trusting forward, cutting oneself free, leaving the past to burn, was always one of the great motive forces of Lawrence's work; it is exactly this to which Lathkill's letter was paying so much half-conscious homage. But sometimes that appeal can come across as the most unsubtle of seducers' gambits, as when Viedma, in *Quetzalcoatl*, says to Kate, who has just told him she must 'go home',

> 'You have no home,' he cried passionately. 'The past is a grave to sleep in. Home is where you tie the new threads of your life, to weave a new pattern. That is home, even if you are houseless. And that is here – here – '[5]

Morier never speaks 'passionately' to Carlotta. But when he muses that 'Perhaps I was the only person in the world with whom she felt, in her uneasy self, at home, at peace', there may be a trace of the need, unmistakable in Viedma's speech, for the man to convince himself as much as convince the woman; it is the man's own desire for a home which starts to seem paramount, a home he suspects only the woman can provide for *him*. Would Morier have paused over this, or shrugged it away, when he read Lathkill's letter and came across the uncanny recycling of his own words back at him? The recycling, the interchange, seems to throw doubt to and fro over both men's arguments; and Morier's claim, that his clandestine mutuality with the other man's wife offers a superior home, with neither roof nor walls, transcending all convention and secreting the profoundest truths of human experience, is suddenly made to sound like the kind of thing people have always said to console themselves for having nowhere to go.

Where does 'Mark Morier' come from? 'Mark' presumably from Mark Gertler, who trained at the Slade School of Art (where Morier and Carlotta's friendship began; called the 'Thwaite' in the story); a working-class student who mixed rather awkwardly with the aristocrats he encountered there. 'Morier' from the author of the Chatterleys' favourite novel, *The Adventures of Hajji Baba of Ispahan*, James Justinian Morier (1780–1849), famous for his travels in the Middle East and, for two years, Mexico: a man of whom it was said that 'he was never at home but when he was abroad'.[6] Lawrence used first-person narrators only rarely, and they tend to be curiously Jamesian, finding themselves called upon to make crucial interventions in other people's lives while remaining in some sense shut out from whatever resolution is effected – Cyril, for example, in Lawrence's first novel, *The White Peacock*, or the anonymous narrator of the 1919 story 'Wintry Peacock'. With an entirely Jamesian ambivalence, such outcomes preserve the narrator's autonomy while beginning to query its value, and the decision to use a narrator of this kind in 'Glad Ghosts' sits interestingly alongside certain preoccupations which Lawrence's letters suggest had been steadily building in him. The previous June he had written to his mother-in-law:

> My sister in Ripley has built a big new house and is *very* proud. Thank God I've not tied a big new house around my neck. . . . One can no longer say: I'm a stranger everywhere, only 'everywhere I'm at home.' That's perhaps even worse – what do you think, Schwiegermutter?[7]

– and at the end of August, to Mollie Skinner, whose brother Jack had recently died:

> There is deep inside one a revolt against the fixed thing, fixed society, fixed money, fixed homes, even fixed love. I believe that was what ailed your brother: he couldn't bear the social fixture of everything. It's what ails me too.
> And after all, he lived his life and had his mates wherever he went. What more does a man want?[8]

These defiant assertions in favour of serendipitous wandering were made while Lawrence was preparing to pack up and leave the nearest thing to a home of his own he had ever had, the ranch at Kiowa, near Taos, New Mexico. Fears for his health had meant that his stay there was never intended to last beyond the summer; he had written of feeling homesick for Europe, and of America's having become too tough and wearing. But one can sense in reading these letters that leaving was more of a wrench than he cared to admit. He must also have been conscious that, given the attitude of the American immigration authorities towards anyone remotely suspected of having tuberculosis, it would not be at all easy for him to return. The concern filtering through into 'Glad Ghosts' with what a home might be, with the conflicting merits of travelling and settling, was fuelled further by his journey to the Midlands that October to see the 'big new house' of his sister Ada in Ripley – *'the new house: it is awfully nice'* – and the less opulent one of his other sister, Emily, in Nottingham; he could hardly not have spent some time reflecting on the huge gulfs, and the surviving connections, between himself and his family and the paths they had taken. It was the first time he had been back since his father's death the previous year; he had recently turned 40; he had come from high up in the harsh, empty landscape and brilliant sunshine of the Rocky Mountains to the dank, wet, chilly, polluted atmosphere and the congested streets of his 'home regions'.[9] As David Ellis remarks, it 'must have been very strange for Lawrence...to look out into the murk of the industrial Midlands from Emily's windows while he was correcting the proofs of *The Plumed Serpent*'.[10]

Writing to Martin Secker, Lawrence affected a comparative indifference to the emotions provoked by this return journey – 'I can't look at the body of my past, the spirit seems to have flown.'[11] Catherine Carswell, however, to whom he had written 'I'm weary of past things...and don't want to look at them', recalled him subsequently confiding to her that 'the horrors of his childhood had come up over him like a smothering flood', and that he wished the whole place could be 'puffed off the face of the earth'.[12] A linguistic repertoire is starting to form here – body, spirit, weary, past; breath choked off or vigorously recovered in 'smothering', 'puffed' – and in other remarks from the same period: 'Cath. Carswell is buried alive'; 'England just depresses me, like a long funeral'; 'So many bourgeois people live on and on, and *can't* die, because they have never been in life at all.'[13] It is a repertoire which already looks to be in search of a ghost story of some kind to develop in, even before Cynthia Asquith actually asked Lawrence to write one, at the end of that October, for an anthology she was planning, to be called *The Ghost Book*; and after she had planted this idea in his mind, the imagery in his writings became more explicit. Baden-Baden, which the Lawrences visited at the beginning of November, was 'nothing but ghosts', a place making him feel it was 'a queer thing, to have a past!'; and when, soon after his arrival in Spotorno, he wrote the essay 'A Little Moonshine with Lemon', he imagined the ranch he had left behind as a place that 'heaves with ghosts. But when one has got used to one's own home-ghosts...they are like one's own family, but nearer than the blood.'[14]

'Like one's own family, but nearer...'. 'Glad Ghosts' marks the beginning of a prolonged reassessment, in Lawrence's writing, of what his father, his mother and his childhood had come to mean to him. The particular rite of passage involved in his having helped, during his stay in the Midlands, to settle what remained of his late father's affairs, must have contributed something to this; a sentence in one of Adam Phillips's essays – not on Lawrence – seems to capture much of the imaginative background of the story: 'The death of a parent is bound to leave one to wonder, one way or another, about parenting; about who, if anyone, one belongs to or wants to belong to; and where, if anywhere, one needs to imagine oneself coming from.'[15] By the time of essays such as 'Return to Bestwood' (1926), 'Enslaved by Civilisation' (1928), and 'Nottingham and the Mining Countryside' (1929), Lawrence's memory of what his family life had actually been like seems to have been completely taken over by safer, more programmatic ideas about what it symbolised, as if he were deliberately building dams against that 'smothering flood' which had threatened to overwhelm him.[16] Especially so, perhaps, in the case of his father – now reinvented by Lawrence as a carefree, raffish Merrie-England gadabout, rather like Mollie Skinner's brother, but penned in, soured and worn down by a nagging, disapproving wife. This reinvention is dominated by a sense of lost or thwarted potential; and in creating Mark Morier, Lawrence was imagining for the first time a man very like himself, with his own attitudes and opinions, actually becoming a father (although in so strangely attenuated a way as barely to be aware of it); a man very like himself, or like a compound of himself and the father he felt he might in other circumstances have had – or perhaps a compound of Lawrence and the man Lawrence's father might have wished *him* to have been. Some form of mourning would seem to be implicated in all this. The story seems to circle around the question of the obligations one owes to the dead, and how one might best meet them or free oneself from them; the narrator sets out to put others to rights while still apparently trailing much unfinished emotional business of his own (his name itself sounds rather like 'remember the dead'), and his narrative as a result sometimes appears only half-conscious of the forces at work in it, or the odd directions in which they might lead. It is just this occludedness that I find most stimulating, this registration by the writing of the trouble its author seems to have had with it.

Haunting in 'Glad Ghosts' is largely a matter of comedy – the story is saturated to the point of carnival with fantasies of passing between things, material and immaterial, of experimenting with alternative roles and powers, being king for a night, crossing gender, swapping wives, speaking through mediums, the whole dream of standing in the other's place and then coming back to oneself anew. But the comedy cannot disguise the deposit of melancholy beneath it: the retrospective brooding, scarcely to be found anywhere else in Lawrence's work, on might-have-beens, losses, and missed chances, and the scourging, straw-clutching feeling that misery and disappointment might be prerequisites of the deepest revelations: 'perhaps, in modern people, only after long suffering and defeat can the naked intuition break free between a woman and a man' (194).

It is in every way a transitional story. It reworks some of the ideas and language of earlier writings, especially stories such as 'The Border-Line' and the unfinished 'The Flying-Fish', the play *David*, and the poem 'Spirits Summoned West'; but one can also glimpse here in embryonic form virtually all the fiction that Lawrence would go on to write. 'Glad Ghosts' moves in the same kind of territory as *The Waste Land*, or *Fiesta*, or 'Leda and the Swan', setting up all the great symbolic connotations for the 1920s of emasculation and impotence, with the land drooping until fertility is restored and a mystic impregnation inaugurates a new order. It dreams of wholeness of being, spontaneously regained through a prototype of what in *Lady Chatterley's Lover* will be called the 'democracy of touch'. But however triumphantly 'Glad Ghosts' proclaims the recovering of health, it seems to me that the details which stay in the mind on reading it tend to be those most intimate with the illness. 'Democracy' and 'touch' are both shaded with scepticism: on the one hand, the class barriers which appeared to have come down look at the end as if they are going up again; and on the other, the most significant contacts between people do not involve 'touch' at all, but are purely mental and imaginative. And at the very centre of the story is a weary, sickly, middle-aged man, Colonel Hale, who no longer wants to care about any of this, who is truly a 'glad ghost' in being happy not to be touched, not to have to bother about sex any more, slumped on a cushion and loosening the top buttons of his pyjamas; waiting, as Lawrence must so many times have waited, for his breathing to come more easily, and for the burden to be taken off him for a while.

## 2

At the cheerless dinner-table at Riddings, the Lathkills' Derbyshire mansion, where Lady Lathkill and Colonel Hale nibble away at unappetising morsels, and the burgundy is sent round with great reluctance, Morier, who has been living overseas, is explaining to Carlotta why he found London so 'dismal':

'I was thinking of the Obelisk Memorial Service.'
'Did you go to it?'
'No! But I fell into it.'
'Wasn't it moving?'
'Rhubarb, senna, that kind of moving. . . . In the rain, a soppy crowd, with soppy bare heads, soppy emotions, soppy chrysanthemums, and prickly laurestinus! A steam of wet mob-emotion! Ah no! it shouldn't be allowed.'
. . . 'Wouldn't you have us honour the dead?' came Lady Lathkill's secretive voice across at me, as if a white ermine had barked.
'Honour the dead!' My mind opened in amazement. 'Do you think they'd be honoured?'
I put the question in all sincerity.
'They would understand that the *intention* was to honour them,' came her reply.
I felt astounded.
'If I were dead, would I be honoured if a great, steamy wet crowd came after me with soppy chrysanthemums and prickly laurestinus? Ugh! I'd run to the nethermost ends of Hades! Lord! how I'd run from them!' (185–6)

Previously the conversation has been as bland as the food, but Morier is stung by Lady Lathkill's remarks into an extraordinary little imaginative eruption: an intense power-fantasy of being hunted without ever being caught, a fantasy which could incorporate an erotic game, with soft and spiky weapons teasing the skin, the tantalising repeated mouthful of the flowers' names, salacious relish curling around the words 'how I'd run from them'; relish as well in a sudden uprising from distant childhood, the sensation of running, as fast as one can, with an expanse of free space ahead, the pure joy of escape, agility, fleetness of foot. In one of the ritual celebrations of the Aztec war-god Huitzilopochtli, as Lawrence would certainly have known, the god's invulnerability was symbolised by a solo runner being chased through the streets by a crowd which could never catch him up, and Morier certainly skips adroitly away from Lady Lathkill's pursuit of him; he allows Johnson's 'Hell is paved with good intentions' to hang, unspoken but implicit, behind what he actually says to her, while borrowing Johnson's imagery to launch a fresh flight of his own. Quicksilver mobility counters monumental weight at every turn; the living shuffle doggedly along while the dead are full of energy and sparkle, reanimated by the pressure of a 'steamy wet crowd' which brandishes over them its insistent symbols of remembrance – the very embodiment of a 'smothering flood': and in the meantime the whole conversation seems driven by a search for an inviolable sanctuary – is there a faint trace of Pascal's thought that only in the tomb could Jesus find peace from his enemies? – a search for a last, 'nethermost' redoubt, where nothing could reach or disturb you.

All the motifs which fed in to the writing of the story intriguingly converge here, almost too many things clamouring together – flown spirits, mothers, resurrections, tributes, partings, England. At the same time, one could perhaps say more simply that instead of engaging with the perfectly serious point put to him, about the needs and motives of the bereaved, Morier has deliberately conjured up, in a profoundly grief-stricken household, a facetious vision of the dead fleeing in disgust from their mourners. Lawrence was sufficiently occupied with these concerns to have worked with them again, in the short and brilliantly concentrated story 'Smile', written during a day or two's break from 'Glad Ghosts' that December. In 'Smile', a man called Matthew, whose wife is dying in an Italian convent (the characters are obviously based on Middleton Murry and Katherine Mansfield), travels from England to see her, working himself up along the way into a suitably tragic state, even reciting to himself some lines from Thomas Hood's 'The Death-Bed'; Lawrence had used them himself in one of his letters exactly fifteen years earlier, when his mother was dying.[17] Matthew arrives too late; his wife is already dead; but when he sees her corpse he finds to his horror that he cannot help smiling, and that the corpse seems to be smiling too. As in Morier's outburst about the remembrance service, the stress here falls partly on the contempt the dead would feel for the hypocrisy of those mourning them, and partly on a wild collocation of histrionic grief, supernatural manifestation, and sexual comedy. Matthew tries to be earnest and dignified in the presence of death, but he cannot take his eyes off a young nun's 'creamy-dusky hands, that were folded like mating birds, voluptuously'; 'out of the fathomless Hades of his gloom, he thought: What a nice hand!'[18] Meanwhile, 'the Mother Superior set two of the candles straight upon their spikes, clenching the thick candle with firm, soft grip, and pressing it down' (75). Again, everything seems to exchange attributes with its opposite, so the living man's face is 'changeless' (72) while the dead woman's keeps changing; the nun's hands, 'like birds nesting in couples' (75), transfer an image of marital togetherness to the solitary and the celibate; the candles around the bed 'quivered warm and quick like a Christmas tree' (73); the funereal is dishevelled by mischievous living instincts. Like many other Lawrence stories, especially those satirising Murry, 'Smile' makes fun of the embarrassing differences between what the body wants and what the mind thinks is required of it, almost to the point of implying that Matthew's grief is completely fake. But it stops short of this, to suggest instead a truth that escapes Matthew himself, that bereavement can encompass some bewilderingly contradictory impulses, and there is no need to feel guilty or ashamed of them – a compassionate message mysteriously sent, via the smiling corpse, from the dead back to the living.

In 'Glad Ghosts', however, this injunction to accept one's reactions honestly is taken into a much more complicated emotional landscape. Morier speaks in an aggressively tactless and provocative way in his dinner-table conversation because he is attempting the drastic shock treatment he believes this family needs, and which he has been sent for to provide. Ever since the war, the Lathkills have been living in permanent gloom, brought on firstly by the loss of their children, and secondly by the oppressive presence in their home of the ghost of Lucy, Luke's mother's oldest friend, Colonel Hale's first wife. Between them, Lucy Hale and Lady Lathkill completely dominate the household, the former by haunting it, the latter by arranging spiritualist sessions to pick up the other's messages. Lucy has already instructed her husband to marry again, and has selected an unsurprisingly inhibited young woman called Dorothy to be the replacement wife, but she has also ordered the Colonel not to consummate the marriage, nor to do anything else that might indicate even a modicum of interest in moving his life forwards. During one recent séance the medium reported seeing the initials M.M., denoting 'someone thinking of your family. It would be good if he entered your family' (184), and the younger Lathkills, with Luke's mother's reluctant blessing, have asked Mark Morier to come, to see if he might tempt a second ghost, the benevolent family ghost, into making one of its rare visits which, according to legend, always restore the family's fortunes. Luke and Carlotta have effectively given Morier *carte blanche* to express himself as freely as he likes; but even so, the mixture of insolent disdain and smokescreen evasiveness in his reply to Lady Lathkill suggests that she may have unwittingly touched an obscure nerve. He never quite succeeds – the story never quite succeeds – in silencing all the reverberations of what she says. Years before, when the Lathkills' twin sons were killed in a road accident, Morier 'learned the news late, and did not write to Carlotta. What could I say?' (179). This comment seems to be pitched somewhere between delicacy and self-regard, as if it were more important for him to consider the calibre of the thing said at such a moment than to make a simple commiserative gesture. When he refers to the 'Obelisk', it is hard not to think that he does so just because everyone else would always have known it as the Cenotaph.[19] What could have made him want to be so aloof and guarded? In his recoil from the Armistice Day crowd, he seems not to regard them as 'real' mourners at all, but as wrapped in Freudian melancholia, incapable of disinvestment from the lost object; his remark, 'Ah no! it shouldn't be allowed', sounds like a robust version of the moralising impulse which, as Kathleen Woodward has argued, lies in the middle of Freud's account of 'healthy' mourning, the sense that the bereaved owe it to the rest of humanity to get over their sorrows as quickly and tidily as possible.[20] And in imagining this crowd in relentless pursuit of its quarry, Morier, rather like Freud again, sees such excessive displays of grief betraying an unacknowledgeable, repressed hostility towards whatever is being mourned – 'soppy emotions on top, and nasty ones underneath' (185) – and that, as 'Smile' more good-humouredly suggested, successful therapy would have to begin by exposing this. But isn't something else leaking into his disgust with them as well, a bitter sense of having been let down by those who professed to love him, a longing for the fellowship and communal feeling which only seems available by way of these hideous parodies?

Lawrence himself never witnessed an Armistice Day service. But the story seems to have taken something from the account of the 1925 ceremony which was printed in *The Times* under the headline 'The Great Silence', and which Lawrence appears to have read in Spotorno (he was originally going to call his story 'The Ghost of Silence'):

> The great crowd was as still as it was silent... nothing but the wind was moving... 'Clearly some greater power was at work than the official request that silence should be kept'... Such a stillness could only come from the heart of the people determined for those two sacred minutes of commemoration to be silent, to be still; a people which for once needed not study to be quiet, for quiet came upon them from within.[21]

Remembering the amount of work which the word 'still' is made to do, not only in 'Glad Ghosts' but in many other of Lawrence's later writings, and his belief in the importance of voluntary submission to one's inner promptings, one would suspect that the behaviour reported here might well have struck him as a bizarre travesty of everything he most valued. In any event, 'Glad Ghosts' certainly gains much of its momentum from its satirical treatment of remembrance rituals and spiritualism, the two most prominent features of the national reaction to mass bereavement. The Cenotaph and the séance were places where mourners could gather, compensating a little for the absence of graves to visit, since so many of the war dead had no clearly defined resting-place. Both forms of gathering also effectively bypassed the official Christian practices whose consolations were widely felt to be inadequate in the face of such incomprehensible losses; the Cenotaph itself, originally a wood and plaster mock-up hurriedly made ready for a victory parade in July 1919, owed much of its popular appeal to its unadorned, abstract design, which seemed to offer something to all religions and none, and it was largely as a result of pressure from the public that it was rebuilt as a permanent structure.[22] But Lawrence, acutely alert to any tinge of coercion, seems to have been primarily interested in the ways in which such commemorative occasions, intended to assuage sorrow and give it meaning, could be unscrupulously manipulated by those concerned to prolong and take advantage of others' feelings of guilt at having survived. Morier's combative reaction to Lady Lathkill's apparently innocent remark may reflect a deep suspicion of her motives; might she have been implying, not only that the dead would take a tolerant and affectionate view of an inept performance, but that the very ineptness could actually reinforce a covert message of the performance, that those who remain could never match up to the level of those who are gone? This is a message that must have permeated English life in the 1920s in many more ways than have left traces; it comes through again in the Window Fund episode in *The Virgin and the Gipsy*. (It may be worth mentioning here that, in re-imagining his relations with his family, Lawrence became interested again in his own erstwhile survivor-guilt, as the younger son carrying the burden of hopes once invested in his dead elder brother; this becomes a prominent motif in 'The Lovely Lady' and in the second and third versions of *Lady Chatterley's Lover*, but it was part of the imaginative milieu of 'Glad Ghosts' as well, since the character of Luke Lathkill was heavily derived from Herbert Asquith, whose elder brother Raymond was killed in the war.)[23] Lady Lathkill's dabblings in the occult seem expressly designed to keep Dorothy feeling subordinate and under permanent obligation to Lucy, her predecessor in the role of Hale's wife; and needless to say, Lady Lathkill herself maintains an insidious precedence in the household over her own son's wife, its ostensible mistress. But unlike in other families of the time, no attempt ever seems to be made to contact the spirits of those loved ones who died suddenly, prematurely, and far from home – Carlotta's twin sons, for example, killed in a car-crash in America; the Lathkill séances are designed simply to help the ghost of Lucy prevent her widowed husband from coping without her, and the messages which arrive are the complete opposite of the cheerful encouragements to move on and not live in the past which, by all accounts, were the kind most commonly transmitted by the spirits.[24]

But the whole situation at Riddings is the complete opposite, indeed an aggressive parody of what might have been 'normal' for an upper-class family in the 1920s. Not only are the household's losses pointedly *not* war-losses, but they just as pointedly invert the losses that convention would have expected: men have survived, while women and children have perished, the children through accident and illness, and Lucy Hale at home while her husband was safe at the Front. It is one of the many sardonic inversions, like that of the Christian preference for spirit over flesh, around which the story is organised; another, when Lathkill suggests that his guests should have a dance after dinner in place of the usual evening spiritualist session, may have been prompted by a report a little further down the same page of that issue of *The Times*, of dance-goers at the Albert Hall who spontaneously decided to stop dancing and to hold an impromptu remembrance service instead. Nonetheless, one might feel that the textual impulse here was again pushing a little beyond the merely sardonic, towards something more mysteriously vindictive. Morier admits to having had the 'effrontery' to sing a French army drinking song at the table while Lady Lathkill, who disapproved of meat and alcohol, was still finishing her 'celery and nut salad' (188); but there would also be a different, unremarked kind of effrontery to his singing it in the presence of two men, Lathkill and Hale, who, unlike him, had actually been soldiers. Morier had already claimed that the private understanding he shared with Carlotta made them 'rather like two soldiers on a secret mission in an enemy country' (175) – a curious attempt to annex for his own self-glamourising use a notion of military romance just about as far removed from the realities of the late war as could be imagined; perhaps every man really does think meanly of himself for not having been a soldier? The song itself, meanwhile,

> Voyez! voyez! voyez vous bien
> Que les d'moiselles sont belles
> Où nous allons!
> (188)

is full of swaggering seduction-fantasies, rapidly projected, during the after-dinner dance interlude, on to the unhappy-looking Dorothy. Morier again mentally savours some soft brushing of the skin: 'I was conscious of . . . the sparse black hairs there would be on her strong-skinned, dusky thighs' (193), and he imagines her being so starved and desperate for sex that, between himself and Lathkill, 'it was a question of which got there first' (195) – conveniently displacing the real source of the two men's conflict. Dorothy's air of listless despondency evidently contributes to her erotic appeal, although Morier prefers to think that she is not simply being pale and interesting but is somehow actively colluding in his vainglorious fantasies, acknowledging the exposure to him of her inner self: 'She knew, with the heavy intuition of her sort, that I glimpsed her crude among the bushes' (194–5).[25] This extraordinary sentence, with its suggestions of Susanna and the Elders, even of Diana and Actaeon, flickering in and out of Morier's seemingly obsessive fascination with pubic hair, also appears to be carrying an awareness of how disconcertingly arousing the spectacle of female vulnerability and distress can be, even how much male arousal might depend on it (sex between Connie and the gamekeeper first occurs in just such circumstances, and the concept of 'tenderness' in that novel is deeply implicated in them): the kind of connection between grief and desire, sowing in tears and reaping in joy, which Morier's narrative keeps obliquely in view while finding it difficult to be open about. Meanwhile, 'her sort' – a phrase in which the voice of Lawrence's mother is suddenly audible through the misogyny and class venom – adds a little to the peculiar *sansculotte* vengefulness which seemed to mark the text from the beginning. There is a French element among all the other elements in Morier's name, maybe recalling Morel in *Sons and Lovers*, a name reflecting Lawrence's father's belief that there was French blood in his ancestry, going back to revolutionary times. The French army song had the call 'Cassons les verres nous les payerons!' (188), which sounds as though the troops were exulting in a newly acquired, specifically post-revolutionary capacity to enjoy the freedoms of the rich, since in the older dispensation of mainland Europe soldiers were never expected to pay for any damage they caused in the first place. Morier says of Carlotta's paintings that 'even she didn't expect them to start a revolution' (174); of himself that he 'should never be king till breeches were off' (178); of the two of them that theirs was a '*liaison . . . dangéreuse*'; of Carlotta again that for all her professed loathing of her own class, her unconscious tics of manner 'proved that the coronet was wedged into her brow', a line which seems to be thinking of just the kind of injury a *sansculotte* might wish to inflict; and even his vision of the Cenotaph ceremony had its mob, its pursuit, its frissons of predatory feeling, its censorious cry of 'It shouldn't be allowed'.

## 3

Reading the line with 'her sort' in it, I do not think it too far-fetched to see both Lawrence's father and his mother – or at least, his 1925 versions of them – inhabiting the same sentence: Gallic cocksureness infiltrated in its secret recesses by Puritan asperity. In the central action of 'Glad Ghosts', the successful exorcising, through a loose alliance of the three men, of the spirit of Lucy from Riddings, what is being imagined is a utopian cleansing of post-war England, of which the great house is a kind of microcosm, from the repressive influence of its mother-figures, and the re-establishing of masculine supremacy. But it is hard enough for the text to clarify what masculinity might actually be, let alone to set it to any effective work, and the struggle for control of the house is beset with comic and unresolved gender-confusions. For a start, the mother-figures, Lucy Hale and Lady Lathkill, both appear to be strange composites of ghost, wife, mother and man. Lucy was certainly much more like a husband or a mother than a wife to the Colonel: '"You might say, she married me . . . I suppose she mothered me, in a way"' (190). Descriptions of Lady Lathkill sometimes employ the male pronoun – 'staring at me fixedly . . . as a hawk, perhaps, looks shrewdly far down, in his search' (182); 'Lady Lathkill ate in silence, like an ermine in the snow, feeding on his prey' (186)[26] – and sometimes stress the immateriality of relationship with her: her voice 'came across' (186), she can be felt 'far off . . . stirring and sending forth her rays' (205), she 'steered heavily past me as if I didn't exist' (189), ominously turning Morier himself into a ghost for a moment. Quite as much as the real ghost with which she allies herself, Lady Lathkill is able to ignore barriers, or insinuate herself through them. Rita Felski, in *The Gender of Modernity*, suggested that among the competing forms of religious comfort at the time, spiritualism might have had a particular appeal to women, not only because the 'purported attributes of femininity – impressionability, sensitivity, passivity – were deemed the ideal qualities of a medium',[27] and the forms of behaviour usually disparaged as irrational or over-emotional were seen as sources of authority and trustworthiness, but because spiritualism could offer empowering fantasy-images of the female, at least in disembodied form, moving with ease across the boundaries and demarcations of the patriarchal order. 'Glad Ghosts' seems to have had something like this in mind when Lady Lathkill comes back to the dining-room, before the men have finished their port:

> Lord Lathkill burst into a loud laugh, then was suddenly silent as the door noiselessly opened, and the dowager's white hair and pointed, uncanny eyes peeped in, then entered.
> 'I think I left my papers in here, Luke,' she murmured.
> 'Yes mother! There they are! We're just coming up.'
> 'Take your time!' (193)

The white hair and the eyes seem to have become detached from the rest of her and floated by themselves, over the threshold of a sacred masculine preserve. There is an intriguing, slightly awed sense here of the ghost-mother's capacity for relentless surveillance, nipping in the bud any activity that threatens to challenge her; the 'loud laugh' that prompted her instant investigation must have been the first heard in that house for many a year.

The men, for their part, have hitherto been so unconfrontational and timidly solicitous that in the original manuscript the only description Morier could find for Lathkill was that 'he suggested a woman. It was almost like driving with a woman' (344) – a description dropped perhaps because it made the point rather too bluntly. As for Colonel Hale, Morier reserves a special contempt for him, a man who not only refuses to sleep with his new wife because Lucy and the past make 'a higher claim on me' (192), but who is apparently completely incapable, despite having reached the rank of Colonel, of doing anything without the help and permission of the women who terrify him. The contempt seems to involve a little of the exasperated disappointment Lawrence often appears to have felt towards the victims of war trauma – 'Well, then I got buried – shell dropped, and the dug-out caved in – and that queered me. They sent me home' (190) – that they had somehow failed to rise to the privilege of a near-death experience, and had regressed into infantilism, instead of being truly resurrected into a far-seeing detachment from petty cares, like, say, Gethin Day in 'The Flying-Fish', or, much more equivocally, Eastwood in *The Virgin and the Gipsy* (or, perhaps, that they had exposed the possibility that infantile regression and far-seeing detachment might be uncomfortably close neighbours).[28] Morier's attempt to encourage Hale and

Lathkill into a kind of officers' mess conspiracy, a drink-induced bombastic defiance of female rule, telling them that '"I'd just face her, wherever she seemed to be, and say: *Lucy, go to Blazes!* – "' (193), always seems as much concerned with his own needs as with theirs, with a yearning like that in his French song for camaraderie and summary gestures, as if the masculinity he were trying to reinvigorate only existed in his envious regrets at having missed it – a yearning that sits uneasily alongside the actual experience of these wounded veterans. And when Lathkill is eventually inspired to follow Morier's lead, it is not on account of anything he actually says; it is Morier's body language that makes the crucial impression:

> 'Do you know!' (Lathkill) said. 'I suddenly thought at dinner-time, what corpses we all were, sitting eating our dinners! I thought it when I saw you look at those little Jerusalem artichoke things in a white sauce. Suddenly it struck me, you were physically alive and twinkling, and we were all bodily dead. Bodily dead, if you understand. Quite alive in other directions: but bodily dead.' (200)

What did he see in Morier's look? Horrified loathing, epicurean quizzicality, even an instinctive pull towards something on the plate resembling a magnified view of the first inseminated stirrings of life? A spark has passed, from one man to another – a living contact, to counter the spirit-contacts between the women: spirit-contacts which, Lawrence argued in his essay on Hawthorne's *Blithedale Romance*, could only ever transmit 'little clots of vibration' from 'dead *wills*', fragments of 'disintegrated consciousness'.[29] The live spark is more profoundly transforming for those alert to it, more mysterious than any intervention from the beyond; far creepier, too, with so much envy, rivalry, implicit ridicule and submerged homo-eroticism crackling in it. It has nothing to do with the will, it cannot wittingly be set going, and it can convey a different message from the one its initiator might have had in mind; instead of confronting the threatening female with anger and violence, as Morier wished him to, Lathkill finds a new compassion for those like himself whose sexual and emotional lives have fallen derelict:

> 'I *do* understand poor Lucy!' said Luke. 'Don't you? She forgot to be flesh and blood while she was alive, and now she can't forgive

herself – nor the Colonel. That must be pretty rough, you know, not to realise it till you're dead. ... But fancy having a living face, and arms, and thighs. Oh my God, I'm glad I've realised in time!' (200)

His new sensitivity to the body leads him to prescribe a course of action for the Colonel quite unlike the one Morier had suggested:

'Why can't you feel kindly towards her, poor thing! She must have been done out of a lot, while she lived. ... Was your body ever good to poor Lucy's body ... her poor woman's body, were you ever good to that? ... That's why she haunts you. You despised and disliked her body, and she was only a living ghost. Now she wails in the afterworld, like a still-wincing nerve. ... Why don't you, even now, love her a little, with your real heart? Poor disembodied thing! Why don't you take her to your warm heart, even now, and comfort her inside there ... ?' (202–4)

Hale seems to take these proposals literally. 'Then, deliberately, but not lifting his head, he pulled open his dressing gown at the breast, unbuttoned the top of his pyjama jacket, and sat perfectly still, his breast showing white and very pure' (204–5) – looking almost as much as if he were about to suckle a baby as to allow a spirit access to his heart, as if one way for men to recover their lost pre-eminence were to incorporate female capacities into themselves, and effect a fantastic inversion of the mother–child relationship which had dominated them. Both here and in Morier's alternative plan, to send Lucy to Blazes and thus fulfil all one's raging wishes at once, the drive to defeat the mother-figure appears bound up with an intense nostalgia for the maternal body, a nostalgia which, as Fiona Becket has pointed out, recurs throughout Lawrence's writing, and is extraordinarily prevalent in this work.[30] Some form of male appropriation of maternity is implicit in the urge to be 'born again' (204), to become, like Lathkill, 'another creature entirely' (204) and bring new existence into the world; the idea threads its way through Luke's hectic address to the bewildered Lady Lathkill:

'Oh, Mother, thank you for my limbs, and my body! oh Mother, thank you for my knees and my shoulders at this moment! ... Oh mother of my body, thank you for my body, you strange woman with white hair! I don't know much about you, but my body came from you, so thank you, my dear . . . mother of my face and of my thighs!' (207)

She listens aghast as her son, exulting in his rediscovered corporeality, not only acknowledges her procreative role but seems himself to be conferring new life upon her, re-endowing her with the fleshly form she had tried to transcend; the son giving a second birth to the mother. He dispels her ghostly powers by seeing her at last, not as an enveloping and ubiquitous presence, but as a physical object, occupying a point in space which he could move towards or away from, something with which relationship might develop; she tries to fight back – '"Hadn't we better go?" she said, beginning to tremble' (207) – but too late; she comes down that night with a 'sudden illness' (209).

Morier takes a back seat during these crucial proceedings. He watches enthralled, but he never explicitly endorses Lathkill's exorcising strategies. He still wanted to say "Lucy, go to Blazes!" The differences between the two men come sharply into focus: Lathkill conducting Lucy gently home, Morier forcing her violently away. In his speeches to Colonel Hale, Lathkill projects on to Lucy his own yearning for shelter and benign maternal protection, turning her into a lost child, with words like 'wails', the reiterated 'poor', the phrase 'love her a little'; he implicitly offers the conventional view that ghosts only go haunting out of discontent with things left undone in life, and that, as with unfulfilled patriarchs like himself, all they really want is to be at home, at peace. There is no room here for the possibility that Lucy might at last be enjoying some 'male' prerogatives, freedoms like those of the Mexican *macho*, in Octavio Paz's account the patriarch's alter ego, coming and going whenever he likes, subjecting his household to periods of tyranny interspersed with unexplained and prolonged absences.[31] For Lathkill, Lucy longs to relinquish any such freedoms: '"Why don't you take her to your warm heart . . . and comfort her inside there?"' (204). But Morier had said '"Why, Colonel, don't you turn round and quarrel with the spirit of your first wife, fatally and finally, and get rid of her?"' (192). Why not sever the bonds between you, instead of caressing them long after they have started to throttle you both? Why deprive her of her freedom to form new bonds, and to sever them in their turn? Let her become another ladybird, or one of Morier's fellow-wanderers through Hades (Blazes, after all), in the mood of the 1920 poem 'Medlars and Sorb-Apples', wanderers who purify themselves by turning their backs on all who might once have had a claim on them:

> Going down the strange lanes of hell, more and more intensely alone,
> The fibres of the heart parting one after the other
> And yet the soul continuing, naked-footed, ever more vividly embodied
> Like a flame blown whiter and whiter . . .
>
> The exquisite odour of leave-taking.
> *Iamque vale!*
> Orpheus, and the winding, leaf-clogged, silent lanes of hell.
>
> Each soul departing with its own isolation,
> Strangest of all strange companions,
> And best.[32]

Here, too, the underworld is a paradoxically revitalising place, where the soul is 'embodied', feeling the joyful sensation of contact between the feet and the ground, and where the words of final farewell, Eurydice's *iamque vale* from Virgil's fourth *Georgic*, are no longer tragic or grief-stricken, but thrilled and expectant, full of the promise of newness emerging from decay. But although in his address to his mother Lathkill seemed to accept that severance was the precondition of renewal, in his advice to Hale he was still encouraging an encryption of the lost object within the self, the kind of psychic manoeuvre which Abraham and Torok have discussed, an identification with the lost object so complete that one would never be able to 'get rid' of it; 'real' mourning becomes impossible, and the melancholia which Morier had tried to dislodge is bizarrely reinstalled, in the names of 'home', 'breast', and 'mother': '"The Colonel's breast is white and extraordinarily beautiful, Mother, I don't wonder poor Lucy yearned for it, to go home into it at last"' (206).[33] Lathkill may, of course, be saying all this cynically, to ensure that the Colonel is fully occupied so as to leave Dorothy free for himself, an interpretation which nothing in the story could conclusively discount; but either way, even in their joint victory, the traveller and the settler continue to look in different directions. The gender-entanglements moreover still persist; men who assert their authority by pretending at some level to be women are giving the authority back in the moment of reclaiming it, while Morier's ideal masculinity seems most nearly exemplified in the behaviour-patterns of the female ghost he is supposed to be attacking.

## 4

The Colonel, shocked when Lathkill accuses him of neglecting Lucy, exclaims: '"She had everything she wanted! She had three of my children"' (203). This is a remarkable thing to be saying in the company of Carlotta, who has lost all three of hers. Critics have claimed that the Colonel's statement signals his failure to appreciate the true importance of sexual fulfilment,[34] but what is surely more interesting is that in saying this he appears simultaneously to have forgotten and to have brought to mind the real source of the grief in the house. Suddenly all the arguments and skirmishes over Lucy seem like distractions, anaesthetising a deeper wound that has not yet been treated. Something similar occurs with Lathkill's obsessive reiteration of the phrase 'flesh and blood'. He wants it simply to mean 'the body', in line with his new, spark-inspired insistence on the primacy of bodily over spiritual needs.[35] But he repeats the phrase so often as to appear magnetised by its other meaning, the family relation; almost as if he were defying this meaning to register. When he says, for example, 'We've been forgetting that we're flesh and blood, Mother' (199), what is now being remembered at one level still seems to have been forgotten at another; more arrestingly still, in the original manuscript he was made to say at one point, '"There's no doing anything with Mother ... Her flesh and blood has passed away"' (350). Lawrence cancelled this, but brought the phrase back again later, into the revised letter at the end of the story, where Gabriel is now described as 'flesh and blood of our ghost itself' (210) – as if only with the birth of a new child can the repressed meaning of the phrase be allowed to emerge openly, underlining how powerfully that repression had been contributing to everything Lathkill had said earlier.

The only time he directly mentions his lost children is in the course of a rapturous speech to Carlotta, when he suddenly says,

'"And the children, it is as well they are dead. They were born of our will and our disembodiment"' (201). This is close to what Sue Bridehead steeled herself to say when she went back to Phillotson in Hardy's *Jude the Obscure*, although Lawrence's text implicitly inverts, again, the Christianising element: 'My children – are dead – and it is right that they should be! I am glad – almost. They were sin-begotten.'[36] Lathkill is presumably thinking that it is 'as well' for the children that they should be dead, since being so unpromisingly born they would never have amounted to anything; and 'as well' for us, since we are better off not having to trip over these reminders of our unhealthy past all the time. Would Carlotta, who remains silent throughout, have agreed with this assessment? When Don Ramón was 'reborn', in *The Plumed Serpent*, he came to think of his sons as being the children of his 'old' body, and thus no longer counting, but they were at least still alive, and even he would hardly have expected their mother to feel the same as he does. Is Lathkill trying obliquely to console his wife, with Morier's talk of the Cenotaph fresh in his mind, by implying that the children died that we might live? – exactly as Sue Bridehead had gone on to say, 'They were sacrificed to teach me how to live. . . . That's why they have not died in vain!'[37]

'And the children, it is as well they are dead'. It sometimes seems as if the whole of 'Glad Ghosts' had been written so that somebody could speak that line. In December 1925 Lawrence was by no means fully reconciled to having Frieda's children in his life – Elsa and Barbara came to visit them at home for the first time, at Spotorno – and much of the writing he produced in this period appears spurred by an ambivalence, not just towards the two girls themselves, but towards Frieda's undisguised delight at having recovered her 'flesh and blood' after so long, at having had restored to her a little of what life with Lawrence had taken away. It would have left him, one might fairly guess, feeling somewhat displaced, in the middle of writing a story about restoration and displacement. 'Glad Ghosts' seems determined to play down the importance of children in a woman's life, and odd passages in the manuscript which might inadvertently have suggested otherwise were carefully rewritten. For example, on a visit to the Lathkills' years before, Morier had been taken to see the nursery:

They were two boys, with their father's fine, dark hair, . . . He had put out his cigar, and leaned over the cots, gazing in silence. The nurse, dark-faced and faithful, drew back. Carlotta gazed at her children steadily. (344)

Lawrence changed the last sentence, writing instead 'Carlotta glanced at her children, but more helplessly, she gazed at him' (179). Everything which a gaze creates the time to brood over, whether it be love, hope, or anxiety, is redirected towards the husband, and away from the children; they are now given a mere glance, as if nothing is to be allowed to distract from or dilute the primacy of the adult relationship. The half-implication in the original passage, that the children might one day offer Carlotta some compensation for the difficulties of being married to a man whom the war has clearly left emotionally damaged, is eradicated, or made into the most fleeting of hints, changing the atmosphere of this moment completely. And a later scene, from the beginning of Morier's current visit, seems to be haunted by an unacknowledged memory of that one:

> Carlotta ... had sat herself down in a chair by the fire, and put her feet on the stone fender, and was leaning forward, screening her face with her hand, still careful of her complexion. I could see her broad, white shoulders, showing the shoulder-blades as she leaned forward, beneath her dress. But it was as if some bitterness had soaked all the life out of her, and she was only weary, or inert, drained of her feelings. It grieved me, and the thought passed through my mind that a man should take her in his arms and cherish her body, and start her flame again. ... She would have to restore the body of her life, and only a living body would do it. (183–4)

Why does he say 'some bitterness', as if he were pretending not to know exactly what has saddened her? It is the first time she, Morier, and her husband have been in a room together since that night by the cots. His remark, 'it grieved me', is the closest the word 'grief' ever comes to being mentioned in the text, and Morier only uses it to describe his own feelings about the grieving woman, uses it in the vicinity, as it were, of the place where it ought to be; like the Colonel talking about 'three of my children', Morier suddenly becomes a conduit for vibrations of which he seems unconscious – one of a number of ways in which this story of ghosts and mediums works to make apparent elements to which, in its trance, it is not itself attending. 'Screening her face with her hand', coupled shortly afterwards with 'shading her eyes with her hand as she looked at me' (184), leaves open the possibility that Carlotta might have been less concerned with her complexion – and with the 'adult' life to which such a concern would alert us – than with hiding the fact that she was in tears; a possibility which the very narrator whose words raised it seems unable, or unwilling, to notice.

Sometimes in Lawrence – it happens again in the *Chatterley* novels – the impression is given that the actual child-figures are being squeezed out to enable the adults to appropriate the idea of 'childhood' for their own use. When Morier dances with Carlotta:

> Her warm, silken shoulder was soft and grateful under my hand, as if it knew me with that second knowledge which is part of one's childhood . . . as if we had known each other perfectly, as children, and now, as man and woman, met in the full, further sympathy. (194)

He makes that fascinating shoulder of hers sound like a faithful dog recognising its long-lost master. Touch reawakens the child in the adult:

> I was glad to have Carlotta again: to have that inexpressibly delicate and complete quiet of the two of us . . . for this hour at least, it was whole, a soft, complete, physical flow, and a unison deeper even than childhood. (195)

Lawrence originally wrote 'as deep as childhood' (346). I would guess that he had the climax of *The Mill on the Floss* at the back of his mind here – at the front of his mind when finishing *The Virgin and the Gipsy* a few days later: a profound, longstanding mutuality rediscovered in the middle of the flood ('I felt as if I were resisting a rushing, cold dark current' [196]), and breaking through everything that had conspired for so long to obscure it. If it is now 'deeper' than childhood, it may be through the intensifying effect of subliminal recollection, like a Wordsworthian 'spot', or because the melting sensation evoked really goes back beyond the period of sibling or playmate togetherness (Morier and Carlotta didn't, of course, know each other as children), to the primary unison with the mother – the hunger, once more, for the refuge of the maternal body, as if one could start again with everything still possible. The woman's touch may not, in the end, be uniting her with the man at all, so much as reconnecting him with buried feelings in himself to which she ultimately has no access.[38] Increasingly, the vocabulary Morier applies to his relationship with Carlotta draws from the 1923 poem 'Spirits Summoned West', in which Lawrence called out to the ghost of his mother:

> Come back then, mother . . .
> It was only I who saw the virgin you
> That had no home . . .
>
> *Come, delicate, overlooked virgin, come back to me*
> *And be still,*
> *Be glad* . . .
>
> Inside my innermost heart,
> Where the virgin in woman comes home to a man.[39]

Lathkill used almost identical patterns of thought and image in his compassion for Lucy. When Morier gazes again at Carlotta, he sees her 'looking like a girl again, as she used to look . . . only now, a certain rigidity of the will had left her, so that she looked even younger than when I first knew her, having now a virginal, flower-like *stillness* which she had not then had' (204; emphasis in text). What the son claims for himself in the poem is transferred across to and between the men in the story, the visionary capacity to see back through the woman to the girl behind her, with all the potential still intact that has been stifled in her subsequent life. And the recurrent emphasis on 'virgin', with that characteristic sliding effect which Fiona Becket has called the 'productive liminal space between the metaphorical and the literal',[40] invests this vision with a curious variant of oedipal desire: to stand in the father's place, by tracking the mother back to an explicitly *pre*-maternal state when only the father could have known her; to imagine her as she could have been before the insentient father clouded her life with his. Maybe a trace of the guilt attached to such imagining works through to the story as well, since in Morier's case it is dancing which effects this resurrection of the woman's unclouded life, dancing which creates the 'flow' and the 'unison' in which differences of class and outlook temporarily disappear; and it was the father, Arthur Lawrence, who was the accomplished dancer, who attracted Lydia Beardsall by being 'alive and twinkling', his robust physicality speaking to something in her which the years eroded, but which he may still have been able to resuscitate a little – on the odd occasions when the children could be got out of the way.

If this privileged vision, seeing the girl behind the woman, is shadowed by the suspicion that it really belongs to someone else, in the story everyone is in someone else's place, everyone's territory is under threat, and it often seems as if one's desires can only be imagined as being enacted by others – a form of imagining that also shields one from the desire's full impact. Towards the end of the passage about Carlotta's sadness by the fire, Morier says that 'the thought passed through my mind that a man should take her in his arms and cherish her body' (184); Lawrence originally made him say 'I wanted to take her in my arms and warm her with life' (344). In that shift to the third person, that delegating of Morier's desire to an imaginary surrogate who could more legitimately realise it for him, lurks a sense that it would be a taboo too far, even for such an iconoclast as Morier, to admit openly that the sight of Carlotta in distress is sexually arousing to the point of making him want to give her *his* child, to become a father himself, to take advantage both of the vacuum which her lost children have created and of the grief which has made her vulnerable. The desire for fatherhood, in counterpoint with the implicit disremembering of the other man's children, does seem to exert a pressure on the text in proportion to the text's reluctance to address it directly. It nestles inside the closing sentence of the fireside passage – 'She would have to restore the body of her life, and only a living body would do it' (184) – where the slippage between the usages of 'body' leaves it uncertain whether it is a lover's embrace or a new child that would 'do it'. And the question of what might actually have happened during the nocturnal encounter that led to the birth of Gabriel is even more elaborately circumvented:

> I must have gone far, far down the intricate galleries of sleep, to the very heart of the world. For I know I passed on beyond the strata of images and words, beyond the iron veins of memory, and

> even the jewels of rest, to sink in the dark Lethe. . . . And at the very middle of the deep night, the ghost came to me, at the heart of the ocean of oblivion. . . . How I know it, I do not know. Yet I know it with eyeless, wingless knowledge.
>    For man in the body is formed through countless ages, and at the centre is the speck, or spark, upon which all his formation has taken place. (208)

Even in this obscurantist rhetoric, the 'galleries', 'iron veins' and 'jewels' hint at a passing beyond the mineral layer which was the collier father's territory, through the Kristevan maternal *chora* where contact is non-verbal, instinctual, in search, again, of the original amniotic stirrings of life. There is a slightly comical pause of uncertainty as to whether what is found there is a 'speck' or a 'spark', a minute particle of solid matter or something fiery and mobile; whether or not it could be held steady, in the hand or in the gaze. And as the mysterious coming-together continues, there is more of the familiar Lawrentian insistence on a 'darkly naked' knowledge, beyond conscious definition:

> I know she came even as a woman, to my man. But the knowledge is darkly naked as the event. I only know, it was so. . . .
>    And then I was aware of a pervading scent, as of plum-blossom. . . . And even with so slight a conscious registering, *it* seemed to disappear. . . . That knowledge of *it*, which was the marriage of the ghost and me, disappeared from me . . . as the scent of the plum-blossom moved down the lanes of my consciousness, and my limbs stirred in a silkiness for which I have no comparison.
>    . . . I wanted to be certain of *it*, to have definite evidence. And as I sought for evidence, *it* disappeared, my perfect knowledge was gone. I no longer knew in full.
>    Now, as the daylight slowly amassed, in the windows from which I had put back the shutters, I sought in myself for evidence. And in the room.
>    But I shall never know. (209)

Morier seems half-sorry and half-pleased that there are no surviving traces. On the one hand he implicitly rebukes himself, like Orpheus after turning round, for losing by not trusting; and on the other, he sees the very absence of traces as a guarantee of the special, Biblically accented value of whatever it was that occurred. At the same time, a different anxiety seems to have crept in under the linguistic armature, as the urgent search for 'evidence' almost begins to suggest an illicit proceeding to which he would not *want* any surviving traces to link him. Sentiments so often accompanying the coming into being of a child, the urge to guard something precious, the turn towards the dawn, the sense of the miraculous intersecting with the everyday, are displaced here upon an unnameable *it* as it departs, in a scent of fruit, going down the lanes in an 'exquisite odour of leave-taking', moving out of reach and making no further demands. Lathkill's closing letter, immediately following this passage, seems to bring some of this cluster of feeling back to Morier in more sarcastic forms – Dorothy's child is referred to as 'it' ('By the bleat of the little thing, I know its father'), and the imagery of dawn is shifted on to the Colonel's pigs, in their 'first red-gold flush'[41] – reinforcing, as everything else in the letter does, that strained ambivalence about the whole business of becoming a father which was lodged in Morier's closing comment on the events, 'I shall never know.' Pathos, in being forever debarred, or relief, at not having to face any repercussions; it does seem to me that buried somewhere in these thickets is a lament for the children that Lawrence knew he would never have.

Morier is finally identified with the ghost, or rather possessed by it, as he lies passively, in the feminine role, and it comes to him; each absorbed or, as it were, incorporated into the other, so that he finds himself becoming father and ghost in the same instant. It enables him to have an entirely dematerialised contact with Carlotta, in which he takes none of the physical initiative which had dominated his imagination all evening; a contact in which, despite Lathkill's impassioned call for them, there is in effect neither touch nor sensuality – indeed sensuality marks the breaking of the contact, as scent fills the nostrils and the limbs stir silkily after the perfect moment has already passed. Morier's ghostliness also enables him to slip away intact in the act of fathering, as what occurs is a kind of immaculate conception in which it is the father who remains unviolated, traceless, impalpable, with none of his power passing out of him through the other's touch into the child who will take his place; the Lathkill family ghost, trailing its plum-blossom scent, brings the outdoors into the home and creates the space to escape through. What Morier calls the 'marriage of the ghost and me' is the last carnivalesque fantasy of being everything and everywhere at once – being the one who stays and the one who goes, intimately linked to the home but always free to leave it; being both aristocrat and commoner, patriarch and *macho*, protecting one's offspring and indifferent to them; being both spirit and body, man and woman, changing sex and substance at will so that the child can be called 'ghost-begotten' (210) – being everything that Morier has to give up wishing for in order to be the other; and it seems at once the mark of trusting forward, letting the future take care of itself, and the mark of a wistful, doubt-haunted ineffectuality, that the text should imagine for him a fatherhood built upon post-coital desertion, with no continuing entanglement with either mother or child, without commitment, without risk, and without love.

## 5

By now the story seems increasingly to have *The Winter's Tale* in mind, with its romance-apparatus, the return of Spring and the mixing of the seasons, warmth brought to the frozen world, the grafting of base-born on to noble stock, the miraculous resolution of sexual jealousies, and the same little shadow over the ending, the question of whether the gains could ever really compensate for the losses; Perdita is found, but her brother Mamillius does not come back.[42] Lawrence had Uncle Oscar press just this kind of question in its most woundingly explicit form at the end of 'The Rocking-Horse Winner', the story written in February 1926 to replace 'Glad Ghosts' in Cynthia Asquith's anthology: 'And even as [Paul] lay dead, his mother heard her brother's voice saying to her: "My God, Hester, you're eighty-odd thousand to the good, and a poor devil of a son to the bad"'.[43] In another of Lawrence's formulations, children were always already ambiguously compensating for what their forebears had to relinquish; this was his theory of the 'grandmothers' dream', whereby each generation was regarded as the product of its grandmothers' secret desires for a different life, a different emotional climate, desires passed down from mother to daughter and finally bearing fruit in the grandchild. Lawrence first presented this idea in the essay 'Making Love to Music', and again at greater length in the 'Autobiographical Fragment' to which Keith Sagar gave the title 'A Dream of Life'. 'We are the embodiment of the most potent ideas of our progenitors, and these ideas are mostly private ones, not to be admitted in public, but to be transmitted as instincts and as the dynamics of behaviour to the third and fourth generation'[44] – children, male children especially, with their parts written for them in the womb, parts imagined years before they could ever be acted. The kind of man Lawrence's own mother really wanted, for example, was not one like himself, whom she nurtured explicitly to make up for the deficiencies of her husband, but one who in her eyes would blend the best features of both son and husband, while filtering out the worst – a man from the new, 1920s generation:

> They are jazzy – but not coarse . . . a bit Don-Juanish, but . . . without brutality or vulgarity. They are more elegant, and not much more moral. But they are still humble before a woman, especially *the* woman!
> It is the secret dream of my mother, coming true.[45]

The ironic tone introduces what sounds like routine resentment at the advance of feminism, at an insidious triumph that has caught men off guard and left them feeling robbed and helpless. But there is something more rueful and elegiac here that seems to look back to the world of 'Glad Ghosts' – the musing over what connects us to our dead, and what our chances might be of escaping their pursuit; the sympathetic feeling for all the life that can only ever be lived vicariously, for the frustrations that cannot be redeemed in our own time, and the frustrations of others that we are born to redeem. Lawrence's late writing is increasingly drawn towards wills, legacies, the coming to light of a hidden inheritance – the question of everything we bequeathe, how we mark the future, for hope or for control or for revenge, deliberately or in spite of ourselves: the remorseless question inside the words of Dr Johnson that lay behind Morier's sudden burst of eloquence, and that openly surface in 'A Dream of Life', when Lawrence writes of his mother's desires and ambitions: 'I myself, her son, could see the dream peeping out, thrusting little tendrils through her paved intention of having "good sons".'[46] The identification, in the story and the essay, with the victims of other people's intentions, seems to encompass the widest and most difficult range of emotion: from the confident belief that natural agility and growth, even though it appears at present so much weaker and more fragile, will always triumph over blocks of stone; through the vision of Hades as a place of rejection, disclaiming, and renewal; towards the bitterest suggestion yet, that Lawrence's mother not only made his life hell, but that part of the hell was being forced to watch the first stirrings of something other than himself that he might have been, but that was to come, if at all, too late for him. Maybe the best way truly to 'honour the dead', to give them what can be given of the peace both dead and living crave, before finally letting them go down the lanes they must follow alone, would be to call them up from their graves once more, as the recycling of 'Spirits Summoned West' might imply, and show them at last the whole spectrum of everything that was done and that went undone, both in their lives and in yours.

It could well suit the imagination of 'Glad Ghosts' if Morier's legacy were to turn out to be Lady Lathkill's dream: if, after the husband and son she has had to put up with, Lady Lathkill could see in Gabriel the masculinity *she* always secretly wanted, blue-eyed and aggressive like herself. 'Ghost-begotten and ready-fisted' (210): despite his Christian name Gabriel seems indeed more like a new Huitzilopochtli, also conceived without carnal contact, directly transmitted from the divine spirit to the earth, to rouse the despondent warriors and put to flight the gods of darkness.[47] Gabriel will invert another romance convention, as the child of a *sansculotte* growing up in a noble household, but he may never come to know his real father; only occasionally the signs of his nature will break out, and set him perhaps at odds with those who have cared for him: rescuing him from them, in a way, but hurting him too, never quite being able to feel at home in his home. As the therapist's gift to the family, Gabriel will keep alive the spirit of challenge on which the therapy was based; in the wider fantasy of the story, he is the gift to the homeland, the fruit of a decisive intervention which simultaneously overturns the class divide, sets the cuckoo permanently in the nest, and re-establishes England as a man's country.[48] The cost of this to Morier – a cost which, in the spirit of the Jamesian first-person narrator, he may still persuade himself is a gain – is his own exclusion from the place he has marked; he too has to leave it to others to live his desires, while he falls back among the shades whence he was called, his yearning for Carlotta fulfilled without his fully knowing it, and the comradeship he searched for glimpsed only in the joshing tones of the letter which expels him.

# 3
# 'Sun' and *The Virgin and the Gipsy*

## 1

When, in 1928, Lawrence substantially revised the story 'Sun', which he had originally written concurrently with 'Glad Ghosts' in the last two months of 1925, he made a small alteration to a scene otherwise left largely untouched, the reunion of Maurice with his son Johnny. The line 'the father talked to the child, who was fond of his Daddy', was changed to 'the father talked to the child, who had been fond of his Daddy'.[1] The new text wants to lay more stress on the distance Johnny has travelled from his former life during the time he has spent in the sun with his mother, Juliet. But in doing so it intensifies the ambiguities that already lay in Johnny's first exchange with his father, who has just struggled down the path to the lemon grove in his dark grey suit –

> 'Come, Johnny! Come and say Hello! to Daddy!'
> 'Daddy going back?' said the child.
> 'Going back? Well – well – not to-day.'
> And he took his son in his arms.[2]

Does the boy actually want his father to go back, so as not to threaten the new bond Johnny has been forming with his mother; or is he searching for reassurance that his father will not desert him again, before committing himself to an embrace? There is a slight note of alarm that, as so often in his young life, a fresh lurch of mood is occurring around him to which he will have to react. The exchange continues –

> 'Take a coat off! Daddy take a coat off!' said the boy, squirming debonair away from the cloth.
> 'All right son! Daddy take a coat off.' (1925: 287; 1928: 34)

'Debonair' could suggest an almost precious level of sensitivity, as Johnny seems at once to be recoiling from an unfamiliar sensation, trying to keep his mother on-side by mimicking her hostility towards her husband, and attempting to reorganise the family's emotional dynamics by changing his father into something he hopes his mother might like. It all seems part of the 'queer, magnetic, psychic connection' Lawrence saw lying between children and unhappy parents, children being 'like barometers to their parents' feelings', as if they were instinctively aware how much their own well-being depended on their capacity to read the restless atmosphere surrounding them.[3]

Juliet is usually thought of as one of Lawrence's rare illustrations of positive mothering. The text itself at one point takes pains to endorse this view:

> She had had the child so much on her mind, in a torment of responsibility. . . . Now a change took place. She was no longer vitally consumed about the child, she took the strain of her anxiety and her will from off him. And he thrived all the more for it. (1928: 22–3)[4]

Her newly relaxed attitude is presented as the first of the benefits accruing from her life outdoors in the sun. According to Judith Ruderman, in *D. H. Lawrence and the Devouring Mother*:

> As the story progresses, the child moves, with Juliet's encouragement, physically and emotionally farther away from his mother, while still maintaining a connection with her . . . Juliet lets go of her role as the smothering, overprotective mother and allows her boy successfully to undergo what [Margaret] Mahler, years later, would call the separation-individuation phase of childhood. The story is almost a textbook case of a turning point in a child's psychological development.[5]

One might equally suggest, however that, far from releasing the boy from the net of her own needs and conducting him towards a healthy independence, Juliet continues to use him as an outlet for feelings that have little or nothing to do with him. Her sunbathing appears to heighten her antagonism towards the male sex generally, and makes her both determined that her son should be different, and exasperated at the traces of resistance he shows (the vocabulary implies that her 'will', supposedly taken off him, is still much in evidence – 'She insisted on his toddling naked', 'She wished she could make him come forth', 'She determined to take him with her'). At one point she makes fun of his puzzled anxiety: 'How he mistrusted her, now that she laughed at him . . . she saw in his wide blue eyes, under the little frown, that centre of fear, misgiving, which she believed was at the centre of all male eyes, now. She called it fear of the sun' (1928: 25). It might equally well have been called misgiving over his mother's disconcerting behaviour and his own urgent need to predict and keep up with it; almost a 'text-book case' of Lacan's belief that primary desire is the desire of the Other, that a child's first concern is to find ways of ensuring that the parent will desire *him*, and will continue to do so.[6] Juliet's new serenity, moreover, resembles at several points a regression on her own part into childlike irresponsibility and self-centredness. She dismisses as beneath her notice the economy of money and care that supports her ('she could not write letters. She would tell the nurse to write' [1928: 28]), and cuts brusquely into her husband's affectionate chatter with Johnny as soon as she feels that she has been left out for long enough: '"What are you going to do about it, Maurice?" she said suddenly' (1928: 34). By the end of the story, when her fantasy of having sex with a local peasant has evaporated, Juliet is arguably left even more embittered than at the beginning, and it is hard to feel convinced that any lasting guarantees have been established for Johnny's emotional security; except to the extent that the episode has prepared him for the recurrent likelihood of being discarded in favour of a new interest, or resented as an obstacle to its development – as when mother and child first stumbled upon the peasant together, and 'a biting chagrin burned in her breast, against the child, against the complication of frustration' (1928: 29).

In the 1925 'Sun', Lawrence transferred to the bright Mediterranean coastline many of the same preoccupations he was simultaneously exploring in the drizzling Derbyshire valleys of 'Glad Ghosts': preoccupations with the search for a home which would allow radically new forms of behaviour to take root; with wanting and not wanting children; with experimental crossings-over into other lives or cultures; with yearning for families, breaking with them, seeking substitutes outside the family for what the family had not provided. Lawrence was especially drawn at this time towards the idea of a family or a group which has allowed the neurosis of one of its members to organise or determine the way the rest of the family interacts with one another, so that when the neurosis is spontaneously or gradually removed or modified, everyone who has been affected by it is suddenly presented with a difficult search for a new way of living; this interest adds a fresh element to the relentless imagining of parallels and alternatives which already fills the texts produced at Spotorno. It was essentially the ruling idea of *The Virgin and the Gipsy*, a long story written immediately after 'Sun' and 'Glad Ghosts', which I would like to explore a little before discussing some of the ways in which the 1928 revisions of 'Sun' address the preoccupations of the Spotorno period.

*The Virgin and the Gipsy* owes much of its detail to what Frieda's daughters, Elsa and Barbara, who visited Spotorno that winter, told Lawrence about what their life was like at home with their father, Ernest Weekley, and his family. But he would already have been well primed to write the story by an incident the previous October, at his sister Ada's house in Ripley. Barbara wrote years later of how, when she was staying with some Nottingham friends of her father, she had been invited for a meal with the Lawrences:

> We had a pleasant meal at Ada's. It was suggested that I should spend the night.
> I telephoned my hostess, wife of a Nottingham professor. When she told her husband, he was very much alarmed. The idea of my spending a night under the same roof as Lawrence horrified him. Supposing he should happen to meet my father, who was in Nottingham too? Presently his wife telephoned, imploring me to go back to their house. I reluctantly agreed and then went to tell the others.
> Lawrence sprang to his feet, white with rage.
> "These mean, dirty little insults your mother has had to put up with all these years!" he spat out, gasping for breath.

I was dismayed, not knowing how to act. The others were silent, Ada looking a little scornful.[7]

By saying such a thing, Lawrence, wittingly or not, would have drawn the company's attention to Frieda's misery without entirely absolving Barbara of complicity in it, and would in a way have provoked as much as exposed a residual tension between the mother and the child – the idea of which seems to get under the skin of the subsequent story, while on the surface of it lies the question of who is to be regarded as 'mean' and 'dirty', unwashed, opportunistic gipsies, or the pious inhabitants of a rectory which was fully equipped with modern sanitation.

## 2

In Chapter 3 of *The Virgin and the Gipsy*, the sisters Lucille and Yvette, the latter being the 'virgin' of the title, have managed to get away for the day from that rectory, in Derbyshire, where they live with their father, Arthur Saywell, his sister, their Aunt Cissie, and their obese, blind, insidiously dominating Granny – their mother Cynthia having run off, twelve years earlier, with a 'young and penniless man'.[8] The girls and their friends are driving through the Peak District, on the trip which will end with their first meeting with the gipsy, and with having their fortunes told by his wife. They pass the park at Chatsworth, where the deer were 'nestling . . . under the oaks by the road':

> Yvette insisted on stopping and getting out to talk to them. The girls, in their Russian boots, tramped through the damp grass, while the deer watched them with big, unfrightened eyes. The hart trotted away mildly, holding back his head, because of the weight of the horns. But the doe, balancing her big ears, did not rise from under the tree, with her half-grown young ones, till the girls were almost in touch. Then she walked light-foot away, lifting her tail from her spotted flanks, while the young ones nimbly trotted.
> 
> 'Aren't they awfully dainty and nice!' cried Yvette. 'You'd wonder they could lie so cosily in this horrid wet grass.'
> 
> 'Well I suppose they've got to lie down *sometime*,' said Lucille. 'And it's *fairly* dry under the tree.' She looked at the crushed grass, where the deer had lain.

> Yvette went and put her hand down, to feel how it felt.
> 'Yes!' she said, doubtfully, 'I believe it's a bit warm.' (16–17)

Why should Yvette appear doubtful about the ground's being 'warm', when several animals have just been lying on it? Did she really intend to say 'dry', like her sister, but found the word 'warm' coming out as it were by mistake, because uppermost in her mind is the image of the doe and her young, nestling together, with the hart watching close by? The whole scene, down to the view of the great house beyond –

> 'I wonder where the Duke is now,' said Ella.
> 'Not here, wherever he is,' said Lucille. 'I expect he's abroad where the sun shines.' (17)

– seems to be stirring up difficult, barely expressible feelings in both sisters, about having been abandoned by their mother, who had been 'like a swift and dangerous sun in the home, forever coming and going' (5); about things which live on the move and only reluctantly pause for occasional rests. There is a vividly childlike, half-envious, half-resentful curiosity in Yvette's wish to 'feel how it felt', to cross momentarily into another world, where cosiness evidently means more than mere physical comfort, and where offspring could be protected carefully but without any excessive paranoia about the dangers facing them. As the girls drive on, across 'the roof of England', looking 'out over the far network of stone fences, under the sky, looking for the curves downward that indicated a drop to one of the underneath, hidden dales' (18–19), they seem to be instinctively searching for a softer, secret, feminised place, a haven always just out of view, beyond this fenced-in stoniness that has Granny's mark all over it (in this district, everything 'was stone, with a hardness that was almost poetic, it was so unrelenting' [9], while Granny, who is not a native of this country but seems to fit it perfectly, has a face 'like a mask that hid something stony, relentless' [15]): a landscape which resembles a 'naked . . . fist' (18), and which hints thereby at so much that the sisters would like to do, but which only the landscape seems able to express for them. Would Granny be the sole target of their unfulfilled wishes? Or is the vituperation heaped on Granny throughout the story so obviously disproportionate to any threat she actually poses as to signal the vicinity of other targets, obscured behind her looming bulk?

As was mentioned à propos of 'In Love', Lawrence came to believe that the lack of restriction on what the post-war generation were allowed to do was paradoxically draining the meaning from so much of what they did, inciting frustrations that could only find outlets in hyperbole and a vacuously emphatic style of speech.[9] Yvette, Lucille and their friends, 'had nothing really to rebel against, any of them. . . . The keys of their lives were in their own hands. And there they dangled inert' (16). This metaphor is allowed to develop when they meet the fortune-telling gipsy woman. Yvette's arm, which, like the keys of her life, had been merely 'dangling' (17) while she watched the deer, is now 'outstretched' (25), in a new access of purpose, as she 'strode and put something into the gipsy's hand' (25). This 'something' is the two pounds which she pilfered from Aunt Cissie's Window Fund; Yvette has discovered that there is, at last, something to rebel against, and her gesture seems to mark an impulsive transfer of allegiance from one system of values to another. But here as elsewhere in *The Virgin and the Gipsy*, the very neatness with which the symbolism falls into place only seems to point up the messy disorder of the story's real emotional content. The session in the caravan with the 'wolfish' gipsy woman may be awakening Yvette to new possibilities of female power ('There was a stooping, witch-like silence about [Yvette] as she emerged' [24]), sending her back into the world reborn, wolf-suckled. But when the gipsy woman talks with Lucille, there is something painfully discomfiting about the way she unerringly homes in on the girl's most intimate and deep-rooted anxieties, offering Lucille a cynical parody of the maternal soothing she has never enjoyed:

> 'You will marry in a few years – not now, but a few years – perhaps four – and you will not be rich, but you will have plenty – enough – and you will go away, a long journey.'
> 'With my husband, or without?' cried Lucille.
> 'With him – ' (22–3)

Comedy can never fully dispel the pathos at the centre of this. And when, at the end of the scene, Yvette suddenly hands over to the woman forty times the previously-agreed price for the fortune-telling, she too seems to be compressing together a number of half-conscious longings: on the one hand to reject the entire Saywell ethos, of penny-pinching and giving only to the more respectable charities, and on the other to be able to hear a voice like this woman's without having to pay for it, a longing which only the contemptuous abuse of someone else's money seems capable of articulating.

Perhaps one consequence of the mother's disappearance would be a tendency for the child to glamorise anyone who appeared to embody the lost attributes. Barbara Weekley remembered another incident which must have helped to prompt the writing of *The Virgin and the Gipsy*: an argument about her then fiancé, who was being vociferously criticised by Lawrence:

> I sat feeling woebegone during all this. To defend a weak position, I said:
> 'Well, he seems *stronger*, somehow, than I am.'
> It was a lie, and Lawrence looked mystified.
> '"Stronger?" I simply don't see it,' he remarked, 'unless it is in being outside the pale . . . alien to society. Maybe he is in that way.'[10]

Lawrence was clearly struck by this remark – which Barbara may of course have half-consciously designed to appeal to him. He transferred it directly to Yvette, who feels of the gipsy-woman's husband that 'of all the men she had ever seen, this one was the only one who was stronger than she was, in her own kind of strength, her own kind of understanding' (23). But Lawrence, not realising that Barbara was lying, also seems to have formed the idea that it was her family situation that had made her vulnerable to thinking like this, about someone who did not, in his view, remotely merit it; vulnerable because she lacked the kind of parental guidance that could perhaps have teased and challenged her into having second thoughts without leaving her feeling sullen and humiliated. With Barbara, he eagerly set out to supply the guidance himself: '"We shall have to laugh her out of this," he told Frieda. "Where is Barby's *instinct*?"'[11] But in the story which he built from the situation, guidance only becomes available in oblique or equivocal forms. After the 'ghastly, abnormal scene'

(26) with Aunt Cissie over the missing Window Fund money, Lucille says to Yvette:

> 'It's perfectly awful! But you never will think beforehand where your actions are going to land you! Fancy Aunt Cissie saying all those things to you! How *awful*! Whatever would Mamma have said, if she'd heard it?'
> When things went very wrong, they thought of their mother, and despised their father and all the low brood of the Saywells. (28)

It is comforting to think that there is someone out there who might still, one day, avenge their sufferings, or whose hauteur they can at least imitate to keep themselves going (of course, if Mamma had been present, she would not have 'heard it'; it could not have been said). At the same time, it is almost as if Lucille were imagining Mamma being *made* to hear it; even as if, in her attack on Yvette, Aunt Cissie had actually given voice to some of the things Lucille would like to have been able to say to Mamma, things latent in the mixture of protectiveness, *schadenfreude* and exasperated annoyance which her sister arouses in her. Each time the 'thought of their mother' encourages them to despise the Saywells, it can hardly help also recalling why they are being exposed to the Saywells in the first place: a recollection which may have a trace in it of the feeling they had as children, as children do, that they were themselves in some way to blame for their mother's departure – 'they decided that it was because their mother found them negligible' (3) – and that she may perhaps have thought that they had too much of the Saywells in them for her liking. Why else should *both* girls despise their father, at this point in the story?

All manner of painful emotions are at work in this text without always being openly addressed by it. This seems especially so in the confrontation between Yvette with her father over her friendship with the Eastwoods, a confrontation alive with everything the mother's absconding brought about. Primarily, of course, it brought about the reconstitution of the Saywell family, previously scattered and relatively innocuous, but now gathered into a fully charged unit of sanctimonious oppression. Granny, the Mater, has ensured her dominant position by cannily colluding in Arthur's idealisation of his ex-wife: 'It secured [Granny] against

Arthur's ever marrying again. She had him by his feeblest weakness, his skulking self-love' (5) – a weakness whose worst effects one imagines Cynthia could well have been able to curb, had she stayed. Aunt Cissie, having been unexpectedly thrust into a parental role, is given the chance, at her nieces' expense, to recycle some of the meanness of her own upbringing and to gain a little perverse recompense for it. Her whole life has been given up to the demands of her mother, and her attachment now to the cause of the Window Fund, tirelessly raising money to pay for a memorial to those who gave their lives in the war, seems to involve an all-consuming effort to sublimate her rage against the cult of self-sacrifice into which she allowed herself to be inveigled. Hence, when Yvette takes the money for her own use, violating so many sanctities at once, the savagery of Cissie's assault on her – 'You little hypocrite! You liar! You selfish beast! You greedy little beast!' (29) – suggests not only how envious she has become of someone who behaves as she secretly would like to, but that Yvette has prompted her, rather as Lucille was prompted, to say things she really wanted to be able to say to her own mother, and which are desperate to find a more acceptable outlet. All this accumulated household malevolence, always displaced on to the nearest available substitute, seems to be gathered in the climax of Arthur's theatrical tirade against Yvette: '"Say no more!" he said, in a low, hissing voice. "But I will kill you before you shall go the way of your mother"' (63).[12] It is here most of all that the scene appears haunted by what both father and daughter have lost; there might have been a mutually enriching love between them, in which her wayward impulsiveness could have been looked on affectionately and not seen merely as a threat, and at some level, beneath his hysterical and abusive raving, Arthur knows this. 'A numb, frozen loneliness came over her. For her, too, the meaning had gone out of everything' (63). The word 'too' just touches on the joint sadness which the main body of the text, in its eagerness to denounce him (he is called 'a rat', 'a slave', 'base-born'), seems loath to admit – except insofar as the denunciations themselves obscurely register some of the disturbance Yvette is suffering, and her need to find some form of protection from it.

To Arthur, the thought of the Eastwoods is irresistible, however many wounds it reopens: 'A young sponge going off with a woman older than himself, so that he can live on her money! The woman leaving her home and her children!' (61) As M. M. Lally has pointed out,[13] since Major Eastwood is 'five or six years younger' than his lover Mrs Fawcett, the same age-gap as the one between Lawrence and Frieda, it is Lawrence as well as Arthur who is imagining a parallel situation to his own, one in which Eastwood appears to enjoy a host of advantages which Lawrence himself conspicuously lacked in his entanglement with the Weekleys in 1912. This time, the eloping woman has plenty of private money, and the husband has agreed to allow the children, two teenagers, to live with her once she has married her lover; indeed, the husband, Simon Fawcett, appears not to be offering much resistance at all. When we read that Mrs Fawcett's 'honesty' may have been '*too* rational. Perhaps it partly explained the notorious unscrupulousness of the well-known Simon Fawcett' (51), it sounds as if Simon may have been quite relieved to see the back of her, while hinting also at serial mistreatments or infidelities on his part which would have virtually justified his wife's departure and left her lover feeling effectively beyond reproach. All the new couple have to trouble them is a little local ostracism which, if Lucille's comment is anything to go by, will pass as soon as the relationship is regularised: '"I should think, *when they're married*, it would be rather fun knowing them"' (55, emphasis in text). What Lawrence might have given for an outcome as convenient and painless as that! Lally is surely right to imply that the inclusion in the story of a marital breakdown which leaves all the parties to it apparently contented is likely to reflect a mixture of resentment and remorse on Lawrence's part over the turn things had actually taken in his life. At the same time, the Eastwoods' relationship itself appears strangely empty or bereft, almost to the point where the scandal surrounding them provides most of what holds them together, temporarily fuelling the 'sense of outraged justice' (54) on which Eastwood's feelings for Mrs Fawcett are based. In the eyes of Yvette, the Eastwoods' situation seems to embody all her yearnings: the adventure of new life, with a new father, a ready-made family, the sense of being openly at war with everyone else and thus eradicating most of the more difficult emotions. But as soon as she tries to enlist the Eastwoods' help with her own problems, difficult emotions promptly spring up again. The Eastwoods agree about the importance of love and desire, but the way they discuss it suggests that in their case the desire may be all on one side:

> 'But you don't know what love is?' cried the Jewess.
> 'No!' said Yvette. 'Do you?'
> 'I!' bawled the tiny Jewess. 'I! My goodness, don't I!' She looked with reflected gloom at Eastwood, who was smoking his pipe, the dimples of his disconnected amusement showing on his smooth, scrupulous face . . . 'I think,' said the Major, taking his pipe from his mouth, 'that desire is the most wonderful thing in life. Anybody who can really feel it, is a king, and I envy nobody else!' He put back his pipe.
> The Jewess looked at him stupefied.
> 'But Charles!' she cried. 'Every common low man in Halifax feels nothing else!'
> He again took his pipe from his mouth.
> 'That's merely appetite,' he said.
> And he put back his pipe. (58–60)

This reads as a really rather cruel sending-up of the parental advice-session with Barbara in which Lawrence was so keen to engage: the loud mother-figure half-fishing for compliments, half-struggling to understand; the father-figure's complacent pronouncements undercut by the comedy of the pipe; the residual doubt as to how much anyone making such a speech as Eastwood's might actually be capable of feeling. Like Juliet in 'Sun', who 'would take no thought for the morrow' (1928: 28), Eastwood shows no interest in planning forwards: '"I'm perfectly all right today, and I shall be all right tomorrow . . . Why shouldn't my future be continuous todays and tomorrows?"' (58). As one of the 'resurrected men', who was 'buried for twenty hours under snow' (60) during the war, rescued only by chance, Eastwood now prefers to live serendipitously, refusing to fasten himself with care, as Lawrence had put it earlier in 1925 in the unfinished 'The Flying-Fish';[14] but this could equally well indicate that there is nothing inside him with which to make commitments, that he could abandon the relationship as easily as he began it (especially, perhaps, if Mrs Fawcett's children were to strain his equanimity when they came to live with them), and that maybe 'Life's awful!' (60), as Yvette opines in a moment of vacancy, because the man you fall in love with may turn out to have a roving eye, and a fundamental indifference to you, half-disguised under the habits of affection.

Julian Moynahan, in *The Deed of Life*, saw Eastwood entirely positively, as someone whose example can help point Yvette in the right direction; a 'resurrection of Gerald Crich':

> And the destined accident of his death has been reimagined to allow the possibility of a second life beyond the frozen wasteland of the snow valley. . . . If a Gerald can be reborn to wholesome desire we begin to imagine other potential reconciliations. . . . In the Lawrence world grace usually does not, but always may abound. Strictly speaking, *anyone* may come back to life.[15]

But in 'the Lawrence world', talking about desire is decidedly not the same as experiencing it; and talking suggestively about it to an attractive young girl, while the woman who has left her home for you sits listening, anxiously trying to work out exactly what you might mean, is not something that would invariably be thought 'wholesome'. Isn't Eastwood also still 'the fair [man] who means bad' luck, if we can trust Yvette's report to Lucille of the gipsy woman's prediction (25)? There is a persistent feeling in the text that Arthur's judgement of Eastwood, however churlish, might not be entirely wrong, and Yvette is sufficiently Arthur's daughter to have already been thinking along similar lines:

> 'Doesn't every man have to carve out a career? – like some huge goose with gravy?' She gazed with odd naiveté into his eyes.
> 'I'm perfectly all right today, and I shall be all right tomorrow,' he said, with a cold, decided look. 'Why shouldn't my future be continuous todays and tomorrows?'
> He looked at her with unmoved searching.
> 'Quite!' she said. 'I hate jobs, and all that side of life.' But she was thinking of the Jewess's money. (58)

It is curious how like her father Yvette sounds, as if the meeting with this couple has touched a hidden trigger; the bantering geniality of her crack about the goose, and the instinctive covering of her tracks when challenged. Later, when she has been banned from seeing the

Eastwoods, thinking about them helps to release in her the unmistakable accents of Arthur at his most histrionically self-pitying:

> After all, what was the revolt of the little Jewess, compared to Granny and the Saywell bunch! A husband was never more than a semi-casual thing! But a family! – an awful, smelly family that would never disperse, stuck half dead round the base of a fungoid old woman! How was one to cope with that? (66)

The viciousness of Yvette's outburst may indicate how being cooped up with the Saywells for so long is causing her increasingly to resemble them, and thus leaving her in ever greater need of rescue. But one could also suggest that, since her mother's accents are as clearly audible as her father's here – in the remark about 'semi-casual', for instance, which could either be endorsing her mother's presumed attitude or sarcastically indicting it – it is as though the daughter's voice, at its peak of angry disappointment with both parents, were still trying to effect an imaginary reconciliation of them, and were still filled with a yearning to belong which reverberates beneath all the dismissive contempt she expresses towards alien groups and allegiances. This yearning coloured her desire for the gipsy from the outset:

> Her soul had the half painful, half easing knack of leaving her, and straying away to some place, to somebody that had caught her imagination. Some days she would be at the Framleys', even though she did not go near them. Some days, she was all the time in spirit with the Eastwoods. And today it was the gipsies. She was up at their encampment in the quarry. She saw the man hammering his copper, lifting his head to look at the road; and the children playing in the horse-shelter: and the women, the gipsy's wife and the strong, elderly woman, coming home with their packs, along with the elderly man. For this afternoon, she felt intensely that *that* was home for her. . . . It was part of her nature, to get these fits of yearning for some place she knew; to be in a certain place; with somebody who meant home to her. This afternoon it was the gipsy camp. And the man in the green jersey made it home to her. Just to be where he was, that was to be at home. The caravans, the brats, the other women: everything was natural to her, her home, as if she had been born there. (70–1)

The 'home' she imagines would be one in which security and freedom were perfectly balanced: security and freedom which had been the gifts to her of each of her parents in turn, but never together. Yvette's is a version of the dream shared by many characters in Lawrence's fiction, the dream of finding a real community of support, usually through crossing the class or ethnic or racial border that divides you from the place you think is truly your own. But her dream seems to have an extra level of pathos and naiveté to it, in her assumption that sexual desire would not itself be a source of conflict (her phrase 'the other women' points to the very tensions which she imagines being extinguished), and indeed the whole erotic question between herself and the gipsy seems to have been absorbed by the essentially filial emotions which saturate the images she dwells on.

Whether Yvette's sexual desire is ever actually consummated is a subject of much debate among Lawrence's readers. Is she still a virgin at the end of the story? Some commentators, like Carol Siegel and M. Elizabeth Sargent, insist she is; they both read the story as a mythic quest for what Siegel calls 'the Mother / life-source'. For Siegel, 'the physical consummation Yvette experiences with the gypsy man is not sexual intercourse but a literal sharing of vital warmth';[16] for Sargent, 'it seems crucial to the work of this tale that we resist the assumption that the gypsy's salvation and confirmation (Christian terminology intentional) of Yvette in the final chapter (sic) involves lovemaking and orgasm'.[17] David Ellis, on the other hand, sees the dénouement paralleling the one in 'Glad Ghosts', where a single night's sexual contact is both a necessary and a sufficient induction into new life,[18] while for John Worthen, *The Virgin and the Gipsy* recalls earlier works by Lawrence in which 'sexual contact goes before, behind, between the barriers of class'.[19] It seems to me that the scene is infused with too much mischievous comedy for any of the symbolic readings to be entirely watertight – all the shuddering and shivering, the towels so conveniently to hand after all the earlier textual rage against washbasins, and the gipsy's closing letter, with its covert invitation to have another go at what the two of them may or may not have managed: 'I hope I see you again one day, maybe at Tideswell cattle fair. . . . I come that day to say good-bye! and I never said it, well, the water give no time, but I live in hopes' (81). Perhaps Frieda's idea that the story's title should have been something like 'Granny Gone' was a recognition that the drowning of Granny was the only unambiguous feature of the climax.[20] But unlike the ending of 'Glad Ghosts', which for all its implicit reservations did give an essentially positive view of life after the removal of the obstacle, it is not at all clear at the end of *The Virgin and the Gipsy* what form the future might take. Could the Saywell family be reconstructed again, towards something closer to the image of Yvette's desires, now that she has had the vitalising contact with an outsider, and Arthur and Cissie have been suddenly and spectacularly freed from their mother's spell? Julian Moynahan thought so:

> Yvette reposes at the end in the bosom of her family. With Granny gone she and Lucille may well be able to break up and reform the patterns of Saywell family life from a position inside.[21]

Or has nothing really changed, is the old blend of sanctimony and furtiveness set to continue, until the girls can finally make the complete escape which the fortune-teller promised? When Yvette is rescued, 'even Aunt Cissie cried out among her tears: "Let the old be taken and the young spared! Oh, I *can't* cry for the Mater, now Yvette is spared!"' (80). This might support Moynahan's optimistic view that the cycle of family bitterness which Cissie has both suffered and helped to propagate could at last be broken. Or it might, as Judith Ruderman suggested,[22] be another of Cissie's pious protestations, disguising with a show of selfless decency her hatred for the dead woman – even, perhaps, her conflicting feelings over her niece's survival; her words seem to be lamenting her own life in their plea for a just outcome from disaster. Meanwhile, Arthur 'in torment watched his tall, slender daughter slowly stepping backwards down the sagging ladder' (80), the return to him, in the midst of trauma, of what he thought he had lost forever; a mildly erotic vision of a fresh start, all legs and wet hair, which would surely be stirring in him thoughts of Cynthia, of what might have been if he had been released from his mother earlier, of all that cannot now be rescued from the wreckage. And in the midst of the 'contradictory feelings' (79) that lie between him and Yvette, he cannot know that for her this descent down the ladder is a replay of her descent down the steps of the gipsy's caravan, with the same determination never to reveal what passed inside; she has gone too far ever fully to come back. The story seems to walk away from the complications it has set up; everything is left suspended, once the narrative has finished with Yvette's journey towards an understanding of the value of desire and of the reasons why her mother acted as she did. But inside this narrative is always the nagging counter-movement of another one, about the sense of the cost of her mother's doing it, which seems somehow alive in the extraordinary vindictive gloating over the destruction of Granny in the avenging flood: the fantasy of compressing everything that was wrong into one boil and lancing it; the fantasy of the clean break which could never actually occur, a fantasy finessing away all the real lingering damage.

## 3

In 'Sun', Juliet comes to feel an intense desire for a peasant working on the neighbouring estate (the man's name, unlike Joe Boswell's, is never revealed). As the story was originally written, her desire was expressed like this:

> 'And Juliet had thought: Why shouldn't I meet this man for an hour, and bear his child? Why should I have to identify my life with a man's life? Why not meet him for an hour, as long as the desire lasts, and no more?' (1925: 290)

Something has stirred her to want to have his child, rather than just to have sex with him; and no sooner has she had this feeling than she seems to want to protect herself from it, to imagine herself no longer feeling it, having moved beyond it, into a new order of existence where conventionally binding commitments would no longer impinge on her. Watching the man, she appears to sense that *he*, childless, wanted a child: 'One day, when a group of peasants sat under a tree, she had seen him dancing quick and gay with a child, his wife watching darkly' (1925: 290). Like the *padrone* in the lemon gardens, in *Twilight in Italy*, the peasant seems to need to become a father in order to feel himself fulfilled,[23] and Juliet would have already understood that the flow of vitality she sees in the man is yearning towards her, with her proven capacity to bear children; the 1928 text made this point more explicit by adding a new, mildly comical scene in which the peasant first sees Juliet naked when she has Johnny alongside her. But something about the man in his community setting – the refreshment in the shade, the families drawing together, the dancing, the hints of operatic passions and jealousies – seems to touch her in ways she wants to fend off or hurry past: on the one hand a nostalgia for belonging, as with Yvette's dream of the gipsy camp, on the other a fear of being engulfed, an instant, disillusioned awareness of the tensions of intimacy which Yvette had blithely discounted. It is a mixture of envy and alarm which prompts Juliet to her vision of a picaresque future, a vision not dissimilar to Eastwood's, in which the only attachments she has will be those she has freely chosen, and can discard at will.

If she sees, even this fleetingly, how sexual impulses might radically reshape the world, rather than simply reconnecting her with the world as it is, the story begins to anticipate the mood of *Lady Chatterley's Lover*, in which, as David Ayers puts it, 'the moment of passionate experience is also the moment in which as yet unrealised human possibilities can be intuited ... in which a future social dispensation can be felt, in which a different humanity emerges'.[24] The commitment to this in 'Sun' is more tentative, not yet ready to step too far away from 'old world' attitudes. Juliet's euphoric notion of a desire only lasting for an hour seems to derive, not just from her imagining a future full of unrestricted onward movement, but from her half-conscious realisation that an hour at a time is the most that the peasant would be allowed off work; the very form of her thinking threatens to re-establish the class differences which the sex itself would temporarily dispel. But what Juliet mainly seems to want is to have the new child – I think she would expect it to be a boy – entirely to herself, and to raise it from scratch as a designer sun-child, born of the 'procreative sun-bath' which the peasant would be to her (1925: 291). This child would be 'sunned right through' (1925: 280), in the way that Johnny, for all his mother's efforts, could never be, having begun with too many disadvantages. Juliet's position would then to an extent resemble that of Lou Carrington at the end of *St Mawr*, isolating herself from society partly in order to sustain an almost priestessly belief in a true masculinity, one which none of the men she knew had ever really managed to exhibit[25] – except that Juliet, instead of waiting for such masculinity to return unaided, would create it herself, impregnating herself with the best available seed and nurturing the child in new and controlled conditions.

Lawrence seemed to be glancing back at this idea during his 1928 revisions, by introducing a quite complicated mythological reference into the text's closing lines: Juliet

> was bound to the vast, fixed wheel of circumstance, and there was no Perseus in the universe, to cut the bonds. (1928: 38)

Juliet is seen here as a doomed Andromeda, at the mercy of the sea-monster which Maurice seems to have become, hunting her down with his 'little, frantic penis' (38); and the reason there is no Perseus to rescue her is that neither she nor anyone else has yet succeeded in giving birth to one, in becoming the new Danaë who could conceive a new Perseus from the procreative sun-bath, the divine shower of gold, and raise him to be the liberator of the next generation.

I say 'Lawrence seemed to be glancing back', because in the course of his revisions he dropped the line 'Why should I have to identify my life with a man's life?', and the brief utopian gleam of single motherhood was extinguished. In addition, in place of the 1925 sentence:

> And Juliet had thought: Why shouldn't I meet this man for an hour, and bear his child?

he now wrote:

> And Juliet thought: Why shouldn't I go to him! Why shouldn't I bear his child? (1928: 37)

As with the shift from 'was fond of his Daddy', to 'had been fond . . . ', the change of tense from 'had thought' to 'thought' is doing a fair amount of work. In the 1925 text, we do not learn of the peasant's existence until the closing scene of the story. When Juliet sits down to lunch with Maurice on the terrace, and catches sight of the other man with his wife across the gully, the narrative breaks off to interpose a retrospective account of the meetings Juliet had had with the peasant while she was sunning herself in the lemon groves – all of which, including the thought of going to him and bearing his child, had taken place well before Maurice's unexpected arrival. But in the revised text, she has that thought for the first time now, while actually sitting next to Maurice, thinking it as it were in reaction to Maurice's return to her, and to the bitterness she feels at the closing-in of her world. Not only does the 1928 text include much more detail about the peasant, but the narrative sequence is completely reordered, so that we are introduced to him much earlier in the story. Because we have already seen the peasant's effect on Juliet, and hers on him, by the time of Maurice's arrival, the remainder of the 1928 'Sun' is now dominated by the contrast she is silently drawing between the two men; and while the wording of her exchanges with Maurice is left largely untouched, the sub-conversation is heavily modified. The most challenging of her questions, 'And I can do anything I like?', which seemed in the 1925 story to be a rather childish appeal for her holiday to be allowed to continue, now sounds like an attempt to extort tacit permission to have an affair; and since Maurice's reunion with Johnny now occurs almost immediately after Juliet has had her glimpse of the peasant dancing with a child, her abrupt butting in – '"What are you going to do about it, Maurice?"' – seems to go beyond mere attention-seeking to express an acid contempt for her husband's attempts to be fatherly. When she demanded, in the 1925 story, that Maurice immediately reorganise all his business plans in the light of the new situation, it largely reflected her concern not to have her sunbathing rituals interrupted by mundane distractions. Now her demand seems driven more by frustration at Maurice's failure to respond to her physically (in the 1928 version he only starts talking to Johnny at all to cover his embarrassment at Juliet's nakedness), given the difficulty she is having in controlling her indiscriminate craving for sex with anyone who happened to present himself at that moment: 'Inside her, the lotus of her womb was wide open . . . she thrilled helplessly: a man was coming' (1928: 32). Her wish to have the peasant's child seems to be even more deeply expressive than in the 1925 version of her disaffection with everything she already has.

At the same time, in her more peevish way of putting it – 'Why shouldn't I! . . . Why shouldn't I?' – is an awareness that it has all come too late, that nothing of the sort is ever really likely to happen; she still dreams about the immediate gratification – sex with the peasant 'would be just a bath of warm, powerful life – then separating and forgetting' (1928: 37) – but the dream no longer includes that fragile inkling of a new order, 'a new way of life' (1925: 283) to which desire might lead her. There had been a certain grudging serenity about the close of the 1925 text, in the acceptance that Maurice 'was a man, too, he faced the world and was not entirely quenched in his male courage' (1925: 291), and in Juliet's resigning herself to her medium-term prospects: 'Nevertheless, her next child would be Maurice's. The fatal chain of continuity would cause it' (291). It was as if the fantasy-alternative were still vestigially alive in her, in the careful formulation 'next child', leaving the door a little open, allowing herself to believe that her real desire was being deferred rather than relinquished; to believe that life with Maurice was still provisional, that a husband was only 'a semi-casual thing', as Yvette had phrased it, and that she could in the interim call upon fantasy to help make life bearable. But in the revised ending Juliet is left only with rage and victimhood – 'she was not free enough ... so much was against her. ... She could not help it' (1928: 38) – with not even a self-deluding hope that anything new might be able to happen; with so profound a sense of adverse fate, that her very taking it for granted that she would produce another child, that even a single sexual contact would automatically make her pregnant, seems less a pledge to the unknown future than a tribute to the sense of the inexorable, on which so much in the story appears to converge, and which many of the revisions seem to have been designed to intensify.

The revisions themselves were made in quite curious circumstances. Lawrence had evidently been happy enough with the 1925 'Sun' to have sent it off to Nancy Pearn, who handled his work at his agent's (Curtis Brown), and to have seen it published in the Autumn 1926 number of *New Coterie*. But an opportunity unexpectedly arose to reconsider it, early in 1928, when Harry Crosby, a wealthy expatriate American bohemian and avid sun-worshipper, asked to buy some of Lawrence's manuscripts, sending $100 in gold coins as an advance payment. The manuscript of 'Sun', which was clearly one of those that Crosby most desired to have, had gone missing, and the only copy to hand was the printed text in *New Coterie*. Nancy Pearn suggested to Lawrence that he might, without straining his conscience too far, simply transcribe the magazine text in his own handwriting and pass this off to Crosby as the original manuscript. Lawrence agreed to do this, and then went much further; he began by making a careful copy (the first page of the 1928 text is virtually identical to the *New Coterie* version), but before long he was embarking on major alterations to the story, and ended up having lengthened it by a good quarter. He then sent the new manuscript to Crosby with a covering letter, carefully worded to allow it to be inferred that the enclosed text was in fact the original, and that what had been published in *New Coterie* had only been a shorter, censored form of it:

> *Sun* is the final MS and I wish the story had been printed as it stands there, really complete. One day, when the public is more educated, I shall have the story printed whole, as it is in this MS.[26]

Crosby took the hint and offered to publish the 'really complete' manuscript himself, through his Paris-based Black Sun Press (sending as a further mark of his appreciation three more gold coins and an antique snuffbox, much to Lawrence's embarrassment).[27] But this letter would not be the only occasion on which Lawrence would offer a tactically advantageous rather than a strictly accurate comment about the relationship between the two versions of the story. His letter that August to Martin Secker, who had just republished the *New Coterie* version of 'Sun' in the collection *The Woman Who Rode Away and Other Stories*, was extremely economical with the truth:

> A friend in Paris, Harry Crosby, wants to do a little edition of the short story *Sun* . . . He wants to do it because he bought the MS. from me, and found the printed version so much expurgated, he wants to print it whole.[28]

Subsequently, in the spring of 1929, trying to put a stop to the pirating of Crosby's edition in America, Lawrence maintained that the original copyright of 'Sun' should still apply, as the Crosby text was 'only slightly different', or even 'only very slightly different', from the one published in *The Woman Who Rode Away*.[29]

All these remarks were motivated by expediency, and one would hesitate to use them as evidence of what Lawrence really thought of the two versions. Nonetheless, the implication is that he wanted the earlier text to be regarded as essentially the same as the later text, only with a handful of frank passages having been left out. This would be disingenuous to say the least, since in reality his 1928 revisions conducted a near-systematic suppression of elements in the original story that had pointed in directions he no longer wished to follow. As with the final version of *Lady Chatterley's Lover*, which he had completed a few months earlier, no sooner had the chance to publish privately allowed Lawrence to circumvent the official censor, than he started to act as his own censor, ruthlessly cutting out of the earlier form of the work whatever failed to fit his current mood. He had, for example, originally described the sun's influence on Juliet like this:

> She was becoming aware that an activity was rousing in her, an activity which would carry her into a new way of life. (1925: 283)

The phrase 'A new way of life' opens a prospect of unbounded adventure, an exhilarating step into the unknown. But the revised text has: 'an activity which would bring another self awake in her. . . . The new rousing would mean a new contact' (1928: 27). The prospect seems to be reduced merely to a sexual adventure, with the word 'new' now appearing to mean 'the most recent in a predictable series'. The exploratory impulse of the first text – 'the desire sprang secretly in her, to go naked in the sun' (1925: 277) – is again checked in the second: 'the desire sprang secretly in her, to be naked to the sun' (1928: 20). 'To be naked to the sun': one now strips oneself down not to create oneself anew, but to enact a ritualised offering of oneself as one already fundamentally is. In that tiny verbal shift Lawrence seems to have re-imagined what had been a scene of Becoming as a scene of Being; Juliet is suddenly glimpsed as she might appear in what Linda Ruth Williams has described as an 'epiphanal pose', a moment when a figure is seen 'complete' in its 'metaphysical landscape' – Mellors at the washing-bowl in *Lady Chatterley's Lover* is one of Williams's examples, or Don Ramón drinking his tea in *The Plumed Serpent* – an indelible vision in which the essence of Being is spontaneously revealed.[30] The 1928 text takes what originally appeared to be unpremeditated expressions of Juliet's new sense of freedom, and reconfigures them as gestures of worship and submissive acknowledgement, gestures whose meanings are no longer self-generated but which conform to precedent; so that where, for example, Juliet had encouraged Johnny to throw off his inhibitions – 'She wished she could make him come forth, break out in a gesture of recklessness and salutation' (1925: 281), the new version has: 'She wished she could make him come forth, break out in a gesture of recklessness, a salutation to the sun'

(1928: 25), as if breaking out were no longer truly reckless, going where it likes, but were one of the pre-specified responses in a liturgy she is trying to make him learn.

The 1928 descriptions of the sun's effect on Juliet's body also take care to emphasise her passive status. In the original text, the 'connection' between Juliet and the sun had activated a latent power of her own:

> By some mysterious power inside her, deeper than her known consciousness and will, she was put into connection with the sun, and the stream flowed of itself, from her womb. (1925: 282)

The new text has

> By some mysterious will inside her, deeper than her known consciousness and her known will, she was put into connection with the sun, and the stream of the sun flowed through her, round her womb. (1928: 26)

The stream was in her, and her womb was the source of it; now the source is outside, and the stream flows in a different direction. Where the earlier text had 'Now she was vague, but she had a power beyond herself' (1925: 282), the later one gives us 'Now she was vague, in the spell of a power beyond herself' (1928: 26), again removing what little marks of agency or possession Juliet had been allowed. In 1925, 'the true Juliet was this dark flow from her deep body to the sun' (282); the sense here was of a movement upwards and outwards, liberating something previously repressed. In 1928, however,

> The true Juliet lived in the dark flow of the sun within her deep body, like a river of dark rays circling, circling dark and violet round the sweet, shut bud of her womb. (26)

The sun alone now does the flowing; the 'true Juliet' is not the flow, but something held stationary in the other's flow – as if fluidity itself, by convention the mark of the feminine, were being reassigned to the masculine force working upon her (she routinely thinks of the sun as 'he'). Everything of consequence is now being done to Juliet rather than by her; and if the earlier text had intermittently implied that the reawakening of her sexuality might be spurring her towards a new self-sufficiency and independence, the revised text presents her sexuality precisely as an obstacle to that independence, a constant reminder of her incompleteness and subjection. She is confined within the measures of a prolonged fertility ritual, and even her renewed delight in the colours, textures and creativity of nature now seems merely a by-product of her womb's helpless thirst for 'man-dew' (1928: 37).

A good deal of Juliet's rage at the end of the 1928 version derived from her recognition that what she imagined to have been working solely for her benefit was simultaneously working for someone else's, with the sun apparently intent upon re-cementing the family unit rather than dissolving it further. The verbal exchanges between Juliet and Maurice are still tense and edgy, but the sun's influence seems to have dispelled the debilitating physical effect each partner used to have on the other: 'at the caressive sound of his voice, in spite of her, her womb-flower began to open and thrill its petals' (1928: 35). The doctors in New York may have guessed that something like this might happen, since their original instruction to Maurice, '"Take her away, into the sun"' (1928: 19), could imply not only that the husband's companionship would be part of the cure (Maurice, of course, initially *sends* her away), but that the husband might also be in need of some similar treatment. The 1925 text had not pursued this latter idea very far, but when Maurice sees his wife in the sun in the 1928 version he experiences an alarming eruption of sensations himself, so much at odds with his normal timorous reserve as to draw renewed attention to how much the latter may have been contributing to Juliet's debility:

> He felt, in his far-off depths, the desire stirring in him for the limbs and sunwrapped flesh of the woman.... Strange thrills shot through his loins and his legs. He was terrified, and he felt he might give a wild whoop of triumph, and jump towards that woman of tanned flesh. (1928: 33)

It never occurs to Maurice that he himself might bear some responsibility for his wife's malaise; he puts it down to a kind of post-natal depression, an occupational hazard of being female, and nothing to do with him. He can sound both sympathetic and mildly condescending about it:

> He was thinking visionarily of her in the New York flat, pale, silent, oppressing him terribly ... her silent, awful hostility after the baby was born had frightened him deeply. Because, he had realised that she could not help it. Women were like that. Their feelings took a reverse direction, even against their own selves, and it was awful – devastating. (1928: 35)

Post-natal depression is sometimes thought to be a registration of the new mother's unrecognised grief over the loss of her former self, the self she had before she gave birth, and Maurice does at least seem to be trying his best to appreciate Juliet's psychic resistance to so radical a change as becoming a mother brings about. While Hester, in 'The Rocking-Horse Winner', felt spasms of guilt at not being able really to love her children, Juliet's exhausting mood-swings, before she began her sun-cure, between anxiety and irritability towards Johnny, seemed to express a different sense of failure – for Lawrence perhaps a more specifically American sense – of having given birth to something imperfect, a cross to bear which marks her out, so that every moment became a barely disguised plea to have her old life back: 'Even if his nose were running, it had been repulsive and a goad in her vitals, as if she must say to herself: Look at the thing you brought forth!' (1928: 22). There was a small but striking exchange early on between Juliet and her own mother:

> 'You know, Juliet, the doctor told you to lie in the sun, without your clothes. Why don't you?' said her mother.
> 'When I am fit to do so, I will. Do you want to kill me?' Juliet flew at her.
> 'To kill you, no! Only to do you good.'
> 'For God's sake, leave off wanting to do me good.'
> The mother at last was so hurt and incensed, she departed. (1928: 20; 1925: 276)

'"Do you want to kill me?"' – is this just exasperated hyperbole, or a half-conscious recognition of the devitalising effect of an intrusive will-to-care, which Juliet has absorbed from her mother and has been inflicting in turn on her own child, and which seems to harbour so much masked hostility and so many dreams of wrenching oneself free? If a breach with her mother is a prerequisite of Juliet's being 'fit' to receive the healing which the sun can offer, she seems rather to resemble the inhibited, frigid 'Helen' in Julia Kristeva's study of depression, *Black Sun*; a woman for whom the intrusive mother was experienced as a kind of blockage in the body which the ideal lover would clear away. Kristeva's account of Helen's case could almost be a commentary on the role of the sun in Juliet's: 'The melancholy object blocking the psychic and bodily interior [must] literally be liquefied. Who is capable of doing it? An imagined partner able to dissolve the mother imprisoned within myself by giving me what she could and above all what she could not give me . . . a new life.'[31]

Such an all-fulfilling partner, who would make up for everything one felt always to have been missing, would be the narcissist's ideal object, and one of the stories being told in 'Sun' is of the course of a narcissistic pattern of behaviour arising from an initial state of depression. Juliet displays many of the symptoms which clinical accounts of narcissism frequently describe: fascinated self-regard – '"What a wild cat I am, really!" she said to herself . . . "I am another being," she said to herself, as she looked at her red-gold breasts and thighs' (1928: 26–7); feelings of grandiosity – 'though [the sun] shone on all the world, when she lay unclothed he focussed on her' (1928: 23); a hunger for admiration coupled with a certain contempt for those she manipulates into providing it. There is an interesting ambivalence in the story about these displays. Sometimes they appear to be signs of Juliet's gradual emergence from her depression, of her passing through a necessary period of languid withdrawal before successfully coming back to the world; at other times they seem more like defences confirming how strongly the depression still has hold of her. Indeed, the two versions of the story could almost be said to have anticipated the ongoing dispute in modern psychoanalytic circles as to how narcissism should most effectively be treated. The followers of Heinz Kohut maintain that therapy should indeed involve a 're-mothering' of the kind Kristeva's patient was searching for, and that the analyst should seek to create conditions for the patient which mimic 'those which earlier in life would have allowed healthy development to occur';[32] in the 1925 story the accent was on how the sun seemed to be soothing Juliet's troubles, encouraging her exhibitionistic performances, and gently conducting her towards at least a modicum of new tolerance for the realities she had to face. But at the close of the 1928 version, the stress falls so much more heavily on anger than on serenity as to suggest that any such serenity, far from representing the patient's maturity and adjustment, would indicate that the therapeutic work had neither properly challenged her, nor addressed the rage and resentment at the root of her condition – the essence of Otto Kernberg's argument against Kohut, that 're-mothering' merely reproduces the narcissism it claims to cure.[33] Whereas before, the imagery had evoked a beguilingly gentle sympathy between Nature and Juliet's mood:

> She looked down at him, her alert breasts lifted with a sigh, as if a breeze of impatience shook them (1925: 287).

– the mood now comes entirely from within:

> She looked down at him, her alert breasts lifted with a sigh, as if she would impatiently shake the cold shadow of sunlessness off her (1928:34).

In bringing her anger more deliberately forward, in a sense compelling her to confront it (rather as happens for Ciss, sunbathing in 'The Lovely Lady'), the 1928 sun-as-therapist is not soothing Juliet, not offering her, through transference, an ideal version of the narcissistic relationships she already has. It seems instead to be saying to her: whatever you take to have been at fault, your mother, your husband, your child, or the whole condition of Western life, therapy can never right all the wrongs, or substitute for what has been missing; at best it can send you back to the world with a clearer awareness of what the wrongs are, wrongs which are unlikely to change or submit to your desire, and to which a managed rather than a repressed form of anger may well be the most appropriate response.

## 4

While beginning work on 'Sun', in November 1925, Lawrence wrote, in the short essay 'Europe versus America': 'It's a relief to be by the Mediterranean, and gradually let the tight coils inside oneself come slack.'[34] The same month, in a letter to Blanche Knopf: 'The sun shines, the eternal Mediterranean is blue and young . . . the last leaves are falling from the vines in the garden . . . we eat fried chicken and pasta and smell rosemary and basalica in the cooking once more'.[35] There is an elegiac note within the joy of returning; 'Sun' has some similar half-bright, half-mournful descriptions of homely and familiar things, a kind of pathos of welcome that seems to fold the words into iambic rhythms: 'The thin little wild crocuses came up mauve and striped, the wild narcissi hung their winter stars' (1925: 279). So many dreams of recovery and health are invested in the warmth of this landscape, as if it could lend those who lived in it some of its immunity:

> Strange, the vivid wildness of the old places of civilisation, a wildness that is not gaunt. (1925: 285)

Not 'gaunt': not desolate, grim-faced, run to seed; but mysteriously self-repairing. Does Lawrence's arresting phrase have a memory in it of his own face in the mirror, during the worst strains of his illness in Mexico in the early spring of that year, 1925? It is striking, at any rate, that he should have wanted to replace this line, in 1928, with an altogether blander juxtaposition of what endures with what passes away:

> Strange, the vivid wildness of the old classic places, that have known men so long. (1928: 31)

The opening line of the story – '"Take her away, into the sun," the doctors said' (1925: 275; 1928: 19) – looks back to the moment when the consultant from the American hospital in Mexico City told Frieda that, because Lawrence clearly had tuberculosis, she must 'take him to the ranch; it's his only chance'.[36] Lawrence put a less dramatic version of this message into a series of letters on 11 March, 1925: 'the doctor says . . . I must . . . stay in the sun, either here, or go to the ranch'.[37] It is characteristically defiant of him to have turned so intimate and desolate a memory to fresh uses in fiction; it constitutes a particularly striking instance of the openness, in all the Spotorno writing, to the different ways in which an event might develop, the fascination with parallels and surrogates. The authority of the doctor's pronouncement sets all manner of disordered energies – hopes, fears, surmises – into clear form; it marks the moment when an agent becomes a patient, exactly the critical turning-point of many of the fairy tales whose motifs Lawrence adapted in his late stories, where so often a character's fate, for good or ill, is suddenly to discover the hidden, determining processes at work within the life he or she believed they were living randomly. And beneath its pointedly lyrical accounts of reawakening, 'Sun', more especially the later version, evokes with great vividness what it can be like to feel one's body in the grip of an unremitting power, when particular organs seem to be working by themselves, or when sensations one thought had been safely stowed away rise up again unmistakably, with all the risks of hectic disturbance for those who have tried to suppress everything volatile and accustom themselves to a régime of caution. There is a certain wry sympathy here – unusual in Lawrence, and against the grain of everything he normally preached – for the mind's hopeless, rearguard struggle against the implacable demands of the body; rather as in *Lady Chatterley's Lover*, when Mellors, with his own history of respiratory trouble, says rather balefully, after his first sexual contact with Connie: "I thought I'd done with it all. Now I've begun again . . . if I've got to be broken open again, I have –".[38]

'Sun' also drew on another of Lawrence's more painful memories:

> The ship ebbed on between the lights, the Hudson seemed interminable. But at last they were round the bend, and there was the poor harvest of lights at the Battery. Liberty flung up her torch in a tantrum. There was the wash of the sea. (1925: 276; 1928: 20)[39]

In August 1923 Lawrence had written to Middleton Murry, from New York,

> At the moment this so-called white civilisation makes me sicker than ever. I feel nothing but recoil from it. Now I've reached the Atlantic, and see Liberty clenching her fist in the harbour, I only want to go west, to the mountains and desert again.[40]

Lawrence then had been watching his own wife embark for Europe, with the statue of Liberty looking on – the time when he and Frieda, who had badly wanted to see her children again, came as close to parting for good as they ever did (and in her husband's absence, Frieda had an intense intimacy with Murry himself in the autumn of 1923). What would have been a strained and unhappy shipboard parting was re-imagined, at the beginning of 'Sun', as a series of sentimental noises on the part of a couple who are more or less openly glad to be rid of each other. As for the subsequent reunion, Lawrence must to some extent have been ironically identifying with the satirised husband's uneasiness on finding his wife so changed, and the habits of their relationship so challenged; with his less-than-triumphant seeing-off of the rival, and his ignorance of what has been happening while he was away.[41] As if to redress this a little, 'Sun' also has in it a number of reminiscences of Verga's story 'Across the Sea' ('Di là dal Mare'), which Lawrence translated while *en route* to Australia in 1922: the heroine leaning on the ship's rail, brooding on mysteries; the ominous rhythm of the piston-engines; the excited nostalgia for the Sicilian coastline; and the dogged figure of the husband, who cannot finally be circumvented, whose shadow falls over the lovers' romantic interludes and casts an ultimately fatal chill on them. The sight of Maurice on the quay, receding into anonymity, seemed to announce the beginning of Juliet's 'liberty':

> Well, he waved his hanky on the midnight dreariness of the pier, as the boat inched away; one among a crowd. One among a crowd! *C'est ça!* (1925: 276; 1928: 19)

The repeating of the phrase, the addition of emphasis to it, marks a startled, abrupt seeing-anew, a dawning in the consciousness. But at the same time, repetition checks the spirit of adventure; others have been there before, the phrase she discovers was already waiting. The moment of apparent enlarging is also a shrinking-back, from the unknown to the known, enacting in miniature everything the 1928 revisions sought to accentuate. In effect, the whole story is slung between the two poles of Liberty and Fate, two statuesque females at either end of Juliet's journey: Liberty, in her assertive American tantrum, and Fate in the figure of Marinina, the Italian housekeeper, who conducts the newly-arrived Maurice through the wild pathways to the spot where Juliet is sunning herself: '"Down there is the Signora," said Marinin', pointing like one of the Fates' (1925: 285; 1928: 32). Marinina, named after the sea, which Juliet had thought 'deeper than one imagines, and fuller of memories' (1925: 275; 1928: 19), is an elderly woman whose eyes 'had the shrewdness of thousands of years in them, with the laugh, half mockery, that underlies all long experience' (1928: 24; 1925: 280).[42] Fate escorts back to Juliet everything that Liberty seemed to have watched her leaving; it is as if the 'vast, fixed wheel of circumstance' (1928: 38) had turned its full circle without moving forward, and Juliet, having ostensibly gone 'away', was discovering what Birkin had discovered in *Women In Love*, 'You can't go away ... There *is* no away.'[43] The fatal moment itself, Maurice's return to his wife, was intriguingly revised. In the 1925 text:

> Marinin' paused a moment, seeing the naked woman standing alert, her sun-faded fair hair in a little cloud. Then the swift old woman came on down the slant of the steep track.
> She stood a few steps, erect, in front of the sun-coloured woman, and eyed her shrewdly.
> 'But how beautiful you are, you!' she said coolly, almost cynically. 'There is your husband.'
> 'My husband!' cried Juliet. (1925: 284)

The later version begins virtually the same, but then has instead:

> 'But how beautiful you are, you!' she said coolly, almost cynically. 'Your husband has come.'
> 'What husband?' cried Juliet. (1928: 31)

'My husband!' carries just the faintest hint that Juliet might still, for an instant, be rapt in a dreamy wonder, afloat on her own beauty, the majestic landscape and the old woman's seductive announcements. It is as if the sun had all along been preparing Juliet for a ceremonial union with someone new; or as if she were glimpsing, through the actuality of Maurice, the lineaments of the greater thing he could yet be: as she thinks later, 'he was a man, too, he faced the world and was not entirely quenched in his male courage. He would dare to walk in the sun, even ridiculously' (1925: 291). But 'What husband?' seems deliberately to deflate all this; it gives the comedy of the scene a different flavour, takes it more in the direction of Boccaccio, with the note of suspicious alarm, about the peasant, about Maurice, and how much the prying old woman might know. The dismissiveness in Juliet's cry is also the kind that never sounds fully convincing, more of a routine disparagement deriving from 'the deep iron rhythm of habit' (1925: 275; 1928: 19) which besets her marriage, the sound of someone too much married to the man ever to forgo him entirely. As such, it anticipates the detectable note of relief inside her protestations at the end of the 1928 story – relief that tinges these protestations without wholly vitiating them – that, after all, events have absolved her of the need to risk anything truly untried. As Juliet laments her lack of 'courage' (a term the text has transferred over from its 1925 application to Maurice), the narrative voice, into which hers is absorbed, retreats into a kind of imperialist prejudice that sees the corresponding lack of courage in the peasant as a congenital cultural defect:

> He was the type of Italian peasant that wants to make an offering of himself, passionately wants to make an offering of himself, of his powerful flesh and thudding blood-stroke. But he was also completely a peasant, in that he would wait for the woman to make the move. He would hang round in a long, consuming passivity of desire, hoping, hoping for the woman to come for him. . . . And she knew the peasant would never come for her, he had the dogged passivity of the earth, and would wait, wait, only putting himself in her sight, again and again, lingering across her vision, with the persistency of animal yearning. (1928: 36–8)

The reluctance, to put it at its mildest, that such a man would obviously feel about initiating any involvement with a wealthy, married, middle-class American woman, is construed as a timidity towards women in general; while the complacent stereotyping, 'dogged', 'persistency', reinforcing the class assumption that he was there to be made use of in the first place, seems also to expose some of Juliet's ambivalence about the whole project: she would not want him to 'hang round' once she had taken what she felt she needed, and on his side, the single hour of desire that she was planning would for any number of reasons be unlikely to satisfy him. Perhaps in the end it would be the forces of habit, of sticking with what one knows, reasserting themselves in the vocabulary Juliet falls back on, that would offer the best chances of emotional security for Johnny, her son, who has been virtually forgotten by this time. The best chance too, ultimately, for the coming child, resented even before it has been conceived: 'the little etiolated body of her husband, city-branded, would possess her, and his little, frantic penis would beget another child in her' (1928: 38), the word 'beget' loaded with a special grudge, that what for the father may be the satisfactions of dynastic continuity and fulfilment should be experienced by the mother as self-erasure and shackling.

Tinged with relief or not, these closing lines seems to enact the last shrugging-away of the surgery fantasy which the Spotorno stories had addressed with different degrees of optimism, the fantasy that a single, vigorous intervention from outside could at one stroke rescue one's being or restore its lost wholeness. The emphasis falls instead on the image of Juliet, with her husband beside her, the two of them more divided in their inner lives than ever, drinking coffee on the terrace and gazing across the gully at the peasant and his wife eating their own midday meal on the mound opposite: an image filled so simply with Lawrentian aching for an inaccessible other world, beyond the 'fixed wheel of circumstance' (1928: 30); the impossibility of ever really crossing over, to the bread and the wine in the wheat-field, the little white cloth on the ground, the mark of the sacramental in every gesture, the communal tie transcending private wrongs and disappointments. Between here and there is always the 'wild gully' (1928: 30), where the two sides meet but fail to mingle, retreating back up their own slopes; an Etruscan vision in miniature, of the banquet and the dancing on the opposite hill, where the city of the living faces the city of the dead, each searching the other for a comfort neither can give.

# 4
# Parkin's Wedding Photograph

## 1

In the first of the three *Lady Chatterley* novels, Constance catches sight of Parkin's wedding photograph almost as soon as she enters his cottage. Hanging on the wall over the dresser is

> an enlarged photograph of a young, fairish man with a rather thin, sticking-out moustache and square shoulders, and a woman, dark and with frizzed hair, wearing a black satin blouse and a big lace collarette. She looked common.[1]

The photograph does not occupy Constance for long. It is late evening, she has come there for the sole purpose of spending the night with Parkin, and as they pass hastily through their awkward preliminaries – his offer of food, her few minutes' perch on the sofa – the first question the photograph prompts her to ask, 'Do you ever see your wife?' (98), sounds rather like a parody of polite enquiry on the part of a well-bred visitor. The sight of the photograph appears rather to reassure than to disturb her. It is certainly less disturbing than one might have expected, since at moments like this in Lawrence's work, whenever a woman in love comes into some form of contact with her predecessor in her beloved's affections, the thought of Poe's 'Ligeia' never seems far away, with its theme of the relentless parasitical hold of the first woman, the first relationship, over the second, and Lawrence's appalled fascination with the man's tacit encouragement of this. The photograph must in some manner have reconfronted

Constance with anxieties she had already felt about what it meant for her to come to the cottage, what kind of threshold she would be crossing. She had shrunk from the place before, from the atmosphere of 'wife' and 'marriage' it seemed to exude: 'The cottage with the kettle and the tea-pot always on the hob! No, Constance had no desire at all to feel its homeliness and its tight intimacy. She wanted to stay outside' (29). Despite having said to Parkin 'I want to be your wife, *really*' (77–8), she had been distinctly uneasy about his apparent assumption of property rights in her, and about the symbolic bigamy it seemed to involve: 'He had a wife. What did he want another for, if only in the wood?' (96). And once she is inside the cottage, the cramped dimensions themselves seemed to be conspiring to turn her every move into a replica of someone else's. She follows Parkin up the narrow stairs to bed – 'Probably the other woman had followed him like this' (98) – with a sensation not only of being a trespasser on another's territory but of being fitted into a pre-existent mould, a sensation disconcertingly aggravated by the movements of his hand while sleeping:

> And she knew that at first he must have slept with his wife like that, because his hand came like a child's, and gathered her breast and held it as in a cup. If she moved his hand it came back while he slept, by instinct, and found her breast, and held it softly enclosed. (99–100)

His body, released by sleep to its own devices, seems to be searching hers again and again for traces of the woman he used to know, while at the same time reaching back beyond either of these two towards the unloving, rejecting mother, for whom successive female bodies may have more or less comfortingly substituted. Perhaps the photograph over the dresser was saying 'You too!' But however much it may be contributing to the process whereby Constance feels herself being depersonalised, drawn into another's orbit, the photograph also has a soothing effect on her. She comes to believe that even from so brief a scrutiny she 'had understood a great deal, looking at the "enlargement" of a bold woman in a black satin blouse, and that young man with the square shoulders and defiant eyes' (99). The 'bold woman' appears incriminated, summed up, all her deficiencies put on view; the man's emotional injuries are given a clear history.

Everything that threatened to press in upon Constance is held for a moment at a safe distance, and in the midst of so much that is alien, of the deep estrangement between the classes that causes so many untrustworthy perceptions, the photograph creates for her a little haven of privilege and control.

It would be possible, though, to be aware of two slightly different images in this photograph, oddly superimposed upon each other, sliding in and out of focus. The image Constance claims to have 'understood' is the image of a predator alongside her unwitting prey, who, by gazing in the same direction, is failing to notice the danger next to him. But the other image is of a couple, as distinct from the separate individuals who comprise it; a couple with the whole course of their relationship, everything that brought it into being and doomed it to fail, somehow already inscribed on their features. When this image comes to the forefront, the viewer is overtaken by a sense of mortality; the past and the future are telescoped together, the wife appears not monstrous at all, but just as hopeful and as defenceless as the husband, and the photograph becomes a revelation of vulnerability in the moment of taking a decisive step. Could this also be part of what Constance has 'understood', as she lies awake that night, reflecting upon the truths which people involuntarily betray, in photographs or in tics of manner – does this second image ghost in underneath and help give those reflections their strange blend of complacency and humility?

After all, her reflections themselves seem equally self-betraying, just at the point where they, too, are aiming to be decisive:

> So this was what it was to be a wife! How implicitly he made a wife of her, even if he had got her only for this one night! The curious united circle of the man and the woman! It was a kind of prison, too.
> No, not a prison! If one thought in that way, it was really a prison to have a body at all. If one wanted to be so tremendously free, one must evaporate into nothingness. That hard little freedom of a separate, completely separated individual, that was worse than a prison. It was just a nail through one's heart. (100)

In the context of the adultery she has just committed, the arrangement of the vocabulary here seems to be giving a peculiarly callous twist to the cliché about being a prisoner in one's own body, the sort of well-meaning remark frequently applied to the severely disabled; a cliché which Clifford's own caustic banter had in its way summoned up that very morning, when he came outdoors in his motorised wheelchair, saying '"Stone walls do not a prison make"' (83). Her trance-like recall of the phrase 'not a prison' seems to be bringing a trace of guilty sympathy for Clifford into the moment when she is most vehemently repudiating everything she takes him to stand for. Such involuntary recall also gives a glimpse of the sheer hatefulness of living day after day with an invalid whose verbal dexterity is all he has, and who pours his words over his wife at every opportunity, in his relentless effort to convince himself that his existence still has meaning and that in some way, somewhere, all his losses could still be redeemed. Wouldn't her mind be inevitably clogged up by the incessant fall-out from this, from the endlessly repeated debates about binaries and contraries, soul and body, white horse and black horse, the relative merits of each thing and its opposite? One of the things the novel so fascinatingly does is to suggest some of the insidious effects of excessive proximity to a man like Clifford. Constance at one point thinks of herself as being 'paralysed with fear', with no apparent recognition of what she is saying (she is in France, far away from him, going over the pros and cons of her conduct – 'I don't feel guilty or wrong. On the contrary, I feel it is right' [131] – and sounding more like him than ever). All through the novel other people's hurts or injuries seem to exert a special magnetism, repeatedly stirring up in the able-bodied an unsatisfied rescuing, nursing instinct, an instinct both aroused and frustrated by Clifford's condition, and which offers, rather as the photograph did, a way of finding one's bearings in situations which might otherwise leave one wholly at a loss – a magnetism working even on Duncan Forbes, as he fusses obsessively over Parkin's reluctance to wear a scarf in the car (190–8). And in the later versions of the text, the idea of castration seems increasingly to mesmerise whatever company Clifford has around him, so Tommy Dukes for example finds himself talking in front of everyone, Clifford included, about cutting his own penis 'clean off' (*Lady Chatterley's Lover*, 39), while Ivy Bolton describes to Constance with fascinated relish not only the spell of impotence her husband Ted suffered, but Bertha Coutts's public declaration that Parkin's own penis ought to have been cut off and sent on to her as something between a trophy and a memento

(*The First and Second Lady Chatterley Novels*, 407). When, eventually, Parkin (Mellors, in *Lady Chatterley's Lover*) openly taunts Clifford about his inability to function sexually, it comes almost as a relief, as if a spell cast over them all has at last been broken. But by introducing and, as the revisions develop, strengthening the idea that Clifford would have come to be virtually the person he is even if he had not suffered this injury, the novel seems to be pulling back, slightly shamefacedly, from one of the most radical features of its original conception, its willingness to explore the full reach and variety of the blighting effect which war-disability could visit on all those touched by it – unless the idea that his injury didn't really alter anything is really Connie's, one of her ways of coping with the barely tolerable feelings to which the real situation exposes her.[2]

Half-conscious memories of Parkin as well as of Clifford find their way in to Constance's nocturnal reflections; the mingling of the two men sees her mind working in much the same way as Parkin's hand as he lies next to her, instinctively tangling two women together as he sleeps. The curious image she uses to round off her train of thought, 'a nail through one's heart' – curious in combining suggestions of killing and of fixing the heart permanently to one place, as though the two amounted to the same thing – looks back to the nails she and Parkin had hammered into a tree the previous afternoon, to pledge their fidelity '"for good and a'"' (79); and the image seems despite herself to resurrect all the uneasiness which that half-solemn, half-ludicrous moment had stirred up in her. It is as if all the time she is arguing herself towards accepting the surrender of her separateness, the surrender which life with Parkin seems to demand, the words she uses to argue with are working against her, setting up a kind of sceptical counter-argument inside the one she is actually conducting. At the same time, rather than indicating a troubling doubt about where passion is taking her, the way these residues of the previous day are resurfacing in her brain may indicate just how ruthlessly passion is sweeping up everything in its path, and recycling it all for its own use. One of the most consistently striking aspects of Lawrence's writing is its ability to register this to-and-fro, shuttle-like pulsing of the mind in crisis. In the first *Lady Chatterley*, however, it seems to have something specifically to do with the experience of marital breakdown: with the transitional period in which one longstanding and apparently settled relationship is being gradually superseded by another, and in which a whole repertoire of psychological and emotional tricks comes into play to help deal with the upheaval.

This is not a subject which Lawrence had ever really explored before (he had glanced at it in *The Trespasser*), but perhaps falling in love at a relatively advanced age, when the upheaval is altogether more problematic – Constance is 27, although she often behaves as if she were 37 – may be the condition that most intensifies this characteristic shuttle-rhythm. One will have had sufficient experience of life to be suspicious of oneself, while being at the same time more susceptible to refreshing astonishments; so one could find oneself veering wildly between the two Lawrentian positions, between the rational, unimpressed, worldly self, and the self transfiguringly enfolded in Dionysian forces: clutching in thrilled panic at the promises of the latter, while staring with exasperated incredulity at one's own superstitious and adolescent behaviour. In addition, all the little defensive hypocrisies and delusions are activated, like the workings of an emotional immune system, whereby the different selves between which one is sliding, the sceptical and the mythically charged, can each be used as temporary refuges from the more difficult or painful perceptions of the other. In this regard I would want to say that the scene in the first *Lady Chatterley* immediately after Constance's nails-in-the-tree adventure, when Clifford comes out on to the terrace to meet her as she comes back from the wood, is as moving and true as anything Lawrence ever wrote. It has such a wonderfully subtle mixture of full and empty words, real feelings and self-regarding or tactically advantageous ones, and it so beautifully catches the sense in which their years together have produced that strange delicacy of cynicism which alerts each to the other's need, and supplies on schedule the means to relieve it, that it was scarcely necessary for Lawrence to underline it all like this:

> But she wept in a burst flood of distress. And underneath she was rather happy. She wept in her old and very sincere grief for Clifford. And underneath she was rather happy because she had knocked her nail in beside the other man's nail and had promised to go to his cottage to spend a night with him.
>
> The grief, too, seemed older, shallower, less radical than the other, the adventurous sort of happiness. (82)

When, only a few weeks after first writing these passages, Lawrence revised them for the second version of *Lady Chatterley*, he took all this out: all the nuances of overlapping tension, and the sense of the invisible filaments that lie so intricately between husband and wife. Virtually nothing is left of the interplay of happiness and grief, the happiness making the grief possible, or of the elusive feeling in the earlier scene that Clifford *knows*, but is still at the stage where he can protect himself from the full impact of knowing, is as it were rehearsing for what knowing might be like. The revised scene is imbued instead with sick misery, contempt and self-righteous resentment.

Lawrence clearly set out to make Clifford increasingly less sympathetic as the rewriting developed. Various comparative studies of the three versions have discussed this.³ He took the risk here of making Constance considerably less sympathetic as well, choosing this of all moments to reprimand her husband's self-pity: '"If you want to die – well really – don't burden other people with it. . . . I *hate* Hamletising men!"' (*The First and Second Lady Chatterley Novels*, 400). But one reason for Lawrence's turning this scene into something so much more abrasive than its original may have been the decision to place it after Constance (now Connie) has seen Parkin's wedding photograph, rather than before; after she has seen the essence of a bad marriage made so brutally visible, impatiently cutting through all those filaments which merely disguise that essence from those who are living in it. Perhaps the transmutation of the photograph-scene, the transmutation to which I want to try to respond, begins with the question of timing, of what meanings an incident might have had if it had occurred at another point, with different traces feeding into it. In the second *Lady Chatterley*, Lawrence not only reverses the sequence of those two events, the encounter with the photograph and the evening return from the wood, and sets them both much later in the narrative, but he splits what was originally one scene into two. Connie's nocturnal reflections on what it means to be a wife, themselves considerably altered, are separated off from the photograph-scene, and moved to a later occasion, when she is reminded of the photograph by the sight of the almanac with which Parkin has replaced it. The photograph-scene itself is totally re-imagined, organised in the second version of the novel around three new elements: Connie this time lets Parkin know she has seen the photograph; she wants it to be immediately destroyed; and the pressure she applies to him to do this turns the moment into an implicit trial of his commitment to her. Meanwhile, in the course of a rewriting in which so much is added to the text, the scene of hammering the nails into the tree is cut out altogether – as also is the remark about 'a nail through one's heart'.

Tony Pinkney, in his book *D. H. Lawrence*, argued that the nails-in-the-tree scene was one of a number omitted from the final version of the novel, *Lady Chatterley's Lover*, on the grounds that the mythic or ritual dimensions of such scenes were too 'modest', too self-consciously artificial, for Lawrence's 'more grandiose apocalyptic projects' – projects in which the entire novel became mythical, with the result that myth-making itself as a human activity could 'no longer be separated out as a topic for debate in its own right'.[4] This would not explain, however, why the nail scene was omitted from the second version of the novel as well, while other such incidents were retained, like the breast-cupping gesture which Pinkney mentions in this connection. Nails and nailing frequently recur in Lawrence's work, often in connection with trees, always connoting a horror of fixing down; perhaps the best-known instance is in the 1925 essay 'Morality and the Novel', itself the clearest statement of Lawrence's view that the novel as a form is quintessentially concerned with the pain and discomfort of transitional states: while religion, philosophy and science all 'want to nail us on to some tree or other', the novel resists this; it 'gets up and walks away with the nail'.[5] Crucifixion imagery becomes more and more explicit towards the end of this essay, recalling an old preoccupation, reaching at least as far back as 'The Crucifix Across the Mountains' (1912), with bodies that were 'locked in knowledge, beautiful, complete... one with the nails', wisps of rhetoric which all seem to curl again around those few lines in the first *Lady Chatterley*.[6] With this, too, come intimations of the Roman terror in the German forests, something one feels is never far away whenever trees and humans meet in Lawrence – the living, bristling otherness of the forest made more alarming by the thought of the skulls nailed to the trees as offerings to the wood gods: a thread picked up in the second *Lady Chatterley*, when Parkin inspires in Connie 'a certain fear, as of the wild men of the woods whom she remembered in old German drawings' (460).[7] Perhaps the nails-in-the-tree scene was felt to be laden with too much baggage, more than the moment could comfortably support.

But whatever Lawrence's reason for discarding the scene, its ruling motif surreptitiously returns in the new version of Connie's encounter with the photograph, bringing right into the centre of the second novel the idea of a conspiratorial bond, emphatically sealed by some symbolic violence; as if there were still a search in the novel for a ritualistic commemorative gesture, that would bestow upon a relationship a sense of durability beyond the ephemeral excitements of its beginning – a gesture that would privately perform a similar function to that performed by a wedding photograph in the public world. One can still hear, faintly reverberating, Parkin's plaintive call, in the lost nail-scene, for '"summat as'll keep . . . for good and a'"' (78–9), his succinct abbreviation of the marriage service; for some token of the security and reassurance each partner craves from the other. And at the same time, the pathos of desire deepens, as such would-be mutual affirmations draw in too many meanings to be stabilised, too many separate nuances for the two people in turn; so that for every gap between them that closes another one opens.

## 2

There was never any suggestion, in the first *Lady Chatterley*, that Constance wanted the photograph to be destroyed. But now she only looks at it for a few moments before saying '"Why don't you burn it?"' (393). All the circumstances of her catching sight of it are different. She has not, as in the first novel, only just arrived at the cottage; nor is it almost dark. She has been there for most of the afternoon, moving around the rooms, finding out where the utensils are kept, making tea and drinking it, and eventually dozing off in Parkin's lap, without apparently having noticed the photograph at all. This seems a scarcely credible oversight, given the size of the thing – so big that when Parkin comes to smash it up he has to break the cardboard backing 'again and again' (393) over his knee until the pieces are small enough to fit on the fire – and given how little else there is for so normally inquisitive a woman to look at. Lawrence seems to have tried to make her oversight just credible enough by moving the photograph, from its original position over the dresser, to the wall by the front door, where it is slightly less obvious, and behind her rather than facing her when she comes in. Nonetheless, he makes her pass through this door more than once – she goes to the threshold to throw the rinse water down the path (387); he sits her at the table facing the door, and he subsequently makes her walk back to the door in order to close it. Maybe the sunlight coming through has a temporarily blinding effect. Primarily, though, she seems to have become so absorbed in her experiment with the role of 'wife', and the kinds of semi-automatic movement that go with it, clearing dishes, washing up, making tea, that she acts like someone so completely habituated to her environs that she no longer notices their component parts, any more than Parkin himself does: 'it was years since he had even seen' the photograph (392).

She wanted to use this afternoon as a rehearsal for a future state of togetherness with Parkin. She has been trying to imagine herself as the person she might become, once the two of them had passed beyond their passionate, honeymoon period, and established the familiarity and the shared history which will lie on the far side of it. She has turned down Parkin's offer of sex. What is important to her is that this should be a dummy run for an ordinary day, a day in which she could immerse herself in commonplace tasks, feeling the security of being liked by her man rather than merely wanted; and instead of the 'latent desire' he expects to see, Parkin can only find 'another sort of wistfulness in her look' (388). She has come to the cottage straight from hearing Ivy Bolton talking at length about her husband Ted, and about how the warmth of touch can leave its mark on the body long after the actual touching has ceased; how two people could remain quite mysterious to each other, even a little enviously so, could be conscious of disagreement almost to the point of incompatibility, yet be united by touch, touch which does not so much dispel the mutual mysteriousness as reveal it also to be a source of joy. This story has made a strong impression on Connie, as has Ivy's sense that established society regards touch and its mark as radical threats, and is implacably hostile to them: '"And even *that* they'd kill if they could," she said fiercely. "They'd like to kill his very touch that he left inside you. If they could!"' (385). The feelings aroused by Ivy's remarks become part of Connie's mood, so that she comes to the cottage primed both to transport herself mentally beyond the things she is currently at war with, and to attack them with all her force wherever they impinge on her. All through her afternoon's wife-fantasy there is a swell of anger waiting to burst, and there is a more 'wistful' yearning to accelerate all the processes of change that need to occur for her to arrive where she would like to be, for everything that presently exists only in glimmerings to be brought to an achieved state. Might this not suggest, as it would certainly have suggested to Bachelard in *The Psychoanalysis of Fire*, that the idea of burning is already in her mind, only waiting for the trigger to release it?[8] Since these acceleration-yearnings are the kind characteristically provoked, in Bachelard's view, by hearthside contemplation ('the fire was red, rather low, the bar dropped, the kettle singing' [386]), the phoenix-vision of the absolute passing away of one condition and the spontaneous birth of another, Connie's wish for the photograph to burn does seem to involve the relieving of pressures generated prior to her seeing it, so that her seeing it becomes not just a stark interruption but in some sense the appropriate climax of her reverie. There is a clear reminiscence of her feelings the previous winter, when 'as she looked round her room, she longed to destroy it all, smash the whole thing to smithereens: smash up Wragby, burn it down, anything, anything to erase it and wipe it out of existence. . . . The exquisite relief it would be, if she saw it in flames, and then in ashes' (254). But the real fire that she is about to light, the burning photograph, appears to be setting off imaginative transmutations more intricate than a merely nihilistic rage. Perhaps part of her is watching her own marriage burn, the levelling effect of the flames enabling her for a moment to think of her marriage as equivalent to Parkin's; perhaps her rebellious passion for Parkin will be the fire that finally destroys Wragby; perhaps inside this web is a memory of Bertha Mason from *Jane Eyre*, a thread of memory running through the second *Lady Chatterley*, attaching itself to the figures of Bertha Coutts and Connie in turn, and making the burning of the rival's image a violent crystallisation of all the replacement-anxiety with which the sequence originally began.[9]

If burning the photograph offers a kind of interim compensation for the failure of other things to burn, it seems to draw in a chain of associations with the late war, and with the ways in which the war intermittently surfaces in the novel. On Connie's part, her outburst against Wragby ended by bringing into the open an idea implicit in a number of Lawrence's earlier writings, that the real problem with the war was that it had not been destructive *enough*, that too many things had managed to survive it. The war seemed to have raised hopes for a truly fresh start and then disappointed them:

'If something would happen that would *really* destroy the world. . . . But what would be the good of dying, as all the men had died in the war, and leaving the world still wagging, as foul and even fouler than before!' (255) The fact that the photograph is still up on the wall in the first place is itself a graphic representation of that unfinished business, of all the obstacles that remain in place when they might have been swept away. The sight of it could hardly help evoking in Connie all sorts of unpalatable feelings about Clifford; feelings similar to those that must have invaded her that same morning, when Ivy, describing how Ted had died, had drawn a connection between personality and fate so emotionally necessary to her that she seems to have forgotten it was Sir Clifford Chatterley's wife she was talking to: '"He wouldn't take care. He was like some of those lads in the war, going off gay and lively. And they were always killed first"' (383). And from Parkin's point of view, the photograph would certainly have a sardonic relationship with countless other pre-war wedding photographs that would at that moment have been gazing out into rooms from which one of the partners was missing. By 1923, when the novel is set, such pictures would have already begun to acquire their special historical pathos, as records of an irretrievable innocence, of the moment before the world broke apart, the last optimistic flurry before the blunder into disaster; as Philip Larkin put it, 'The thousands of marriages / Lasting a little while longer': in this case, though, the photograph rather parodies such pathos, as for Parkin it was the marriage that was the disaster, while the war, which left him virtually unscathed, offered a convenient opportunity to escape the disaster.[10] The novel here is a little reminiscent of 'Glad Ghosts' in its acerbic treatment of the contemporary conventions and pieties, a treatment which appears to occur almost inadvertently and of which both texts seem only partly aware.

As he starts to break the photograph to pieces, Parkin pauses a moment to look once more, and passes sentence on it all: 'A man's a fool!' (393). Jude Fawley probably felt much the same when he burnt the photograph of himself which he had given to Arabella on their wedding day, and which, after she left him, he found on sale in a shop window.[11] Part of Parkin's folly lay in having allowed himself to drift into a whole way of life without questioning whether it was really what he wanted, the way of life of which wedding photographs on display in the living room are among the presiding symbols, occupying as they do a halfway position between being private commemorations and being public shows of support for the established order, images of social integration.[12] Connie's question, '"Why do you have it?"', touches a little nerve of defensiveness about this: '"I don't know! Folks does have 'em!"' (392). When she goes on to suggest (with her usual electrifying carelessness, given that the war only ended a few years earlier), that such photographs '"always look like dead people"' (392), there is a hint in her words not just that the figures look stiff and mummified but that they have a haunting, almost accusatory effect, as if present life were being scrutinised by these old, unchanging, always-young faces for the expectations it had failed to fulfil, or the standards it had failed to meet. Perhaps Parkin, who had erased the photograph from his mind, now finds on being re-alerted to it that it so graphically concentrates all the intimidating and repressive forces that had shaped him as virtually to incite an equivalent aggression against it – an aggression stirred up the more for his having been re-alerted in such a recriminatory way, by a woman whose entry into his life is igniting so many uncomfortable feelings that had been lying relatively dormant.

In the second *Lady Chatterley* the photograph is not seen as a valuable source of insight into its subjects; it is primarily a piece of furniture, ugly, heavy, 'horrid'. We are given details of all the materials used in making it – brown paper, backboard, thick card, glass, metal sprigs, gilded and chocolate-coloured plaster; the stress is on the sheer there-ness of the thing, as a chunk of resistance symbolising all the other tightly layered resistances which the lovers will have to encounter. It takes a considerable effort for Parkin to smash it, and the attention drawn to hideousness and effort brings the latent comedy of the scene into the open. For a moment we can see, among all the other things we can see, a hen-pecked middle-aged man, prodded out of his afternoon doze by a woman's imperious demand that he deal with a household chore he has put off for as long as possible: '"Do burn it now!" she said' (393). A sudden shaft of mockery falls over the vision of future togetherness which the novel had just before so lovingly set up, full of sunshine, peace and warmth; Parkin, who after all has had a long morning's journey to Uthwaite and back, finds himself flung from his armchair of 'pure forgetfulness', forgetfulness which, the narrator rather ominously tells us, 'is perhaps the best experience of life' (392), by a woman's insistence that he remember, remember all sorts of things which he seemed to have successfully blotted out until she came along. Perhaps it is still the case that 'a man's a fool'? When he says, of burning the picture, '"If I'd ever looked at the thing I'd a' done it long enough ago"' (393), it sounds like a petulant claim to be master in his own house and to fend off the sense that the woman has already taken over. But the element of mockery also brings a more hopeful intimation into the scene, of something the two of them would not quite yet be ready to welcome: of how they could come to make a relationship out of their clashes, out of the eccentric match between her egotistical obliviousness to others' sensitivities, and his affronted, exasperated, grudgingly admiring reliance on a woman's energy to get him going; there is a glimpse here of something unusually *affectionate* in Lawrence's treatment of his fictional characters.

Immediately after this, however, is an instant almost of trepidation, as if they had both suddenly become conscious of the momentousness of what they were about to do:

> He rose rather stiffly, stood on a chair, and lifted down the heavy, dusty picture.
> 'Not worth while dusting it now!' he said.
> 'You can save the frame if you like,' she said, 'though that's ugly too!' – It was! – a chocolate-coloured moulding with a gilt pattern.
> 'We'll save th' glass,' he said, 'an' that's a'!' (393)

Parkin's first remark has a weirdly elegiac note somewhere in it. Does Connie say what she says because she has picked up this note? Does she worry for an instant that she might have presumed too far? Or is she remembering Ivy's reaction to the japanned work-box in the attic at Wragby – '"Why it must have cost pounds and pounds"' (356) – and thinking that the working classes, instinctively more prudent than she herself needs to be, might jib at sacrificing anything that still had some value? All at once there seems to be the kind of embarrassed distance between people that so often in Lawrence immediately follows a moment of agreement.[13] And this tremor of hesitation in the face of finality is marked by one of those characteristically Lawrentian interjections – 'It was!' – which nervously break the spell of realism and destabilise the vantage-point from which we are watching; effecting in this case a strange, last-minute illumination of what is about to be destroyed, an intensified farewell look. It is as though one had reached a point where disposing of anything, even something detested, becomes too heavily meaningful to be done without a certain discomfort. Possessions, fittings, fixtures which create miniature worlds around them, generating ties of people and place, ties expressed in everyday rituals like dusting, fending off the continual accumulation of decay – these are little salients in the long, attritional contention between the traveller and the settler in Lawrence's writing: ties and rituals that can seem contemptibly restricting and petty in one minute, and enviably sustaining in the next ('It was a kind of prison . . . No, not a prison!') The ambivalence towards such objects and possessions may have become more pronounced since the earlier great set-piece about it, 'A Chair' in *Women In Love*, as age and frailty take their toll, and the scope for changing life and circumstances starts to narrow down.

Ambivalence certainly permeates the account of the japanned work-box, a scene which does not occur in the first version of the novel. By providing an equivalent disposal-scene in the Chatterley household to the photograph-scene in Parkin's, this addition seems engaged not only with the patterns of symmetry and contrast, but with some extra compulsion in the second novel to explore the dynamics of clearing things out. The description of the box oscillates between an enthralled appreciation of Victorian craftsmanship, and a horror at what it actually produced (a horror made more explicit in the revised version of this scene in *Lady Chatterley's Lover*). The entire culture from which Connie is seeking to liberate herself seems to be somehow crystallised in this box – in particular, by the way it exemplifies the curious nineteenth-century obsession with providing close-fitting cases for everything: 'as if', as T. J. Clark has put it, 'an object did not properly exist for this culture until it sat tight in its own interior', either to be protected from 'the general whirl of exchange', or because each object 'was felt to be so wonderful in its own right that a separate small world should be provided for it, like a shell or calyx'.[14] Connie gives the box to Ivy Bolton, and finds the older woman's obvious delight in it both amusing and slightly repellent. But of course for Ivy there would be a strong subliminal connection between this treasure-chest of ingenious secrets, each snug niche keeping its tiny content safe from adulteration, and all the thoughts of babies, cribs and illegitimacy that just this minute arose from the discussion of Connie's pregnancy prospects; it is hardly surprising that Ivy should be thrilled and flustered: '"Oh, my word! Why it's lovely! It perfectly fascinates *me!*"' (356). The box appears to have been intended as a travelling-case, but it expresses, through the very perfection of its design, so overpowering a sense of the compartmentalisation of life, the anticipation of every contingency, that even if it were not 'that unhandy in-between size! Such a big thing to pack in a trunk: and impossible to carry unpacked' (355–6), it would still have an utterly desolating effect upon the hopes invested in Lawrence's kind of travelling, the hopes of coming upon something genuinely fresh and unknown. It could be that, as Michael Squires implies, Ivy's enshrining of her long-ago life with Ted has cut her off from the chance of emotional renewal – a melancholic encryption leading ultimately to her perversely maternal coddling of Clifford – so that this box would speak directly to her psychic investment in things sealed away and preserved, taken out for occasional caressing.[15] On the other hand, it may simply be her professional life as a nurse that the box calls out to, a connection that would bring quite different feelings into play: about how while for the able-bodied this box would have the chill of the coffin on it, for the invalid it might represent exactly the order and comfort and ready access to simple necessities which he or she would rely on every day; about all that can be signalled by clearing things out of one's attic; or about what it would mean to be always lugging around with you this cumbersome parody of an Etruscan burial casket, with the little things needed for the last journey.

In the late essay 'Pictures on the Walls' (1929), Lawrence exhorted his readers to make frequent changes to their domestic environments, on the grounds that décor can become not merely stale but positively harmful, life-sapping, constrictive: 'If only people would be firm about it, and rigorously burn *all* insignificant pictures, frames as well, how much more freely we should breathe indoors.'[16] The last phrase gives a touching glimpse of how far advanced his tubercular illness was. The essay is animated by a great relish for burning, which comes to mean more than just an efficient method of waste disposal; rather a ritual purification of the air, as if the place in question were always a combination of shrine and sickroom, and the business of life – explicitly, the 'woman's business' – were the continuous warding off of ominous atmospheric forces: as if burning the pictures and photographs you have had for too long effected a kind of superstitious, pre-emptive victory over the looming power to hurt with which all objects and attachments potentially threaten you. Something like this may come to mind when Connie, in the third and final version of the photograph-scene, says '"One should never keep such things!"' (*Lady Chatterley's Lover*, 199). Lawrence certainly seems to have been alert – Constance, in the first novel, was implicitly alert – to the ways in which photography was reawakening in the modern world the primitive instinct to identify the image of a thing with the thing itself, and thereby gain a magical power over it – such that in our time, as Susan Sontag has pointed out, the defacing or destruction of someone's photograph has become, if not quite the equivalent of sticking pins in a wax doll, the especially ruthless way of dismissing that person from one's life.[17] Witter Bynner records an occasion in Chapala in 1923 when Lawrence seized some photographs of Frieda's children from her hands, tore them in pieces, and trampled them on the floor – a story which Bynner may have maliciously embellished, but which from other reports of Lawrence's behaviour would be by no means improbable.[18] Such demonstrations gain much of their force from the sense of a sacramental atmosphere to which the violator is paying a perverse tribute. Proust was responding to the same idea in the scene at Montjouvain, where the narrator comes across Mlle Vinteuil and her lover desecrating her father's photograph as part of their sado-erotic foreplay.[19] That scene, and the scene in the second *Lady Chatterley*, convey an interestingly similar sense of the way this special, 'magical' property of photography becomes involved in one conspirator's tempting or testing of the other, to see how far the other is prepared to go; and both scenes, also, convey a sense of how the very readiness to go that far seems to reveal something alarming and inaccessible about the other conspirator, just when you thought the two of you were drawing closer: for Connie, even a shadowy premonition of danger, in Parkin's ruthless and systematic obliteration of what once had mattered to him.

3

A little earlier that afternoon, Connie had tried to advance her wife-fantasy by asking Parkin's Christian name, and telling him to call her 'Connie'. These familiarities, however, were quickly aborted:

"What am I to say to you, Connie?" he said, in a funny artificial way.
"It does sound not quite right, somehow," she said.
"We'll call one another by no names," he said hastily. (391)

His discomfort with calling her 'Connie' might indicate a residual class awkwardness. Or it might suddenly have come to him what she appears to be too self-absorbed to notice, that he has used this name before, because it is his daughter's name, one which presumably he and his wife had chosen for her between them.

Parkin and Constance's first real contact with each other had actually been by way of this child, who, when Constance asked her name, had 'peeped at her with dark, wilful, resentful eyes', and said '"Connie Parkin"' (15) – the only time the name of Constance's destiny is pronounced in the novel, as though to mark from the outset how whatever she acquires will have to be taken from someone else who already has it. The original version of the meeting between the two Connies is subjected, in the second novel, to as radical a revision as the photograph-scene, and one that takes it in a similar imaginative direction. But in its first, understated form, the scene was already emotionally complex and resonant. Constance had been walking alone in the wood, attempting to calm the barely suppressible ferment of frustration and malevolence which life with Clifford was stoking in her. She heard a gunshot, 'as if in echo of her own feelings' (14), followed by the sound of a child crying: 'She hastened forward, all her disconnected anger fastening upon the supposition that someone was hurting a child' (14). Much of that anger derived from the condition of being both childless and continually subject to clinging childlike demands – 'there was always Clifford. He required her attention and occupied her feelings almost as young children would have done' (13); the scene she is entering, in which villain and victim would appear to be clearly distinguished, seems to be offering her a chance to lash out, as well as to effect a heroic rescue. But this small measure of psychic relief is cut off almost immediately by Parkin's terse explanation of what has happened:

'Why I shot that there old Tom cat, as has been havin' his own way in here for a month or two. ... An' my little gel here, she thinks she must needs scraight for him.' (14)

Deprived of the focus it wanted, her anger starts to disconnect again:

> She gently wiped the face of the motherless child with her handkerchief. It was obvious the little thing was afraid of the man, her father. Constance felt a resentment against him. No wonder his wife had left him. Constance felt that he did not really like his little girl. (14)

She thinks through the grid of her own preoccupations: an envious yearning for a guilt-free abandonment of one's husband, checked, in emotionally coercive expressions like 'motherless child', by a sense that guilt is inescapable – the guilt seeming to pass to and fro from wife to husband and back again. The speed and simplicity with which Lawrence's writing takes us into the insides of people is again notable, and perhaps not noted sufficiently often. Constance's resentment against Parkin is aroused not just by his rough treatment of the child, but by his open display of exactly the kind of hostility towards being encumbered which, in her case, has to be kept hidden – a disquieting inkling of mutuality which, as she leads the girl home, she tries to push firmly away: 'He disliked women, and despised them. He was merely stupid' (15).

The new version of this scene in the second *Lady Chatterley* illustrates Lawrence's extraordinary commitment to re-imagining what he had already written, poking up sparks from what he had seen smouldering in it. The girl is now nine or ten years old rather than five, and plays a much more active part; her father's voice, far from being 'strangely caressive' (14), snarls menacingly from the beginning; and instead of explaining the situation straight away to pacify the angry woman, Parkin deliberately turns up the heat:

> 'What's the matter? Why is she crying?' demanded Constance peremptorily.
> The man's eyes narrowed, and for some moments he did not deign to answer, but looked into Constance's blazing eyes with a narrow, glittering little look of derision.
> 'Yo' mun ask 'er!' he said. . . . Then she exclaimed, rather breathless:
> 'I asked *you*!'
> . . . 'Ay! Ah know yo' did! But 'er's none towd *me* why 'er's scraightin', so 'appen *yo'd* better ax 'er.' (257)

The emotions aroused by the incident now seem completely disproportionate to any rational appraisal of it; and there is such a peculiar mixture of contemptuous familiarity and distance in the adults' treatment of each other that they start to look less like irritable strangers than like a separated couple, using the moment when their child is returned from an access visit as a chance to inflict some verbal wounds on each other, while the child insinuates itself between them in a well-practised search for advantage.

There is an affinity with the photograph-scene, in the way that a shadow from the absent wife seems to fall so much more darkly over the revised version than the first; an intimation coming partly from the girl herself, old enough now not just to be in her father's way but to have a pronounced manner of her own, and from the note of weariness in her father's annoyance, a hint of all the other times he has had to put up with this. There is affinity also in the delay in Connie's seeing what in the first version had been seen immediately, the photograph or the cat; a delay creating room in both cases for momentum to gather steam before being checked and diverted by a sudden revelation. Here, Connie's frustration at the scene's not going to plan, and at the other characters' not playing quite the parts she had assigned to them, gives rise to a full-blown attack on the girl, who is regarded not, as in the first novel, as simply a 'bold-eyed child' (16), clumsily self-conscious, but as 'a sly, false, impudent little thing, already full to the brim with tricks' (259). The attack is made the more disconcerting by the narrator's starting it before Connie does, as if voicing her thoughts before she were quite ready to admit them. This aspect of the scene certainly sets difficulties for the reader. Obviously, the pieces of nine-year-old female behaviour which the narrator variously describes as 'a false sort of plaintiveness', 'affected plaintive pitifulness', 'the "superior" trick', and 'false airs and ways' (258–60), are largely the results of the girl's astute adaptation to the emotional world in which she finds herself, a world of adult hatreds, parental desertion, and a little compensatory spoiling by her grandmother, where the only affectionate attention she ever receives is likely to be offered at someone else's expense. Equally obviously, Connie is enraged and humiliated by the way in which the girl's naively exploitative manner exposes the more cynically exploitative element in her own, since it was Connie's 'false sweetness' that prompted the girl to see what use could be made of it, and it was Connie who, throughout the scene,

> was play-acting. Or if she was not play-acting, if she really did feel a motherly distress at the weeping of the child, at least she was trying to find some occasion to turn and rend the man. (257–8)

We are brought close here to the kind of sceptical and even rather hysterical suspiciousness, in Lawrence's later writing, towards virtually any profession of concern for another's suffering – concern which is always felt to have dubious motives, and seen at worst as a form of collusion in the suffering, almost a desire to have suffering inflicted so as to be able to lament or avenge it. But for all this, the reader can still feel gripped and drawn in by the uncomfortable emotional turbulence in this scene, where the attack from all sides is mean and unjust, and the girl is nonetheless intensely dislikeable – where indeed all three characters can arouse such volatile mixtures of sympathy and dislike that justice is hard pressed to keep up.[20]

That turbulence is encapsulated in Connie's closing pronouncements on her namesake: 'How he disliked that brat of his! She could sympathise with him there! It was an unattractive piece of femininity, that one! . . . Crying over a "pussy", and as hard-hearted a little piece of goods as ever emerged!' (261). Of course, one is never more angry with others than when one knows oneself to be at fault, and Connie's struggle with her conscience makes itself felt in the oddly discrepant phrase, 'piece of goods', a phrase which does not seem to belong to her at all; as though, in trying to justify coming down on the side of a man's brutal deriding of a child's innocent distress over a dead cat, Connie were forced to move out of her own linguistic register and borrow an expression from much nearer his. And there is so much loneliness in what she says, in the way her internal monologue seems to be appealing to a community of the like-minded to which, unlike Hester in 'In Love', she will never actually belong. All Connie's contemptuous summing-up is filled with craving for an uncorrupted feeling, for something real and vulnerable which would not abuse her protective instincts, nor leave her mortifyingly conscious of the corruption already within the instincts themselves – the craving which led her to approach the girl in the first place, inviting such a wounding rebuff, and which now leaves her holding the word 'pussy' in inverted commas, like something repellent being taken away with tongs.

It is interesting that she should try to distance herself from the word like this, since it began its textual life as her own word, in the first *Lady Chatterley*. In that version of the scene, she had already seen the cat's corpse before asking the girl what the matter was, and this seemed the most suitable way of coaxing a five-year-old: '"Don't cry! It was a nasty bad pussy that scratched the little bunnies and killed them"' (14). In the second version, it is the girl who says 'pussy' first, and Connie, unsure what is being referred to, picks the word up, looking to establish a feminine bond against the man. But comic puzzlement quickly takes over, vaguely brushed with innuendo: '"Shot a pussy? Did he shoot your pussy?"' (258).[21] Parkin relishes his moment of theatre:

> 'There's the cat! There! If anybody wants to be sorry for him! He's fat wi' Sir Clifford's young rabbits and bods, if that's summat to be sorry about!'
> Constance involuntarily looked round. There stretched out under the brambles lay a large rusty-black cat with a big head, and amazing flat flanks. Dead, the creature looked like a piece of offal. . . . Constance didn't like the look of him. (259)

She isn't about to let Parkin triumph; she turns her back on him and attempts to re-form her uneasy bond with the girl. Again, the dynamics of the scene at this point are quite different from those in the first version. Whereas there Constance had taken the child away with her, however haughtily, for the benefit of both the child and Parkin, here she ignores Parkin altogether and takes the child in an attempt to score off him. Her self-satisfaction only lasts a few minutes, however; she has lumbered herself with a long, disagreeable trudge to the cottage, and her subsequent attack on the girl is clearly augmented by her annoyance not only at this but at not having managed to land a sufficiently annihilating blow on the father. And there is a further strand in the tissue of mockery, in the way the utter deadness of the dead cat seems simultaneously to echo and to ridicule the metaphorical notions of deadness that had been obsessing Connie immediately before she heard the gunshot: shouting silently at Clifford, 'Can't you see you're half dead, and you'd be much better wholly dead? . . . Hanging on to the raft in a dead weight' (255); thinking of herself as 'just another carcase, horrible' (255), of 'the strangle-hold of the death-breathing air' (256), of how 'her heart and her deeper self' were 'bound in a dead, iron frost that never yielded' (256); utter deadness, the image of violent obliteration, lying almost overlooked at the centre of the ferocities and insincerities of this sole encounter between these three people, and eloquently speaking to each of them in turn.

The younger Connie now effectively vanishes from the text. The only time she is mentioned again is in Clifford's letter about the reappearance of Parkin's wife, and her foiled attempt to snatch the child back: 'The daughter, being kitten of the cat, bit and fought so hard that she received a smack in the face which sent her into the gutter' (*The First Lady Chatterley*, 128). Revising this, Lawrence altered two points. The girl now 'bit her mother's *hand* with such force that she received . . .' (*The Second Lady Chatterley*, 502, my emphasis) – a girl of nine or ten biting her mother's hand would seem to involve a more disturbing set of motivations than in the case of a struggling five-year-old. Also, the mother now 'seized upon her own daughter, as that chip of the female block was returning from school' (502): a detail which Lawrence could hardly have added without remembering Frieda's forlorn vigils, many years earlier, outside schools in London, in the hope of seeing her children who had been ordered to ignore her; and the bitter rows this provoked with him as to who was to take precedence in her life. After this, the text is silent. In neither version of Connie's visit to the fight-damaged Parkin at his mother's house is the child mentioned at all, although we have been given to understand that she lives there; neither on the weekday evening of the first version, when one might have expected a five-year-old to be somewhere nearby, nor on the Sunday morning of the second, when a nine-year-old who had wanted to stay to help her grandmother with the cleaning (259), might normally have been found helping with the cooking. But her disappearance seems to leave a strange mark on the text. In the first version of Connie's visit Parkin is described three times in the course of a single page (144) speaking to her 'as if to a child', and while these phrases are removed from the scene in the second version, their mood is remembered in the account of Connie's anxiety over Parkin's health: 'She saw in him the danger of death. She felt it in her heart, as children sometimes do' (522).

As seemed to be happening in 'Glad Ghosts', child-coloured elements pass between adults in the house of the missing child, as if the inner story of this moment were that the one had to be erased for the other to develop (in the various imaginings of the lovers' future, one consequence goes completely unaddressed – that Parkin without a backward glance will have abandoned his firstborn child, a child on whose behalf, for all his antipathy, he has hitherto exercised some rudimentary paternal care). The scene is in addition curiously dominated by the kitchen fire: heat and flame drawing everyone towards it. In the first version, Parkin's mother, interrupted on her baking-day by Constance's unexpected arrival, 'crossly' screens the fire on her guest's behalf with a piece of sheet iron, which Parkin, not considering anybody else's comfort, subsequently unhooks with his bare hand, injuring himself in the process:

> He reached forward, and with a quick, cat's-paw movement jerked the screen by its brass handle and unhooked it from the stove-bars. But it burnt him, and he let it drop with a clatter. . . . He now stared into the glow of hot coals, red-hot, that half filled the grate. (143).

His body again seems almost instinctively searching for a symbolic focus for his feelings: he wants the fire to say something about the anger he finds hard to articulate, about the radical energy which his wife's unlooked-for return appears to have whipped up; about the absolute nature of the change from his old condition to his new, from gamekeeper to factory worker and committed Communist; almost to provide, through the pain of hot metal, an anticipation of his new life at the foundry; to concentrate into one irritable twitch of the hand his renunciation of domestic ties and all that reminds him of them (as in one of the passing evocations of Lawrence's childhood which punctuate the novel – 'Constance little knew how familiar the clang of the little metal fire-screen was to Oliver' [142]). In the revised novel, many of these fire-born feelings are transferred directly over to the photograph-scene, while this kitchen episode works itself out rather differently. Apart from one brief inspection of the meat in the oven, Parkin takes no notice of the fire, while this time it is his mother's way of attending to the fire which concentrates all *she* would like to be able to say; coming downstairs after having been sent to make his bed, she darted into the room, rushed at the oven, looked at the meat, turned it, shut the door, snatched the screen from before the fire, set it aside, and taking the poker, eased the red fire carefully near the oven, so that the black coal above began to smoke dense yellow under the bonnet, then leaped into flame. Whereupon the old woman set the screen before the fire again, and immediately darted the lid off the iron saucepan, peering into the steam. And all this time she had not even noticed the presence of her son and of Connie: or had refused to take notice. (521)

Her performance effects a pointed, sarcastic commentary on their clandestine passion and its disrupting of the domestic order, while the writing, with rather lovingly nostalgic detail, extends the first novel's recollection of the colour, sound, and claustrophobic bustle of the working-class kitchen. And at the same time, the very attention drawn to the old woman's food-salvaging operation, with its implicit reproof – I suppose I am going to have to do everything myself! – seems to be tracing in the air the outline of the missing girl, who would normally have been there, helping with all the jobs that are going neglected; the recurrent conjunction of the fire in the grate and the old connections from the past, in the see-saw play of summoning and obliteration.

'Kitten of the cat', 'cat's-paw movement' – the tom cat is one of a series of feline images, distributed across both versions of the text and transferred from one character to another, until in the end Connie herself, who was the 'tiger-cat' who 'wants a mate, though the mate will probably devour his own offspring' (*The Second Lady Chatterley*, 250), seems to take over the tom cat's role. In a gesture ostensibly designed to feminise Parkin's utilitarian world, she sprays his handkerchiefs with scent – a piece of territorial marking half-consciously inviting the attention of potential rivals. At first the tom cat and Parkin seemed to belong together, feral, renouncing domesticity, reverting to their original natures, in a little sequestered masculine enclave of keeper and poacher, accepting as it were without complaint the harsh justice of the hunters' rules by which they live. We came upon the two of them at the moment when Parkin sensed that their enclave was being trespassed upon and contaminated by a female sentimentalism which could neither be countered nor placated by his appeal to that justice: '"Tha doesna want him to bite a' th' little bunny-rabbits, does ta, an' then eat 'em? . . . He wor a bad 'un. Look at him, an then cry for him. Look at him!"' (14). It is by no means unlikely that Parkin may have deliberately shot the cat in front of the girl, in aggressive defiance of the threats to the ordering of his world which are beginning to hem him round. In the second version of the novel, when Connie first comes to the hut where he is working, a half-memory of the shooting incident works its way into her view of Parkin as a pure-bred creature defending against adulteration: he 'guarded the wood like a wild-cat, against the encroaching of the mongrel population outside' (302), while the tom had seemed to her 'a rather fine, if mongrel poacher' (259). Having had, since the shooting incident, her searing vision of Parkin's body as he stooped over the washing bowl, she regards him at this point as a figure out of Fenimore Cooper, one of the last of the precariously surviving true race (with the sense, too, that his daughter would be one of the mongrels, a cross between the pure and the impure). But Connie is not aware that at the moment of her imagining this she is herself the encroacher, exposing the very fantasy of purity and seclusion which attracts her. She brings with her not just the taint of femininity from which he had tried to escape, but the taint of ownership, of the whims of the wealthy which make possible and at the same time circumscribe the life of outdoor solitude and self-sufficiency which he has been living. A gamekeeper's existence, as a servant offered a little domain of licensed mastery, is every bit as 'mongrel' as a poacher's. Especially in times of economic depression and heightened class resentment, anyone occupying the position would attract hostility from both sides: his own class would see him putting his local knowledge at the service of the enemy, while his employer would suspect him of sympathising with the poachers and working in secret to undermine the landowning interest. There would moreover be an inescapable sense of corruption and futility built into the work itself. The woods and spinneys to whose rhythms the keeper appeared so enviably attuned would actually be maintained by an entirely artificial form of land management, in which all natural predators of the game being reared would be ruthlessly controlled; such instincts as the keeper may have had either for the hunt or for nurturing would be warped by the sterile paradox of killing to preserve and preserving to kill. Whatever satisfactions his way of life offered would greatly depend upon his being able to hold all such paradoxes at bay; but here, the initial gunshot, the sound intended to say 'keep out', has the effect, by attracting Connie's attention, of inviting in the forces which breach distinctions, which make him freshly aware of his dependency, and distract him from his 'warpath instinct' (350): it is the last violent, would-be simplifying thing we see him do before smashing the photograph to pieces.

## 4

I think that this sense of a belated, misfiring, rearguard defence, of something false and corrosive which can also be psychologically soothing, may be remembered in the last and in a way the most mischievously inspired element in Lawrence's rethinking of the photograph-scene: the decision to shift the introduction of the chopping signal from one part of the text to another. In the first *Lady Chatterley*, Parkin's suggestion of a signal is linked directly to the hut, where the lovers first realised their mutual passion:

> 'Goodbye!' she said, to get away from the peculiar hypnotising spell of his fox-red eyes. 'I shall come to the hut.'
> 'If I'm not there,' he said, 'yer might chop a bit o' wood, so's I s'll hear, yer know. I s'll hear.' (61)

What would be running through her mind were she ever to do this? (She never does, in the first novel, unless in one of the missing sections of manuscript.) The sound she would make would remind her of the hammering that drew her towards him, when he was knocking together the coops: 'She liked to see him stooping, doing the rough carpentry' (31). Lawrence had used the vision of the man absorbed in manual work before, in *The Virgin and the Gipsy*, as a signpost on the road to female sexual awakening – tinker's hammering – and here more explicitly it creates a sense of refuge and calm for her, the proximity of order and purposeful concentration which 'made her feel *she* was working too' (31): an image drawn again from Lawrence's childhood, the memory of the father bent over small household tasks in 'Paul Morel' and *Sons and Lovers*, transferred over to Constance to evoke for her a lost sense of the reliable, almost of the omnipotent – 'I s'll hear, yer know. I s'll hear' – in which she could feel she was beginning again with everything still in front of her.[22]

But Lawrence's revisions give the chopping signal an entirely new set of coordinates. In the second *Lady Chatterley*, Parkin's suggestion is made immediately after the photograph-scene, when

> Suddenly, out of nowhere, he said to her:
> 'If you want to come to th' hut and I'm not there . . . take the hatchet and chop a bit o' wood. I s'll hear you – an' Flossie will. Chop a bit o' wood on th' block, you know. We s'll hear that.' (396)

The suggestion is now prompted by the sounds he has just been making while chopping up the heavy photo frame – the sounds not of building, shelter and security, but of destroying, scattering and breaking free.

Perhaps Lawrence felt that any association of the sound with the coop-building was no longer acceptable. The second novel certainly makes it more difficult for the reader to forget, in the idyll of rustic woodwork and handfuls of corn, that these pheasant chicks are being raised to gratify Clifford's obsession with death, the perverse underside of his exultation at having survived the war: 'the strange, awful thrill he felt when he saw a bird ruffle in the air, and make a curving dive' (228). The need now may be for a private lovers' code that is in no sense implicated in the corruptions and class dependencies of a keeper's working life. But once the chopping signal has been relocated in the way it is, everything encoded in it changes as well. When Parkin started to break the picture up, he did so with a methodical ferocity in which he became almost oblivious to Connie's presence beside him, and certainly oblivious to his earlier concern that they might be seen or heard together ('"But th' door is wide open, an' if anybody chanced to come afore we 'eered 'em!"' [391]). He carried the heavy frame outside, with Connie following, and loudly set about it with his axe. Afterwards – and the sequence does have a post-orgasmic feel to it, as if his exertions had partly relieved the frustration caused by Connie's refusal to have sex with him – he seemed to lapse into a gruff self-sufficiency, talking about how easily he manages his house without a woman's help, and appearing content and even a little eager for Connie to go back to Wragby: '"Shall we be going, then?" he said . . ."Shall we be going?" he repeated' (395). And when he sees the daisy she has threaded on her dress, his concern about their being discovered is renewed in a rather more self-centred way than before; he is extremely reluctant to endorse her desire to publicise their intimacy even this discreetly – '"Folks'll tell where you've been"' (395).

From her point of view, the emphasis is on how 'curious' (394) his behaviour had become on account of the photograph, and how unimportant to him she had suddenly been made to feel. There is a strange edge to his inviting her to replay, whenever she wishes to call him, the moment when a sense of liberation, of passing into a new life, coincided disconcertingly with this withdrawal from her, this sense of the persistence of an emotional world into which she cannot fully enter. For her to pick up the hatchet would not be to commemorate the first moments of their passion, as in *The First Lady Chatterley*, but to return her each time to the place of contradictions, a paradoxical fixing or re-freezing of the moment, just when consigning the photograph to the fire seemed to have effected a melting of apparent fixities. It is indeed a curious lovers' message which reminds its user of the barriers in the relationship, and how another relationship shadowed the birth of this; a nagging trace of that Ligeia-anxiety which never quite disappears from the text, that the first relationship might somehow still be the important one, the one that is really the source of the energy and intensity that Connie's intervention has merely catalysed. On the one occasion when she does actually use the signal, going on to make a fire at the hut with the wood she has chopped, some of these elements appear to be stirring: the fire in the grate, recalling its earlier connections – '"You feel sometimes," he said, looking at her, "as if you could start out with a hatchet an' begin smashin' the whole place up"' (461); the scene designed to assert a mutual commitment – this time by running naked in the rain and adorning each other with flowers – which still has its little pulses of not-quite-togetherness, slight misalignments of mind. (Connie sets up this wild interlude, which is flanked by Parkin's two spells of preoccupied gazing into the fire, to deflect them both from the thought of her imminent journey to France – her matter-of-fact discussion of which can only inadvertently indicate to him the gulf, once more, between her world and his.) Even the very idea of having her call to him by chopping seems to be motivated, in the second version of the novel, by his preoccupation with safeguarding the space around him. He suggests it after a period of listening with 'trained alertness' (396) for discrepant noises in the woods; he has learned to avoid being taken unawares. Chopping on the block, her message sent out hopefully into the silence, would be the kind of signal which leaves him with all the advantages, of mobility while she has to stay put, of choosing the moment and form of his answer; a little different in this respect from the vaguely Australian 'Coo-ee!', a signal with an implicit antiphonal equality built into it, which Connie shared with Clifford – a last trace of their former intimacy, which she betrays, in a fit of angry contempt, by using it to summon Parkin to help with the wheelchair motor:

> 'I must go,' she whispered.
> 'I shan't come to Sir Clifford,' he said.
> At that moment they heard Clifford's voice, away beyond the trees in the hollow, calling *Coo-ee! Coo-ee!*
> 'Coo-ee!' called Constance in reply.
> Then the keeper said again:
> 'I shan't come unless he shouts for me – I s'll be at th' hut.' She nodded, looking at him over her shoulder as she ran down the hill after Clifford . . .
> . . . The chair tugged slowly, unevenly up. . . . Then she stopped.
> 'You'd better call Parkin!' said Connie. 'He will perhaps be at the hut.'
> 'We'll let her breathe,' said Clifford.
> He waited a while, then started his little motor again. The chair made funny coughing noises, then reeled on a few yards, as if it were sick.
> . . . 'You may just as well call, Clifford! Why waste your nervous energy!' she said.
> 'Any other time, the fool would have been poking his nose in,' said Clifford crossly.
> 'Coo-ee! Coo-ee!' she called.
> And almost in a moment, Parkin came striding down the slope. (414–17)

Parkin seems almost to have been waiting in the wings to hear her demonstrate her transfer of allegiance in front of Clifford, who is himself too absorbed in his own frustrations to notice.[23] But although the chopping signal appears to mark as decisive a repudiation of Parkin's past as this way of calling to him does of hers, it would still seem to be dominated by some private business of his own, rather than by the pledge made to the lover; it would still seem to be reminding her, whenever she lifted the hatchet, of everything about him of which she could not be sure.

## 5

Parkin's concern to guard his space against intrusion might extend even to his most ostensibly intimate confessions; the account he gives, shortly after this, of how his sexual anxiety originated in his catching sight of Bertha's pubic hair, is so fluent and composed as to sound more like an attempt to prevent the question from being probed any further than a real exposing of wounds. In any event, the development of the novel has taken us a long way from the point where Constance was able to feel that studying her lover's photograph gave her an almost motherly insight into psychic tensions which he was unable to articulate. In *The Second Lady Chatterley*, there is no suggestion of her studying the photograph at all, let alone drawing any empowering inferences from it.[24] And in the final version of the photograph-burning scene it is Mellors, rather than Connie, who studies the picture first, pre-emptively imposing his own reading on it: '"Shows me for what I was, a young curate, and her for what she was, a bully," he said. "The prig and the bully!"' (*Lady Chatterley's Lover*, 199). Connie does demur from this a little, feeling that by the look of her 'the woman was not altogether a bully', but she sees nothing in the portrait of Mellors himself to contest his view of it.

Lawrence again altered the sequences as well as the details of the events. In *Lady Chatterley's Lover*, there is no chopping signal, and the photograph-scene is little more than a perfunctory pretext for Connie to ask questions about Bertha; questions which, in the second novel, had been held back for a later occasion. The afternoon tea in the cottage living-room, which had then led up to the sighting of the photograph, now occurs separately and earlier. Indeed, in the third novel Lawrence actually has Connie visit the cottage three times, once to the threshold and twice fully inside, before she finally manages to notice the photograph at all. The mood she brings with her to the scene is not the mixture of wistfulness and anger that had been aroused by Mrs Bolton's story, but a more straightforward irritable resentment, brought on by Clifford's behaviour when Mellors pushed the wheelchair – resentment which leads her to carry on rather petulantly interrogating Mellors about his sexual attitudes long after the conversation seemed to have naturally died, almost causing a quarrel. Almost nothing survives, in this photograph-scene, of the sense of the momentous, of the undercurrents of mutual vulnerability and defensiveness, or of the play of trespass, reassurance and betrayal, which seemed to have been set going by the original encounter with the photograph and Constance's first, solitary, hidden, anxiously tender contemplation of it.

But one idea that is remembered, that was latent in the discarded chopping signal, is of a Bertha seemingly brought back to life by the steps taken to erase her. The wild violence of her return becomes more intense with each rewriting, and the rather quaint, code-of-honour duel between Parkin and his wife's champion is replaced, in the end, by Mellors' imagining with relish the summary justice he would like to visit upon her (as indeed upon swathes of his compatriots): '"A raving, doomed thing in the shape of a woman! If only I could have shot her, and ended the whole misery! It ought to be allowed"' (280). The possibility that hovered over the second novel's photograph-scene now becomes harder to discount – that the main effect of Connie's intervention may actually have been to flush the gamekeeper out of cover, and to stir up all those dormant passionate antagonisms between him and his real or imaginary enemies – passions to which she herself remains curiously tangential. Elizabeth Fox, in an article in *Études Lawrenciennes*, went so far as to argue that the most important relationship at the end of *Lady Chatterley's Lover* was Mellors' relationship with himself, with the idea of his own manhood – Connie having served to reinvigorate both the manhood and the opposition to it which enabled it to be defined more clearly. In Fox's view, the letter Mellors writes to Connie at the end of the novel is 'more a salute to himself and to his connection with a phallic power' than 'a missive to Connie that foresees a happy ending for the couple'.[25] Certainly, in Mellors's earlier letter, one sees how relieved he is by the simplicity, at last, of being found out and hunted down, and by the chance he is given to exult, both in his enemies' discomfiture and in the emergence in himself of an anarchic, boat-burning persona who deliberately throws his own affairs into turmoil:

The cat is out of the bag, along with various other pussies (*sic*). You have heard that my wife Bertha came back to my unloving arms, and took up her abode in the cottage: where, to speak disrespectfully, she smelled a rat, in the shape of a little bottle of Coty. Other evidence she did not find, at least for some days, when she began to howl about the burnt photograph. She noticed the glass and back-board in the spare bedroom. Unfortunately, on the back-board somebody had scribbled little sketches, and the initials, several times repeated, C.S.R. This, however, afforded no clue until she broke into the hut, and found one of your books, an autobiography of the actress Judith, with your name, Constance Stewart Reid, on the front page. After this, for some days she went around loudly saying that my paramour was no less a person than Lady Chatterley herself. . . . Sir Clifford . . . asked if I knew that even her ladyship's name had been mentioned. I said I never listened to scandal and was surprised to hear this bit from Sir Clifford himself. He said, of course, it was a great insult, and I told him there was Queen Mary on a calendar in the scullery, no doubt because Her Majesty formed part of my harem. But he didn't appreciate the sarcasm. He as good as told me I was a disreputable character who walked about with my breeches buttons undone, and I as good as told him he'd nothing to unbutton anyhow, so he gave me the sack, and I leave on Saturday week, and the place thereof shall know me no more. (269–70)

It is striking how closely his style of writing resembles Clifford's. There are the same ironic clichés, the same affectation of distaste lying thinly over the malicious enjoyment (the way he pauses to name Connie's book, for example, a well-known catalogue of sexual exploits which he seems amused to find her evidently having acquired before her marriage) – as if by way of his vicious combat with Clifford something of the other's manner had mingled with his own. The burning of the photograph has now become the principal catalyst for the lovers' expulsion from the wood. For the first time in the three novels, the keeper's wife actually finds out that it is Lady Chatterley who is the other woman, and she finds out because in this version Mellors, his pragmatic instincts well to the fore, decided to save the backboard as well as the glass. But one has to wonder what exactly is being called into play when a married woman uses the backboard of her lover's wedding photograph as a doodling pad – on some unspecified occasion when she must have wandered into the spare bedroom with a drawing implement handy – and then signs the results with the initials of her maiden name. There would seem to be a scarcely manageable overload of meaning in this moment, a piling-together of so much that had been suggested in the earlier forms which the associated scenes had taken: territorial marking, discreet or cruelly triumphant; the wiping-from-the-record of both marriages at once; the element of filiality in Connie's relationship with the gamekeeper, that seems to draw out her nostalgia for the security of her adolescent, pre-war, family-sheltered life – to most of which overload one would imagine her completely oblivious, the vacancy of her doodling state allowing it all to work through her. Isn't there a hint of the sacrilegious still surviving in these final, strange refinements of the story of the photograph, whether we take Connie's behaviour to constitute an openly callous breaking of taboos, or an instance of her characteristic vague carelessness, whose repercussions suddenly come to matter? Mellors' account in his letter seems to carry with it a hankering for the sacred, for a sense of something larger than themselves hovering above even their most heedless actions. By way of the photograph, the lives of all four principal characters are brought, just for once, suddenly into juxtaposition, and we have a glimpse of how things might appear from the standpoint of their humiliated victims; on one side is the lovers' egotism – the hideous brittle insouciance of the letter, the sense in it that destiny is watching over them – and on the other side the surrounding world, of pain, failure, loss, emotional havoc and impotent vindictiveness, which touches and is touched by everything they do, and to which both of them struggle to remain contemptuously indifferent (judging by Connie's main reaction to this letter, her expression of annoyance that 'there was not a word about herself, or to her' [270]). Perhaps, too, in that brittleness, that indifference coming under increasing pressure from the sensitivity it is obliged to block out, one could also glimpse the psychic cost to the lovers of keeping up this level of disengagement from humane sympathy and fellow-feeling – a foretaste of how the repressed might return with the same indefatigability of pursuit which Bertha herself has demonstrated.

## 6

In the first *Lady Chatterley*, the reality of Parkin's desire only became truly apparent to him after the third sexual encounter:

> Parkin ... after coming back to the hut where she had been, and sitting there in silence, his hands folded between his knees, gazing out into the night, at the stars that seemed slippery between the boughs of the oaks, and seemed, somehow, like the body of the woman; after gazing a long time motionless and thoughtless into the night, as if all the night were woman to him: at last lay down on the straw in the hut, and wrapped in a soldier's blanket, slept immovable. (43)

The sensation of peace here seems the deeper for including much that might normally disturb it. His familiar landmarks are so flooded with the sense of the other that he can no longer see them steadily. They pulse in and out, near and far, until the gaze has nothing on which to settle – an experience evoking awed bemusement (with the faint suggestion of the birth of Christ playing over the last cadences); a trace, at 'slippery', of routinely misogynistic suspicion; and a reminiscence of the war, of a sentry's vigil, full of longing, anxiety and grateful relief: but all the potentially disruptive associations are folded in to a negative-capable acceptance of uncertainty and loss of control. As the rewriting develops, the novel has less and less use for this kind of lyricism. In *The Second Lady Chatterley*, while a more prosaic, restless version of this passage is retained, the transformation of the environment by passion took a different cast, and it began immediately after Parkin and Connie first had sex:

> When she was gone ... he waited in the darkness under a tree on the knoll, whence he could see the lights of Stacks Gate. ... The lights at Stacks Gate and at Tevershall seemed wickedly sparkling, and the blush of the furnaces, faint and rosy since the night was cloudless, seemed somehow aware. A curious dread possessed him, a sense of defencelessness. Out there, beyond, there were all those white lights and the indefinable quick malevolence that lay in them. (330)

The thought of the war, of exposure and refuge, the hut, the soldier's blanket, which seemed to belong so naturally to the imaginative coordinates of the original passage, has now given rise to a sense that the coming of the woman is like the launching of Verey flares, lighting up the previously obscure battlefield and searching out friend and foe alike. Increasingly, the emphasis falls on the clarifying of what he sees, the preparing of the ground for action, rather than on the faint challenge offered to vision itself, in the first version of this moment, by the sense of being absorbed within a quivering, vibrating cosmos which takes away one's powers to measure it. The Lawrentian hero is never lastingly content to *be*, as his woman invites him; he has to *do*, often in recoil from the new awareness of his being to which she has brought him.[26] And by the time of *Lady Chatterley's Lover*, the stars have disappeared completely, and the gamekeeper in his blanket can no longer sleep in peace:

> He went to the top of the knoll and looked out. . . . There were hardly any lights, save the brilliant electric rows at the works . . . an uneasy, cruel world . . . flashing with some rosy lightning-flash from the furnaces. . . . He went to the hut, and wrapped himself in the blankets and lay on the floor to sleep. But he could not, he was cold. And besides, he felt cruelly his own unfinished nature. (*Lady Chatterley's Lover*, 143)

# 5
# Strange Women with White Hair: 'The Lovely Lady', 'Mother and Daughter', 'The Blue Moccasins'

### 1

One of the snippets of information which Luke Lathkill included in his letter to Mark Morier, at the end of 'Glad Ghosts', was that his mother, Lady Lathkill, had been so stimulated by the birth of her grandson Gabriel – or what we presume she has allowed herself to believe is her grandson – that she spontaneously abandoned everything that made up her previous identity, and converted instead to the cause of the young. For an elderly woman to do this is almost unheard-of in Lawrence. Luke's comment expressed a little of the general astonishment: 'Even Mother doesn't look over the wall, to the other side, any more. It's all this side for her now.'[1] In the first version of the letter, Lady Lathkill's change of heart had been detailed more graphically: 'Mother ... has already settled upon [Gabriel] her small estate in Northumberland ... which she had previously willed away to the Psychical Research Society' (352) – that is, not only had she given up all her longstanding interest in spirits and séances, but she had pooled together the divided family assets and relinquished her claim to a separate, female financial interest. The 'ready-fisted' infant has fulfilled the grandmother's dream, leaving her nothing further to wish for; and in the euphoria of this conclusion, her relationship with her old friend Lucy, which had lasted so long and which on both sides of the grave had occupied all her loyalty and devotion, is simply thrown aside without a backward glance.

The story, as Mark Morier tells it, wants us to regard this throwing-aside as a sudden burst of enlightenment on the old lady's part, whereby the relationship with Lucy, artificially prolonged by spiritualism, stands revealed as a corrupt impediment to real relationship, or, at best, a false substitute for what had been missing. It could be argued that the reinstallation of patriarchal power, through the birth of a male heir, was the secret tendency of Lady Lathkill's behaviour all along; that her occult rituals, with their concern for exact obedience and for messages which brooked neither argument nor delay, were really unwitting efforts to compensate for the true sources of authority which the household temporarily lacked. On the other hand, her obsessive dedication to keeping Lucy's presence in front of them all, finding for Colonel Hale a replacement wife to perpetuate Lucy's influence on him, organising and preserving everything in the household as she imagines Lucy would have wished it, might suggest that part of what was motivating her was a displaced or screen mourning for her lost grandchildren – the condition which, as I tried to imply earlier, pervades that story, but from which the story itself does its best to turn away: so on either of these counts the arrival of the new grandson would bring Lady Lathkill's hidden wishes to light, and allow the screen relationship to be discarded. But sometimes – I am remembering again Parkin's wedding photograph – the very ruthlessness with which something is jettisoned can leave it strangely irradiated for a moment, just before it disappears from view. We could have a sudden glimpse of what the relationship between Lady Lathkill and Lucy might have been before its symbolic meaning for the story took it over: a simple friendship between two women, maintained over many years, and kept going through grief by every means available; the survivor's life sustained and given value by her dedication to the memory of her oldest friend, for the sake of the world they had shared together. If any of this reaches the surface of the text, it is only to stand as the perverse or even vaguely prurient counterpart of what, between Morier and Carlotta, was presented as entirely positive – the idea of a shared past, a connection going far back, which makes itself felt less through words than through gestures, glances, demeanour, modes of tacit and secret understanding which revive that old world and hold it protected. I tried to suggest in my earlier discussion of 'Glad Ghosts' that this was one of the deepest veins of feeling in a story which, wavering between going back and going forward, seemed so obscurely intimate with Lawrence's emotions on returning to Europe in the autumn of 1925. When Lady Lathkill calls out, 'Are you here, Lucy?' (196), is it not possible to hear something that Morier, who finds this call both chilling and hilarious, is not able or perhaps not willing to hear – the defiant, even rather majestic pathos of one for whom the world is momentarily enriched by the echoes of the past vibrating in it? But in this story the business of the old is to relinquish, to efface themselves, not to persist in their outmoded attachments. There is an undertone almost of menace in Luke's comment, 'It's all this side for her now', as if his mother's joy at the birth of a grandson were also a kind of permission to die, a *nunc dimittis* to accompany the other Christmas allusions which play rather mockingly around the names Mark, Luke and Gabriel; in the face of this new vision, Lady Lathkill lets go of every last feature which had made her herself, even to the point, one assumes, of giving up her belief in reincarnation, and her own anticipated return to earth as an animal rights campaigner (192).

Lawrence kept coming back, in the succeeding stories, to questions of age and ageing, in women almost exclusively. The women are primarily presented as grotesque 'devouring mothers'[2] (or mother-figures, like Lina McLeod in 'The Blue Moccasins'), blighting the lives of their offspring; but their own ways of experiencing and reacting to advancing age became a new and quickening focus of interest for Lawrence, somewhere in the corner of the extraordinary and indiscriminate hostility he appears to have conceived, sometime in the mid-1920s, towards elderly women in general.[3] Indirectly related to this is the motif which really unites all the stories I want to discuss, the return or resurrection of the father in the child: the dispelling of female power in the moment when the father's lineaments become unmistakably visible in the child's body. This dramatic moment characteristically effects a posthumous revenge of the father over the mother, triumphantly reclaiming the child as his own and liberating it from the mother's control. Moreover, since what is suddenly revealed is a form of direct transmission from father to child of the genetic essence of the line, the immortal, inherited structure, which is always invulnerable and always in its prime, its appearance constitutes a symbolic victory of the father–child connection, not only over the mother herself, but over all the processes of ageing and bodily decay which it is the mother's lot alone to suffer and exhibit. This motif first surfaced in 'Glad Ghosts', when Luke, at the climax of one of his rhapsodic outbursts, 'rose curiously on his toes, and spread his fingers, bringing his hands together till the finger-tips touched. His father had done that before him, when he was deeply moved' (206).[4] In that story, the language of inherited gesture, the father's chance to speak again, belongs with the other masculine alliances against the female domain of spirit-messages and mediums; but as 'Mother and Daughter' shows, it is not only male children whose bodies can, unbeknown to themselves, become their own and another's in the same moment. And it is not as if the presences of the two parents in the child were being equalised after long years of disparity; once the father has made himself felt again, the mother tends to be completely sidelined, her resemblance to or ongoing connection with her child minimised or denied altogether. Even Luke's histrionic speech of thanksgiving to his mother for having supplied him with his body parts was underpinned by a sarcastic incredulity at the idea that these two people could be in any way related; he seemed to be drawing attention as much to the gulf as to the link between his physiology and hers, when he cried out: "Oh Mother, thank you for my knees and my shoulders... thank you for my body, you strange woman with white hair! I don't know much about you, but my body came from you, so thank you, my dear. ... Goodnight, Mother, mother of my face and my thighs!' (207).

## 2

The ageing, devouring mother takes extreme form in the character of Pauline Attenborough, in 'The Lovely Lady'. Pauline's denial of her real age – she is 72, but in the half-light could pass for 30 – is symptomatic of a more wide-ranging perversion of nature in her, by which she has tried to maintain an iron grip on her grown-up sons. She is by some way the most aggressively excoriated of all Lawrence's elderly female characters, with the possible but by no means certain exception of Granny in *The Virgin and the Gipsy*; Lady Lathkill gets off lightly by comparison. 'The Lovely Lady' exists in two complete versions. Cynthia Asquith, having had some success in 1926 with her *Ghost Book*, began later that year to prepare an anthology of murder stories, to be called *The Black Cap*. When Lawrence sent his contribution, in February 1927, Cynthia thought it was too long and asked him to cut it – whereupon he proceeded to prune so much that the text ended up considerably shorter than she had wanted, although she did accept it in this revised form.[5] It was certainly unusual for Lawrence at this stage of his career to be asked to alter a story which he had obviously regarded as finished, having typed it out himself and made corrections to the typescript, but he took full advantage of the chance to re-examine it, and in the end reduced the text by more than a third.

The changes interest me not least for the hints they offer of certain impulses and drifts of thought that seemed to belong to the original conception, but which may, if the paradox can be allowed, only really become visible once they have been erased or modified. When Ciss climbed on to the roof, to sunbathe in the spot where she will eventually hear Pauline's voice coming up through the drainpipe, she saw, in the first version, 'the great rounded tops of the beech-trees calmly abutting into the upper, cleaner world'.[6] It sounds rather like a reminiscence of one of Lawrence's favourite Northern lyrics, Goethe's 'Wanderers Nachtlied' perhaps, where calm treetops, with the sun about to sink over them, speak of rest and blessing. But for Lawrence, true blessing would be more likely to involve revivification than rest; the sun over these beech trees is full of the warm South, burning vitality and confidence into the body, as if the passing, half-attentive imaginative work in the writing were being drawn towards a moment of miscegenation, of the blending of alien races. This in a story whose 'hero', Robert, is actually, unknown to himself, the fruit of such blending, the child of an Anglo-Saxon mother, Pauline, and a Latin father, an Italian Jesuit priest called Mauro; the reconciliation of northern and southern antipathies, which had been the subject of fantasy but never achieved in 'Sun', and tentatively promised but held in suspense at the end of *The Lost Girl*. When revising 'The Lovely Lady' Lawrence cut out the evocative line about the beeches and wrote instead 'the great elm-tops' (362). It is the kind of compression that seems to imply that what was discarded had been merely decorative – but why change beeches to elms, unless perhaps to spread around Pauline's house something more specifically English, ancestral, protective, like the elms on the Beveridge estate in 'The Ladybird', with none of those overtones of purity and the 'cleaner world'? Compton Mackenzie claimed that Lawrence told him it was the melancholy of elms which had driven him from England; is this seemingly trivial revision alert to something, or not alert?

One could more confidently say that the general tendency of the revisions is to make the condemnation of Pauline more open and direct than it already was. When she dresses in the style of a young Spanish beauty, having 'in some mysterious way,' as Lawrence puts it in his best affronted-dowager's tone, 'saved up her power of being thrilled, especially in connection with a man' (249), the phrase 'saved up' was reset in italics in the shorter version, to put additional stress on the calculating artifice of all Pauline's behaviour. The new text pushes Pauline away to a safer distance, across which she can be more straightforwardly attacked. It is partly that quantities of humanising biographical detail about her are taken out, and partly that the revised version also removes almost all the element of mutually conscious rivalry between the two women, Pauline and her niece Ciss who fight over Robert; the element of identification with the enemy that sanctifies the combat, without which the story simply tells of the worsting of an old woman by a younger one's opportunistic trick, repellent and humiliating. In the original text, Ciss's sunbathing had made her realise, in 'a dim kind of way . . . that Aunt Pauline was really a very fine sport, playing her own game with such perfect athletic skill and isolation. . . . Well why not? People must look out for themselves. . . . Here was a new creed, for Ciss, born of the sun in her' (252). Later, once their battle has been truly joined, the transfer of powers between the two women was made explicit: Ciss 'had stolen some of Aunt Pauline's mysterious strength, and she had it inside herself' (257). All this was omitted from the revised story. The idea of murder on which the story was grounded also began as an unstable energy of longing and repression vibrating between all three characters – energy which had given Robert a 'stiff, murderous mask' (251), and made a glance between Ciss and Robert 'sullen and desperate as murder' (251). But in the new text, murder is merely the crime that Pauline commits: 'It was clear murder: a mother murdering her sensitive sons' (363). The trend is to make Pauline into a more routine effigy in order to draw off and simplify feelings which had originally been more intricately distributed.

It may be that this reflects the ambivalence Lawrence must have felt, by 1927, towards anyone who, like Pauline, was devoting her entire life to disguising the truth about her bodily condition. In the account of his journey to Vulci, in *Etruscan Places*, a journey made in the April of that year, between writing the first and second versions of 'The Lovely Lady', Lawrence was intrigued, almost to the point of impertinent probing, by the mass denial on the part of the locals that they had ever suffered from malaria, despite what he took to be the obvious signs of it in their faces.[7] Certainly the new text of the story retains and, by weeding out some discursive interjections, strongly enhances the attention which the first version had paid to the physical and psychological techniques of denial. There is a half-bitchy, half-admiring fascination with how Pauline does it, sometimes expressed by way of a beauty-stylist's appraisal of her face – 'a lovely oval, and of that slightly flat type which wears best; because there is no flesh to sag' (244) – and sometimes through a more grotesquely alienating account of the 'invisible wire' of which only Ciss was aware, the wire that pulled up the wrinkles on Pauline's eyelids, wrinkles which, 'when the smile sank in weariness . . . would go haggard with the suggestion of geological centuries' (244), as if she were a specimen of something removed from the human order of time altogether (it is also a deft way of bringing the word 'haggard' into the story, in case we missed the allusions to She-who-must-be-obeyed). Pauline seeks as much control as possible, not only over her physical appearance, but over the ordering of the day, the rhythms and habits which she never allows to be disturbed. A bottle of champagne is drunk at dinner every evening – one of Lawrence's reactions, perhaps, to the scene in Ibsen's *Ghosts*, where the mother calls for champagne for her son, served by the girl whose position in the household is so ambiguous: a scene in which the paraphernalia of celebration is nervously brandished over the first stirrings of an unstoppable inner breakdown. By ordering champagne every day, Pauline is denying to every day its chance to be special, toying provocatively with all the longings she is stirring up. The perversity of her will to dominate is so extreme, and so easily satirised, that one could come to feel that a certain pressure is being exerted on the writing by what it is blocking out – that is, what one might think of as the normal reasons why the ageing might wish to suppress the evidence of their age; an anxiety about mortality gathers elsewhere in the text, having been shifted from the place where one might most expect to find it. Sometimes it is expressed through some brilliantly simple, almost cinematic visualisations, as for example when every week Ciss winds up the stable clock on the wall underneath her flat, or when Robert every day pours out the regulation two glasses each for his mother and Ciss before drinking the rest of the champagne bottle himself, or when Robert and Ciss are walking at night through the paddock, 'where the hay, cut late, was standing in cock' (259 – 60), a line changed in the revision to 'cut very late' (350). Or the anxiety emerges more directly, with an unusual, rather Jamesian pathos, omitted from the second story, when Ciss 'asked rather feebly': '"Don't you ever want to *live*, Robert?. . . To love, and to *feel* things. . . . To feel something before we die"' (258) – a last-minute plea to be exposed to the full extent of one's vulnerability, a plea seeming to speak of a deeper preoccupation in the story, lying underneath the more ostensible, *Virgin and the Gipsy*-theme of the stifling of 1920s youth, and 'the intense, impassioned sympathy of the young for one another, when they are overshadowed by the old' (250).

Another concern that was becoming current in the 1920s also finds a way into the text – the psychological impact of feminist progress and the adjustment of gender roles, since a good deal of Pauline's behaviour could be regarded as an extreme case of what the psychoanalyst Joan Rivière called 'womanliness as a masquerade', in a paper of that title published in 1929. Pauline's age-denial is not just a matter of using cosmetics, keeping everything unaltered, and being careful about the light she is seen in. She also affects a fluttery coquettishness whereby she acts the part of a man's girlish subordinate, despite being not only his senior but his superior in intelligence and acumen – acting the part so successfully that when she and Robert sit down together every evening to pore over his collection of old Mexican documents, 'it was as if he were the elder of the two' (250). Joan Rivière argued that this kind of increasingly prevalent behaviour represented an unconscious defence, on the part of professional and career women of the time, against the fear of reprisal from the masculine world they had successfully invaded; an attempt by the women to propitiate male resentment in advance, by reinstalling themselves firmly back into the orbit of male sexual desire from which their working lives might appear to have removed them.[8] There is a striking little subtext in 'The Lovely Lady', to do with Pauline's having made her fortune, before she did 'brilliant war-work, and became a Dame' (256), by dealing in the art market, 'on the basis', as the narrator puts it, 'of her father's collection' (256), so that what had been his hobby, his pride and joy (in the way she herself never was; 'he paid little attention to his daughter' [256]), became a series of smart investments for her, with her uncanny nose for the rise and fall of trends, and her hard-headed opportunism ingratiatingly disguised as good luck. The same business skills seem to be at work in her daily sunbathing ritual, to which she attributes a good deal of her remarkable preservation, but only because the time she spends exposing her skin is calculated with the care of an economist, anxious not to trespass too far, not to provoke what in the story's first version was the explicitly gendered source of her success into exacting retribution:

> 'Not too much sun, any more than too much shadow. . . . Not too much. Enough to absorb vitality; then stop, before the sun begins to absorb one's vitality back from one. Absorb vitality from the sun, but don't let him get hold of you, and absorb *your* vitality.' (254)

This is part of the monologue which Ciss accidentally overhears through the drainpipe, and since it is the same sun which implants in the younger woman the courage to go on to the attack, Ciss unwittingly becomes the agent of a large-scale phallic vengeance which for years has been patiently awaiting its moment, hiding in the recesses of her aunt's life – quite apart from the more conscious guilt which Pauline feels over her treatment of her elder son Henry.

'"Enough sun, enough sex-thrill, enough active interest, and a woman might live for ever"' (254), was Pauline's pithy assessment. The sex-thrill and the active interest both came from her browsing with Robert through his Mexican archives, 'old papers relating to the trial of English sailors before the inquisition at Vera Cruz', and other 'strange horrifying processes against nuns and priests, foreign merchants and travellers in Vice-regal Mexico' (247).[9] Pauline, once she started reading, was 'genuinely thrilled over these weird and often terrible stories. She always wanted to know, to know everything, especially the worst' (247) – always the classic female crime, for Lawrence, compounded by the obvious erotic delight Pauline was taking in the apparatus of terror and the violation of sanctities, all the time looking up 'so eagerly' at the man alongside her, her son, with whom she imagined herself 'a little in love' (247). It was on these occasions, when Pauline and Robert seemed to form their closest bond, and Ciss was politely dismissed, that the latter felt most keenly her exclusion and neglect, and her desire to wrench the seemingly helpless Robert from his mother's clutches. But what are we to say of Robert's own compulsive, unwitting, and occult fascination with the milieu of his secret origins, with Catholic history, the Inquisition, and the transgressive entanglements in these case histories of Saxons and Latins, priests and laity, sexuality and faith? Was it that what had really drawn him to these obscure documents was the trace of his father, trapped inside them like a genie, trying to send coded messages of his whereabouts to the one who might one day set him free? It seems as if a mysterious force were gradually gathering itself, both inside and outside the room where Pauline felt so thrilled and youthfully salacious, and were preparing with elaborate cruelty to expunge her from what she might have believed to have been her most intimate story; a force which the text finally unleashes in the form of storms, lightning and ghostly voices, but which is really the collective recrudescence of the masculinities which she in various ways had threatened or abused.

The first version of 'The Lovely Lady' included some heavy trailing of the mystery of Robert's father. The suspicious whisperings about Pauline, who at the time of Robert's conception was separated from her rather anonymous husband, Henry's father – 'Robert's coming made everybody catch their breath. But then, after all, Pauline's husband sometimes came to tea' (256) – were greatly cut in the new text, as were most of the transparently betraying details of Robert's appearance and manner. In particular what was cut, along with most other points of clear identification between Pauline and Ciss, was the sense in which both women were attracted to Robert because he unconsciously exhibited something finer under a dull surface. Despite his 'creamy-sallow face ... fat and expressionless', Ciss 'found in him a quality of beauty and pure breeding which she absolutely failed to find in Aunt Pauline's loveliness' (246); and for Pauline herself Robert 'was to her truly a wonderful, pure man with a touch of patient nobility. But he was also the ineffectual Robert who waddled a little when he walked' (250). Her fatal persecution of her elder son Henry over his choice of wife followed the familiar *Sons and Lovers* pattern. But in Robert's case it seems different, since here the mother is not really pressing extravagant emotional demands on her second son to compensate for the loss of the first, or for the deficiencies of the father. On the contrary, she is taking advantage of the fact that Robert just sufficiently resembles the man who fathered him as to stir up some renewed sexual vibrations for her to enjoy, while at the same time she regards Robert as 'only an English half-breed' (262), so manifestly inferior to his father as never to challenge the supremacy of the latter's image – the subtlest of insults to both the son and the father, eventually brought into the open when she says to Robert, in one of the few lines from this part of the story which Lawrence decided to keep, that his father 'was far too distinguished a man to have had you for a son' (269–70).[10] Her kind of sarcasm would seek to kill at the root a range of tangled emotions whereby a father might feel himself fulfilled, or disquieted, or touched to the quick by the way his son has turned out – an issue not approached in Lawrence at all often, although there was a curious, slightly overblown moment in *Aaron's Rod* when Jim Bricknell's father 'felt a wild tremor go through his heart as he gazed on the face of his boy'.[11] It is the truth about Robert's father's identity, and the disparaging contrast between father and son, that Ciss hears Pauline accidentally muttering into the drainpipe, and that finally spurs her into taking retaliatory action, speaking back to Pauline through the pipe herself, and pretending to be the accusing voice of Henry from beyond the grave. And with entirely appropriate irony, Pauline was muttering all this in a mixture of English and Italian: with fatal effect, since for Ciss it is the Italian part of the speech, whose meaning is unintelligible to her, which allows her for the first time to hear undistracted the poisonous and repellent caress Pauline puts into her voice; while the English passages supply the material information for the younger woman's subsequent attack. Lawrence is, as usual, unerringly ruthless in creating this perfect retributive moment, where the real engine of the old lady's downfall is her macaronic wandering, in a moment's loss of guard, back to the scene with Mauro which she has stored up all these years, the scene of her too delicious agony, as she calls it in a language her rival cannot understand.

I mentioned earlier how 'Glad Ghosts' and, in passing, the first two *Lady Chatterley* novels, had allowed the question to emerge of what it might be like to become a father and to have no further contact with one's child – the counterpart, in a sense, of an impulse from far back in Lawrence's writing, to imagine growing up in a household from which one's father had absconded, like Frank Beardsall in

*The White Peacock*, and was thus, unlike Arthur Lawrence, unable to disrupt or bring strife into the family on an uncomfortably regular basis.[12] Lawrence had described, in *Sons and Lovers* for example, the familiar process whereby fathers found themselves being excluded from the charmed circle of mother and child, exclusions in which, for the most part, fathers 'half-acquiesced'.[13] He had also hinted at a fascination with an even more radical form of effacement, reprieving and slightly sinister, in his account to Louie Burrows of a dream he had had, of her giving birth to their child, and his immediately feeling that 'I was the one who had to disappear from the scene, and there was a dark shadow in my place.'[14] But Mauro, in 'The Lovely Lady', is perhaps the most extreme fantasy-father Lawrence ever imagined, the one with whom only the most attenuated contact could ever be possible, since he would have automatically disinherited his child from his world in the very act of engendering it; it would be his secret commitment to the flesh he had turned his back on; he would have suffered the turmoil of having broken all his vows, of having fallen under the spell of a woman whose greatest thrill lay in seducing the supposedly pure (as happened to Dimmesdale in Lawrence's reading of Hawthorne's *The Scarlet Letter*); and the father-spark between him and his child would have to do all its mysterious work unaided, purified, and beyond conscious recognition.[15]

Lawrence did in fact know an Italian priest, or rather monk, called Mauro; Maurice Magnus's friend and benefactor in the monastery at Monte Cassino. I think there are some intriguing half-remembrances of Magnus, and of Lawrence's account of him which formed the introduction to Magnus's *Memoirs of the Foreign Legion*, running through the first version of 'The Lovely Lady', and largely cut from the revised text. After all, it was the photograph of Magnus's mother to which Lawrence gave the half-ironic title 'a lovely lady', and since she was supposed to have been the illegitimate daughter of the Kaiser, the secret lineage feeding through to Magnus was as exotic as they come.[16] Is it possible to suggest, without sounding merely facetious, that the author of 'The Lovely Lady' might himself have been found wandering, in unguarded moments, back to some dangerous ground? What would be at stake, in the pressure of those remembrances, would be how comfortably one could live with the decisions one had taken, up to the point of bearing responsibility for someone else's death – Lawrence had written, of his reaction to the news that Magnus had committed suicide to avoid being arrested for debt, 'I could, by giving half my money, have saved his life. I had chosen not to save his life.'[17] It is an issue which seems to me vividly present in the first version of 'The Lovely Lady', and considerably muted in the second. The revised text offers only a token acknowledgement of the inner struggle Ciss had to endure in order to see through the destruction of Pauline which her decision to intervene had initiated. But in the original story, the exhausting swings of emotion were right in the foreground:

> Ciss... wondered whether it would not be better to submit, to yield again to Aunt Pauline, and let the old rule sway again. It would be so much easier, and in a way, so much kinder. – But no! The fight had begun, and now it would have to go on. ... Sometimes [Ciss]... would have done anything to recall those words down the rainpipe. She wept in pure misery and terror of what had resulted. And then again she hardened her heart. Let it be so! (271–2)

Ciss has to deal not simply with her own vulnerability in the face of the pain she causes others, but with two distinct kinds of horror unleashed by her actions. The first is the spectacle of humanity shaming itself, in Pauline's behaviour after she has been condemned: 'wriggling and wriggling and wriggling to get away from the sense of her own guiltiness. And Ciss was determined... she should not escape. She should not emerge once more, for the millionth time, feeling good and blameless' (264). The odd hyperbole of 'millionth', odd because it is difficult to imagine that Pauline had ever felt especially guilty before, let alone that often, suggests how hard Ciss is having to work to wind herself up to her task. It also seems to sound a note of the First World War, the talk of millions, making Ciss's charge against Pauline, of 'forcing her will over others' lives' (264), resemble the charge the 1920s might have levelled at the generals, or at the 'old bitch gone in the teeth', as Ezra Pound put it in an image uncannily remembered in 'The Lovely Lady', when Pauline is described eating strawberries and biting off their stalks, 'showing all her teeth like a vicious dog' (268). As for wriggling, 'let us not try to wriggle out of it,' Lawrence wrote in the Magnus introduction, about the West's collective responsibility for the war.[18] Ciss's second horror is more insidious, the shock and the thrill she experiences on the roof, when she realises that she has inadvertently stepped into the priest's role herself, and has overheard Pauline's private confessions – a ghastly and comical thrill, not far distant from Pauline's own thrills as she helped to decipher Robert's Mexican papers. Perhaps all writers have moments when they are overcome by a comparable kind of panic, at the feeling that they may have penetrated somebody else's soul, crossed into forbidden territory and taken something into themselves which is more than they should have to bear. It is this sudden terror of their having become intimately part of one another that really makes it a life-and-death struggle between Ciss and Pauline, not their rivalry over Robert: something which the second version of the story, with its greater comic succinctness, actually sees more clearly than the first: 'Pauline was sending out her thoughts in a sort of Radio, and she, Ciss, had to hear what her aunt was thinking. How ghastly! How insufferable! One of them would surely have to die' (364).

The courage Ciss needed to survive all this was, in its way, a little like the kind Lawrence attributed to Magnus: 'the lonely terrified courage of the isolated spirit which grits its teeth and stares the horrors in the face and *will* not succumb to them'.[19] Most modern people, according to Lawrence, could not properly realise the horror Magnus went through, in the war; 'we haven't the soul-strength to contemplate it'.[20] The first version of 'The Lovely Lady' seemed to recall this, in the account of Robert's archive of Mexican atrocities: 'There were so many things the modern mind just refuses openly to contemplate' (247). This also was cut from the revised text. More dangerous ground? Lawrence seems always to have been afraid of forming lingering attachments which could not easily be thrown off. It was partly for this reason that he claimed his visit to see Magnus at the monastery of Monte Cassino, in February 1920, had been decisive and symbolic: a successful, once-and-for-all exorcism of the world of the past, of the amniotic beguilements of still and unchanging beauty, and of the temptation to regress. He recalled having said to Magnus, as they looked down from the monastery on to the railway station below, 'one's got to go through with the life down there. ... One can't go back.'[21] Wrenching himself away left him feeling that 'my heart was broken ... the old world ... had come to another end in me'.[22] But not only was this the kind of wrench that was never truly final, that Lawrence would have to go on making again and again, but he would also have been wrenching himself from all that was not made explicit in his account of his relationship with Magnus: the allure, to some part of himself from which other parts recoiled, of a free-scavenging, irresponsible, outlaw existence, unencumbered by any conventional restraint or female pressure. Perhaps that note is also distantly sounded in another passage cut from the first version of 'The Lovely Lady', when Robert discovers his real identity and remarks: 'The only comfort left is to know I am a bastard . . . I am glad. Now I needn't try to be inside the pale' (271).

When Robert first saw Pauline in her state of collapse, after Ciss, pretending to be Henry, had condemned her through the drainpipe, the age-gap between him and his mother, which her witchcraft had previously narrowed to nothing, suddenly appeared even wider than it actually was. '"Why Mother, you're a little old lady!" came the astounded voice of Robert: like an astonished boy, and with all the malice of youth' (267). His mother becomes at a stroke a 'strange woman', as Lady Lathkill had done – an estrangement intensified shortly afterwards, when Robert contemplates her dead body. At this sight, the 'astonished boy' seems to mingle with the priest in him, provoking reflections which combine little emotional spurts with a kind of detached, sermonising connoisseurship:

> Something very childish about the poor dead face, that smote his heart suddenly. And at the same time, that look of wilfulness and imperviousness . . . And at the same time, the pathos of a maid who has died virgin and unlived. It is the contradiction of a woman hardened to her own will; she never lives, she only knows what it is to force life. Because living, for a woman, means the gentle interpenetration of her life into other lives, other lives into hers . . . This was how Robert saw her. (273–4)

His interest in exploring the nuances of what can be said about her, implicit in the repeated phrase 'at the same time', quickly subdues what remains of his sense of personal connection with her. 'At the same time', doubled like this, also hints again at how casually and yet deeply the writing is drawn to the mingling of disparate conditions, among the other miscegenations and illicit crossings in the story (even a passing concern as to whether cousins should be allowed to marry, although Robert and Ciss of course turn out not to be cousins), with Pauline seen as a child, a virgin and a wilful old woman all at once, separate temporal phases telescoped together: as if to the eye of eternity she appeared both complete and unfulfilled, in covert allusion to Keats's 'still unravished bride of quietness', a line which seems to have kept coming into Lawrence's head in these years and which appears again and again in his late writings. David Ellis, in his discussion of this passage, pointed out 'how struck Lawrence had been by the virginal expression on his mother's face when she was dead', and that in 'The Lovely Lady' for the first time he was no longer interpreting that look in 'a wholly positive way. . . . It suggests that he was now blaming Lydia Lawrence more bitterly for the man he had become . . . and doubting that she had cared for him with anything like the fervour with which he had been devoted to her.'[23] I think myself that the blaming is actually much stronger in the revised version of the story, where Robert neither looks at nor muses over his mother's body at all. His closing remarks are now made into explicit accusations, launched at his mother's departing spirit in the peevish and self-dramatising tones of one still possessed by it:

'Do you think your mother ever loved anybody?'. . .
'Herself!' he said at last. . . .'She put a sucker into one's soul, and sucked up one's essential life.'
'And don't you forgive her?'
'No . . . I *know* I've got a heart,' he said, passionately striking his breast. 'But it's almost sucked dry. I *know* I've got a soul, somewhere. But it's gnawed bare. I *hate* people who want power over others. –' (355)

But the original ending had been quite different:

'It is as you say, there must be some sort of a God somewhere, and some sort of divine justice. Otherwise it's not worth having – life. One can go so awfully wrong, without knowing. Nobody tried to keep mother right, when she was a little girl. And she didn't know how to keep me right, when I was a boy. If there's no God of any sort to appeal to, Ciss, you've not got much of a catch in me.' (274)

Ciss, herself the daughter of a clergyman, had expressed her own religious anxieties earlier, saying to Robert that she had a bedrock of trust 'somewhere. ... If I didn't I should feel so awful and guilty' (272). Far from blaming his mother for his troubles, in the first version of the story Robert had seen his mother and himself linked in a common predicament; the resurrected father in him might, through the vehicle of his son's compassion, almost be articulating his own remorse at how the absence of proper paternal care and guidance during childhood, Pauline's and Robert's alike, may have sent ripples of damage through the generations which the father-spark alone would be powerless to repair.[24] Only God the Father, it seems, could ever put right what the human fathers had for whatever reason left undone. By erasing not only all this speech, but all Robert's reflections over his mother's death-bed, the revised story seems to be trying to deny that all the subjects originally prompted by the spectacle of Pauline's body – mortality, doubt, regret, unfulfilment – were really subjects of this story at all. It is strange that Lawrence should at first have named Pauline's house 'Old Brinsley', after the colliery where his father worked, and then left the house unnamed in the second version. But all the alterations of tone and mood cannot wholly dissipate the sense that the vicinity of old age and physical disintegration seems to have drawn up a fear in the writing, that emancipation may have come too late, that childhood damage may have gone too deep for a mid-life rebirth to have any real substance; and that, rather like Lady Lathkill, one may be experiencing an upheaval whereby the whole of one's previous life is rendered meaningless or fraudulent, but there may not be enough time, energy or faith left to find anything with which to replace it.

Perhaps one could read this differently, though, and see a memory of Magnus still haunting the story, in the change between the two endings: the first so extraordinarily downbeat, the second so brisk and uncompromising. Are they facing each other, as Morier and Lady Lathkill had done, in unresolved debate over what it would be to deal justly with the dead, with those closest to us, like our parents, on whom we feel called to pronounce? In the Magnus introduction, Lawrence had asked 'Who dares humiliate the dead with excuses for their living? ... Forgiveness gives the whimpering dead no rest. Only deep, true justice.'[25] In the first version of 'The Lovely Lady', Lawrence had tempered the judgement with a hesitant intercession of fellow-feeling; but the verdict of the new text is hard and unmitigated, offering the condemned not sympathy for what she had lost, but the lonely dignity of what she had chosen.

## 3

The ending of the story 'Mother and Daughter' (1928) is unsettling in a comparable way. One could try to read it in the way it seems, on the surface, to want us to, as a celebration of the defeat of the ageing and repressive mother, this time called Rachel Bodoin, and the liberation of the daughter Virginia from suffocating ties. But one would have quite a struggle to dispose of the nagging sense that things had gone too far for anybody really to feel triumphant, except the sixty-year-old Armenian businessman Arnault, who has insinuated himself into the opportunity that the mutually corrosive mother–daughter relationship finally came to offer him. If Virginia's marriage to Arnault is seen as a successful outcome for her, then again it is as if the mother's behaviour had been directed throughout and unbeknown to her by occult and hidden forces, of which the daughter was the ultimate beneficiary; Virginia's earlier, inadequate suitors had to be scared off by her mother's 'awful female humour', and Rachel's relationship with her daughter had to decline into testiness and acrimony, in order to clear the way for this 'Turkish-carpet gentleman', whom Rachel detests, but who is completely impervious to her mildly racist sarcasms.[26] The re-emergence, to the mother's dismay, of the father in the child, taking his revenge on the mother through the child, is more explicitly detailed here than in the other stories:

> Virginia was her father's daughter. Could anything be more unseemly, horrid, more perverse in the natural scheme of things? For Robert Bodoin had been fully and deservedly knocked on the head by Rachel's hammer. Could anything, then, be more disgusting than that he should resurrect again in the person of Mrs Bodoin's own daughter, her own *alter ego* Virginia, and start hitting back with a little spiteful hammer that was David's pebble against Goliath's battle-axe! (236)

In this case, the child does not enact the father's revenge simply by coming to resemble him, but by deliberately turning away from the mother to search for an alternative father-figure, in a belated, half-conscious attempt to find what had been missing. Virginia seems happy to accept a daughterly role in her marriage to Arnault, after all the years when she has effectively been her mother's 'wife', since she and her mother 'set up married life together' (228) in their Bloomsbury apartment, and entertained in the evenings, sitting 'brilliant and rather wonderful, in magnetic connection at opposite ends of the table' (230). The daughterly role would have some clear advantages; as Janice Hubbard Harris put it, Virginia will have 'a future – a home and a mate', and after years of enervating toil in the Civil Service, 'once married, she will balance her private and public life, allowing each to nourish the other'.[27] Her husband-to-be, the Turkish Delight, as Rachel named him, offers an opulent and scented benevolence: 'Dear little girl, Arnault will put flowers in her life, and make her life perfumed with sweetness and content' (242). At the same time, by marrying into a tribal order in which women have completely subordinate positions, Virginia will have to abandon the equality she is accustomed to and continue indefinitely playing the 'little girl' Arnault takes her to be; she will have to understand that for all her personal attractions she is primarily a calculated financial investment for him, with her business experience and her valuable apartment; she will have to cede precedence to her new stepsons, for whose reception whenever they visit London the apartment is now earmarked; and she will have to regard herself, having once been head of a government department, as a slightly superior grade of secretary-cum-hostess who provides her employer with occasional sexual services. Rachel's hostility towards her daughter's marriage is obviously justified in ways which even her disappointed egotism cannot vitiate. Nor can one be entirely sure of the textual drift here; whether this marriage, this outcome represents the best Virginia could obtain, or whether her coming to believe that this was the best was itself the final wound that life with her mother had inflicted on her.[28] Mother and daughter take their leave of each other in a bitter series of Parthian shots:

> 'I think the Armenian grandpapa knows very well what he's about. You're just the harem type, after all.' The words came slowly, dropping, each with a plop! of deep contempt.
> 'I suppose I am! Rather fun!' said Virginia. 'But I wonder where I got it? Not from you, mother –' she drawled mischievously.

'I should say *not*.'

'Perhaps daughters go by contraries, like dreams,' mused Virginia wickedly. 'All the harem was left out of you, so perhaps it all had to be put back into me.'

Mrs Bodoin flashed a look at her.

'You have *all* my *pity*!' she said.

'Thank you, dear. You have just a bit of mine.' (248)

What seems to come through most strongly here is the need, on both sides, to deny resemblance, to define each as the other's antitype, and to impose these black-and-white finalities on the issue, in order to avoid having to examine aspects of the situation that cannot be simplified so easily. 'You have *all* my *pity*' may have been intended to be a sarcastic, obliterating dismissal. But it could in a way be curiously literal, responding to the vocabulary of inheritance which Virginia has just been using; the mother seeing her daughter at the last as reproducing her own chronic incapacity for pity, and suddenly, even self-sentencingly, seeing herself through the other, stranger and replica in the same moment – a recognition which rather disrupts her attempt to be withering, doubling the emphasis as if unsure where it should most effectively fall.

Either way, the mother's prized repose has trembled a fraction; the whole story has been engaged in a contest for the meaning of the word 'repose'. Rachel, aware of her own 'terrible inward energy' (225), and anxious to conceal it, 'sat with a perfect repose . . . she cultivated repose. Her very way of pronouncing the word, in two syllables: re-pòse, making the second syllable run on into the twilight, showed how much suppressed energy she had' (225). This is 'repose' precisely as Ruskin used the word, to denote the temporary resting of a body whose essential condition lay in movement, a condition intimated by the very quality of the resting. Unlike Pauline Attenborough, Rachel is not interested in sex-thrill, or in pretending to be young; 'repose' for her is the appropriate bearing for a woman past mid-life, the manifestation of a power she is choosing for the moment not to exercise, like 'the dangerous repose of a pugilist' that Luke Lathkill saw in the infant Gabriel. But for Virginia, repose is what you need to be able to obtain when you are tired, and it is a mark not of self-sufficiency but of relationship, of the recuperative shelter which certain kinds of relationship can offer, the maternal body which her actual mother seems not to possess; it was in the 'homeliness' Lawrence found in the curvaceous Etruscan places, with their 'curious peaceful repose', the 'stillness and a softness in these great grassy mounds with their ancient stone girdles',[29] or that Virginia finds in Arnault, with his 'soft still hands' (242) and his 'fat immobile sitting' (238), telling her 'you are so thin, dear little thing, you need repose, repose, for the blossom to open, poor little blossom, to become a little fat!' (242). Repose here would also be the afterglow of fulfilment, predominantly sexual, and exactly what, in Arnault's eyes, Rachel lacks. 'But what, under holy Heaven, are you as a woman? You are neither wife nor mother nor mistress, you have no perfume of sex' (240) – no stored-up warmth in her, of the kind Ivy Bolton had, and Lady Eva, in *The Second Lady Chatterley*, thought she might have had if only she had married a policeman.[30] In the symbolic pattern of 'Mother and Daughter', Virginia is rescued from her mother's fate, as well as from the debilitating effects of the struggle for success in the masculine workplace, by the restorative intervention of Arnault's pre-modern patriarchal values; when he nominates an early wedding day, she replies 'Very well!' (echoing, consciously or not, her mother's 'Very well!' of a few minutes earlier), having been 'caressed again into a luxurious sense of destiny, reposing on fate, having to make no more effort, no more effort, all her life' (247). But in the human pattern, Virginia might also have ended up thinking that his cynical and self-satisfied paternalism represented 'fate' or 'destiny', something to repose on, because the pressures of her way of life have exhausted her judgement, because she 'was amazingly stupid when it came to life, to living' (241–2), because she has always been easily fascinated, and because she never had the kind of father who would have refused, for her sake, to allow himself to be so comprehensively eliminated from the life of his own family.

## 4

I do not think it need be too controversial to suggest that the fairy-tale motifs of these stories, the paternity-revelations, the spectacular come-uppances and petard-hoistings, are discharging some fairly dark psychic material. The more so, perhaps, for Lawrence's having on this occasion given the oppressive mother Rachel a good number of his own characteristics: a capacity to stay unflaggingly interested in her daily household tasks, for example, and a gift for mimicry, whose power over its victims is described almost enviously –

> She had a really marvellous faculty of humorous imitation... really touched with genius. But it was devastating. It demolished the objects of her humour so absolutely, smashed them to bits with a ruthless hammer, pounded them to nothing so terribly, that it frightened people. (230-1)

She also follows Lawrence's precepts in refusing to allow past projects to define or restrict her, an attitude culminating in a speech which one could imagine Lawrence not only approving but virtually making: '"Virginia, don't you think we'd better get rid of this apartment, and live around as we used to?... We had the pleasure of making it. And we've had as much pleasure out of living in it as we shall ever have"' (237). But the prevailing bitterness in these stories of wasted lives and wrong turnings is not the only mood that contact with elderly women can provoke. It was said by way of another such woman that, on the contrary, 'Tragedy is lack of experience'.[31] This was Marinina, in 'Sun', 'a woman of sixty or more, with... dark-grey eyes that had the shrewdness of thousands of years in them';[32] she of the half-mocking laugh and the Etruscan smile, the smile of the old world, whose enigmatic power Pauline tried to imitate, the smile that flashes its indeterminable mixture of sympathy and disdain on the flounderings of the young and the uninitiated, and turns life into a comic theatre whose actors are either ignorant or vainly defiant of the roles given them to perform. Would it be a hazard too far to suggest that the playful lambency of Lawrence's late style, the unpredictable shifts of allegiance, whereby the same character can be treated at one moment with intimate concern and the next with sardonic dismissiveness, sometimes even in the same sentence, might owe something to the outlook of that kind of elderly woman, the kind who takes an amused or sprightly or exasperated view of a scene from which she has herself withdrawn, and to whose fates and problems she remains at bottom perfectly indifferent?

Both the bitterness and the indifference seem equally marked in Lawrence's last completed story, 'The Blue Moccasins', written in July 1928. It is almost soufflé-rich and light, full of teasing allusions to what is stirring underneath it, but carried off with such extraordinary nonchalance that one struggles for a way of discussing the story that could keep faith with this. There is a self-parodying element in Lawrence's reaction to being asked to write something for the Christmas number of a magazine called *Eve: The Lady's Pictorial*; he gives its readers the hero they would presumably have wanted from him, a well-bred, passive, good-natured middle-class man who falls in love at the end, reveals an unexpected vitality and masterfulness, and starts saying things like 'Aye!' and 'Happen so!' But it is at the same time an emotionally difficult story, with a tension even stronger than that in 'Mother and Daughter' between the pantomime simplification of themes and the complex distribution of sympathies. The same pattern is at work as in 'The Lovely Lady' – a youngish woman called Alice Howells helps a youngish man, Percy Barlow, to free himself from a fascinating female of the previous generation, the 57-year-old Lina McLeod. This time the fascinator is the man's wife rather than his mother, even though 'it's quite impossible', as Alice spitefully remarks, 'to think of her as anything but Miss McLeod!'[33] But as with the other stories, the apparently decisive outcome occludes something equivocal; this time, it is unclear whether the old woman really has been defeated, or has retreated from the battle in some relief, conceding victory to her rival while intimating that the prize was not worth fighting for.

In the world of the pantomime play, *The Shoes of Shagpat*,[34] which Percy and Alice perform together while Lina watches, old people are simply villainous tyrants, fair game for any abuse. The young yearn to escape from them, and always eventually succeed, to the loud applause of the onlookers. The blue moccasins themselves are drawn into this symbolisation; they are made to signify the wearer's enslavement, and are repeatedly flung triumphantly aside – 'Away, shoes of bondage, shoes of sorrow!' (199). Percy, in the role of Ali, makes for a comic and distinctly cut-price *Sheikh* (Arnault, in 'Mother and Daughter', might have been created in satirical homage to Valentino; I'll show them what a real Oriental lover looks like!). On stage, Percy's Eastern costume and make-up does for him exactly what Alice's does for her; it allows his body to exhibit the full history of his desires, in his case to take part in a heroic rescue, to be enraptured and seduced; the history which his mind, unlike Alice's, has yet to acknowledge. But in some ways the more striking revelation in Percy's performance is his apparent obliviousness to the likely effect on Lina of seeing another woman kicking the blue moccasins around the stage; especially since he had already lied about their whereabouts when Lina asked him. For her, of course, the moccasins represented the moment, early in their marriage, when Percy said to her that their beautiful blue colour was not so blue as her eyes – a piece of affectionate triteness which had helped her delude herself into believing that the age difference between them need not matter. Lina's intervention from the stalls, more brilliantly dramatic than anything in the actual play, when she stands up just as the lovers are in the middle of their clinch and says 'Percy! . . . Will you hand me my moccasins?' (200), seems to effect a fleeting, pitiful protest, not only against what is happening on the stage, but on behalf of the ageing more generally, forced to watch as so many things that meant so much to them are stolen, trampled over and brutally assigned new meanings, in the inexorable process whereby one generation displaces another. Lina protests against what she, unlike Marinina, cannot yet accept with equanimity: that everything to which she felt most intimately connected should eventually become a prop in that comic theatre, a theatre which allows neither nuance nor nicety, but presents instead only the endless replay of the great symbolic patterns, to which individuals have to submit, and within which all their most anxiously discriminated concerns seem trivial. The cruel shifts of tone in the text keep rehearsing this. The sentiment in this line, for example: 'But sometimes she went to him in his room, and was winsome in a pathetic, heart-breaking way' (194), is brusquely stamped on half a page later: 'she went to him now, to be nice to him, in her pathetic winsomeness of an unused woman of fifty-seven' (194) – where her behaviour is no longer her own, has nothing individual about it, but is merely an example of how women of her age and type behave, the part now allotted her which she cannot choose but play.

The resurgence of the father in the son is given an ironic twist in this story. Percy, 'pliable as wax' (193), ends up exactly where his father was, in a rectory, with a new woman, in whose hands he 'was but as wax' (188). It is curious how so many characters in the late stories, from *The Virgin and the Gipsy* onwards, turn out to be the children of clerics, sons and daughters of the vicar. And for Percy some latent sense of betrayal, over his father's failure to behave in accordance with his standing, seems to get into his furious denunciation of

Lina after she has left the theatre; a denunciation which rather resembles the one launched against Granny in *The Virgin and the Gipsy*, in its excessive disproportion to anything the old woman may seriously be supposed to have done. Throughout his adult life, Percy seems to have been harbouring a slow-burning fuse of resentment against his father, for having allowed himself to be controlled by a woman, Percy's stepmother, and having acceded as a result to what was effectively the expulsion of his son from his home. Now, as Percy pours out his bitterness upon Lina – '"Wouldn't even leave the moccasins! And she'd hung them up in my room, left them there for years – any man'd consider they were his' (206) – it is as if we were hearing echoes of what might have passed between Percy and his father years before: the blustering justifications of contemptible behaviour, and the mean, cringing animosity towards an authority-figure who is safely out of earshot. Blaming Lina entirely for the breakdown of their marriage, Percy leaves unmentioned the difference in their ages, the stumbling block most obvious to everyone else – a silence seeming to betray, among other things, the strength of his need to deny that his relationship with Lina was implicated from the outset with his unresolved feelings towards his family. So much so, that now the excitement of acting with Alice has stirred all his emotions up, he seems to need Lina even more than he did before, as a screen to avoid having to confront the problem with his father, leaving himself free to become like his father, and to enjoy the purely selfish fruits of so being.

Percy had always denied, from the beginning of their marriage, that the question of Lina's age was at all troubling to him. He denied it with an intensity of utterance he never matches again until now: '"Don't talk about old! You're not old!" he said hotly. . . ."You're younger than me, in most ways, I'm hanged if you're not!"' (189). But it remains the unspoken subtext of all that follows; even of his implying that the moccasins had been left in his room for so long that they could be regarded as having passed into his possession by a kind of law of custom. In the first, abandoned version of the story, where Percy's name was Barclay rather than Barlow, everything to do with the age-question was clear-cut. The narrator told us outright that 'it's a crazy thing for a woman of forty-eight to marry a man of twenty-six', and that they could never have a genuine relationship, only try to play roles for each other. 'She didn't quite know whether she was his mother or his little-girl sweetheart or his wife or his aunt or his school-mistress: in a bewildered fashion, she was all these things in turns: and he was in turns her son, her little-boy sweetheart, her husband, her poor nephew, her pupil, and her bank-clerk.'[35] In this version, Percy came to be straightforwardly repelled by his ageing wife's appearance, felt intermittently guilty for being so, and was really thinking of other girls when he made love to her. But in the re-written story, the mood is much more complex. In one scene, oddly reminiscent of a famous moment in *The Waste Land*, the numbed, taciturn war-veteran stares mutely while his wife works at her hair:

> And he would sit there silent, watching her brush the long swinging river of silver, of her white hair, the bare, ivory-white, slender arm working with a strange mechanical motion, sharp and forcible, brushing down the long silvery stream of hair. He would sit as if mesmerised, just gazing. (190)

The play of attraction, repulsion and uncontrolled memory seems so indeterminable as to leave Percy completely lost in the strange richness of what this vision could be saying to him: about his mother and stepmother (the passage is clearly remembering Paul Morel's obsession with his mother's hair-colour in *Sons and Lovers*); about everything he has seen at the Front, the bleached bone-whiteness, the not-quite-alive, uncannily repetitive bodily movements; about the quest for restored youth and beauty on which the old always seem to be venturing, about everything that waits ahead for him – all involved in some hideous, war-generated Angel-of-Death fascination, rather like Colonel Hale's towards Lucy, in which awed devotion, horror and an unacknowledgeable hatred seem to weave their way in and out: 'he would watch her, watch her, watch her, as if she was the ultimate revelation' (192).

Alice, who seeks to shake him out of this, belongs in her own way to the war-damaged generation, which has to settle for what it can get. No doubt she can hear the petulant self-pity in Percy's final outburst – 'Wouldn't even leave the moccasins! And she'd hung them up in my room' – as much as the rage of old Adam which the narrator claimed it was expressing. It was the war, of course, which set the context for all the relationships in the story. Alice's young husband was killed, and she refused, like Connie Chatterley, to take her fate tragically – with the result that a brittle show of normality was imposed on repressed layers of frustration, anger and grief, to make a highly combustible package. Alice's trailing around with her 'a very perky little red-brown pomeranian dog that she had bought in Florence in the street' (192), would appear, given Lawrence's old notion of Florence as the quintessential city of men, to be an obscure comic demonstration both of Alice's instinctive homage to masculinity and her ironic view of its pretensions, together with an anxiety about loss and not wishing to lose anything more; and what she sees when she looks at Lina is a woman who managed to keep her man when others had theirs taken away. Lina was evidently sufficient of a personage to have had some influence at the War Office; she could not pull strings quite so effectively as Pauline in 'The Lovely Lady', who made sure Robert stayed at home for the duration, but she did hold on to Percy until 1916, when, in what was either a careless slip or a piece of gratuitous mockery on Lawrence's part – or was it another half-glance across towards T. S. Eliot? – we are told the young man was sent to Gallipoli; the campaign there had actually been abandoned and all the surviving British troops evacuated by the middle of January. The clash between Alice and Lina is clearly grounded in a competition for scarce resources, a special, war-aftermath version of the impulse behind all the fairy tales of wicked stepmothers who hoard for themselves what ought to belong to others; and in this case the passion to defeat the rival woman, to expropriate her, seems considerably greater than the passion for the man, or in a sense indistinguishable from it:

> Alice ... was worked up now, caught in her own spell, and unconscious of everything save of him, and the sting of that other woman, who presumed to own him. Own him? Ha-ha! (199)

Behind their confrontation is the fear running in the veins of the story, the fear each woman summons up in the other, of growing old and lonely and abandoned; and Percy, with his usual crass disregard for what anyone else might be feeling, cranks up the pressure by saying to his wife, in front of Alice, that his performance with the moccasins '"doesn't really hurt *you*, now does it?"' (204). As if, being female, one could pass beyond feelings, reach an age where one was no longer deemed to have any, and be routinely subjected as a result to blind inconsiderateness or open cruelty; as if part of Percy were still in the pantomime, viewing the aged as mere cartoon obstacles, and the other part in life, needing Lina, for reasons he is unable to be clear about, to appear invulnerable, untouched, far above the ordinary world.

It was because that fear worked itself in behind Lina's love of solitude, of 'the bliss of being quite alone, quite, quite alone' (191), that she came to see the pantomime in the first place:

> As night fell, and rain, Miss McLeod felt a little forlorn. She was left out of everything. Life was slipping past her. It was Christmas Eve, and she was more alone than she had ever been. Percy only seemed to intensify her aloneness, leaving her in this fashion. (196)

It is impossible to unravel the strands of real sympathy from those of jeering mock-sympathy in a passage like this. But when Lina does arrive at the show, she is not only humiliated but energised, quite as much as Alice is by her acting. Lina becomes so angry that she no longer worries about alienating her husband by allowing him a glimpse of her contempt for him, and she no longer feels obliged to play the perfect lady, someone too genteel to react to lies and insults. The drama of the moccasins finally purges her misplaced desire not to be 'left out', re-establishes the positive vision of solitude which she had momentarily doubted, and paradoxically brings about a release from bondage for all three characters. And when Alice invites Percy to spend the night with her at her father's rectory, we are reminded that this is Christmas Eve, the season of renewal, when not only were the old gods supplanted by the young, but the one for whom no room could be found (Lina arrived so late that all the seats in the hall had already been taken) was the one at the centre of the miracle.

## 5

Christmas is the time for gifts, and Percy's attack on Lina turned upon the question of whether the moccasins were to be regarded as a gift from her to him: not only whether property rights in them had passed to him by custom, but whether her having hung them up in his bedroom signified from the beginning that they were now to be considered his own. The question only entered the story during the last stages of revision, since in the original manuscript sketch Miss McLeod hung the moccasins in her own bedroom, unequivocally as a keepsake from her special moment. There would have been a quite different meaning to Percy's removing them in those circumstances. The new element of doubt over giving and taking seems to have set up an unusual uncertainty on Lawrence's part as to how his story should end – an uncertainty to which he drew attention when reading his manuscript to his friends the Brewsters. He paused to ask whether they thought Lina should give the moccasins back and allow the performance to continue, or take them away with her. They thought she should give them back, and Lawrence at first seems to have thought so too, changing his mind at the last minute and writing the new ending in between the crossed-out lines of the old one.[36] If Lina gives the moccasins back, accepting her own redundancy, in a ceremonious handing-over to her younger rival, like the closing scene of *Der Rosenkavalier*, she bestows a kind of blessing on the lovers while leaving them with a provoking sense of obligation to her, which one feels Alice at least would much rather have done without. If on the other hand Lina takes the moccasins away, turning her back on it all in a clean break, she more completely disentangles their lives from her own, while bequeathing them the feeling that they have shamefully abused and humiliated her, a feeling left to work whatever poison it may. Lawrence seems at times to have felt that victors were somehow diminished by their victories – not just because with nothing left to fight against, one's life was deprived of meaning, but that something seemed to die in the soul whenever strength was brought low by cunning. The play *David*, the closest Lawrence came to a tragic presentation of the passing of power from old to young, has Saul's grimly sardonic reaction to the defeat of Goliath: 'Single-handed hath David slain Goliath, indeed! Even without any combat at all';[37] and the image of David's pebble, with the uncomfortably mixed feelings it arouses, crops up several times in Lawrence's later writing. It expressed Rachel's bewilderment at Virginia's obduracy in 'Mother and Daughter' ('hitting back with a little spiteful hammer that was David's pebble against Goliath's battle-axe!'), and it came into the introduction Lawrence wrote for Siebenhaar's translation of Multatuli's novel *Max Havelaar*: 'When Jack fights the giant, he *must* have recourse to a trick. David thought of a sling and a stone . . . *À la guerre comme à la guerre*'[38] – as if it were both salutary and somehow radically frustrating that one could not beat the giant by becoming a giant oneself.

Christmas in Lawrence's writing was always a time of powerful, life-changing transformations. Henry and March are married at Christmas in 'The Fox'; Aaron famously abandons his family at Christmas in *Aaron's Rod*; Clifford Chatterley even suffers his paralysing battlefield injury on a Christmas Day.[39] In *Sons and Lovers* Christmas was especially significant. Not only did Walter and Gertrude meet at a Christmas party and marry the following Christmas, but their family life was at its most intense in two subsequent Christmases: the first celebrating William's homecoming, when he 'had brought them endless presents. . . . There was a sense of luxury overflowing in the house'; the second following William's death, when Paul collapsed with pneumonia on 23 December, clutching his Christmas box, and precariously survived, to see his mother rededicate her life to him.[40] This sequence has in it something of the relentless pattern of retributive justice which becomes so prominent in the ageing-women stories; the figure of Father Christmas, who gives without taking, changing places with his alter ego, the figure of Death, who takes without giving – evasions of the laws of exchange, but evasions doomed in the end to reinforce those laws, like the evasions the Man who had Died condemned in himself and Madeleine:

'You took more than you gave. Then you came to me for salvation from your own excess. And I, in my mission, I too ran to excess. I gave more than I took, and that also is woe and vanity.'[41]

Tremors from the world of *Sons and Lovers*, the world where white hair made so profound an impression, can be traced throughout Lawrence's late work. In the closing pages of 'The Blue Moccasins', the Christmas-transformed Percy seems to have a touch of both Walter and Gertrude in him; Walter, in the eloquence of his physical and the self-important bombast of his vocal display, Gertrude, in her crowning remark, '"If God's not good-natured and good-hearted, then what is He – ?"' (206), which recalls her kitchen-table debate with Mr Heaton, when she imagined Jesus thinking, at Cana, '"What a shame! – all the wedding spoiled." And so He made wine, as quickly as he could.'[42] One might even feel that Lawrence's deepest response to visiting the tombs in *Etruscan Places,* where 'gradually, the underworld of the Etruscans becomes more real than the above day of the afternoon',[43] draws something from the scene of Walter's breakfast, his 'hour of joy', alone in the darkened, draught-proofed room, with just a candle and a few homely implements to cook and eat with, preferring 'to keep the blinds down and the candle lit, even when it was daylight. It was the habit of the mine.'[44] Other strange collocations of death and *jouissance* dominate the striking short essay 'Over-Earnest Ladies', later called 'Insouciance', written a couple of weeks before 'The Blue Moccasins'. This was an account of Lawrence's irritation with an elderly Englishwoman at his Swiss hotel, who exasperated him by talking about international politics while he was trying to sustain 'a direct, sensuous contact' with the 'things that are actually present' to him – these things including, most prominently, two mowers, an elderly man and a young, working close by, in 'the vividness of near green': 'how plainly one hears the long breaths of the scythes!'[45] As when Percy gazed at his wife's 'slender arm working with a strange mechanical motion, sharp and forcible', the writing here seems momentarily mesmerised, so that the full sense of what is happening in it can only emerge considerably later, when the elderly, distracting woman is suddenly seen as an Atropos, carrying her 'fatal shears'.[46] Perhaps the most curiously suggestive of the pieces I have in mind is the poem of July 1929, 'What are the Wild Waves Saying':

> What are the wild waves saying
> sister the whole day long?
> It seems to me they are saying:
> How disgusting, how infinitely sordid this humanity is
> that dabbles its body in me
> and daubs the sand with its flesh
> in myriads, under the hot and hostile sun!
> and so drearily 'enjoys itself'!
> What are the wild waves saying?[47]

Lawrence's source here is not *Dombey and Son* directly, where the dying Paul Dombey puts the question to his sister Florence, but the immensely popular Victorian parlour duet by Joseph Edwards Carpenter, whose opening sequence goes like this:

*Paul*
What are the wild waves saying,
    Sister, the whole day long,
That ever amid our playing
    I hear their low lone song?

Not by the sea-side only,
    There it sounds wild and free,
But at night, when it's dark and lonely,
    In dreams it is still with me!

*Florence*
Brother, I hear no singing!
    'Tis but the roaring wave,
Ever its long course winging
    Over some ocean cave.

'Tis but the noise of water,
    Dashing against the shore,
And the wind from some bleaker quarter
    Mingling with its roar.

*Duet*
No! it is something greater
    That speaks to the heart alone,
The voice of the great Creator
    Dwells in that mighty tone!

Strange that Lawrence's final, uncompromising repudiation of ordinary people's pleasures, the kind his own family enjoyed whenever they could, should be connected with a song he would have learnt at home in Eastwood, with Ada at the piano, the others intermittently joining in.[48] How wryly self-aware would he have been, sitting on the beach at Forte dei Marmi, moving only with difficulty, watching activities in which he could no longer share, drifting half-automatically into thoughts of a boy called Paul, who was excluded from the world by his infirmities, whose one compensation was to have been granted insights and perceptions which his healthy, adoring sister admired but could not follow?

# Notes

## Preface

1 Paul Eggert, 'Comedy and provisionality: Lawrence's address to his audience and material in his Australian novels', in *Lawrence and Comedy*, eds Paul Eggert and John Worthen, Cambridge: Cambridge University Press, 1996, 145.
2 Ibid., 147.
3 I think this aspect of Lawrence is captured as well as anywhere in Geoff Dyer's astute, funny, if somewhat wearingly self-indulgent book *Out Of Sheer Rage*, London: Little, Brown, 1997.
4 The mystery of creation is the divine urge of creation,
 but it is a great strange urge, it is not a Mind.
 Even an artist knows that his work was never in his mind,
 he could never have *thought* it before it happened.
 A strange ache possessed him, and he entered the struggle,
 and out of the struggle with his material, in the spell of the urge
 his work took place, it came to pass, it stood up and saluted his mind.

 God is a great urge, wonderful, mysterious, magnificent
 But he knows nothing before-hand.
 His urge takes shape in flesh, and lo!
 it is creation! God looks himself on it in wonder, for the first time.
 Lo! there is a creature, formed! How strange!
 Let me think about it! Let me form an idea!
 'The Work of Creation', in *The Complete Poems of D. H. Lawrence*, eds Vivian de Sola Pinto and Warren Roberts, vol. II, London: Heinemann, 1964, 690.
5 Details of these reworkings are provided in the introductions to the Cambridge editions of *England, My England and Other Stories*, ed. Bruce Steele (1990), and *The Fox, The Captain's Doll, The Ladybird*, ed. Dieter Mehl (1992).
6 The editor of *Hutchinson's Story Magazine* evidently thought 'The Fox' was too long, although in the event Lawrence only cut about 580 words from the original 8,400. 'The Lovely Lady' was reduced from 13,700 to roughly 7,000. See the introductions to *The Fox*, 'The Captain's Doll', *The Ladybird* (xxii), and *The Woman Who Rode Away and Other Stories*, eds Dieter Mehl and Christa Jansohn, Cambridge: Cambridge University Press, 1995, xli.
7 *The Letters of D. H. Lawrence*, vol. VI, eds James T. Boulton and Margaret H. Boulton, with Gerald M. Lacy, Cambridge: Cambridge University Press, 1991, 269.

8  Tony Tanner, in one of the last essays he published before he died, commented with a beautiful succinctness and clarity on this kind of group interplay in Lawrence's three American stories from the summer of 1924, *St. Mawr*, 'The Princess', and 'The Woman Who Rode Away'. Tony Tanner, review of David Ellis, *D. H. Lawrence: Dying Game*, in *The Times Literary Supplement*, 9 January 1998, 3–4.
9  John Worthen, in his contribution to the collection *Lawrence and Comedy*, 'Drama and Mimicry in Lawrence', discussed the previously little commented-on link between Lawrence's style and his skills as an impersonator. *Lawrence and Comedy*, 19–44.

# 1  'In Love'

1  'More Modern Love', in *The Woman Who Rode Away and Other Stories*, eds Dieter Mehl and Christa Jansohn, Cambridge: Cambridge University Press, 1995, 309. Subsequent page references to 'More Modern Love' and 'In Love' are to this edition.
2  *The First and Second Lady Chatterley Novels*, eds Dieter Mehl and Christa Jansohn, Cambridge: Cambridge University Press, 1999, 418.
3  To mention just a few of these discussions, all of which appeared or were re-published in the same year, 1990: Wayne C. Booth, in 'Confessions of a Lukewarm Lawrentian', suggests that 'In Lawrence's practice, all rules about point of view are abrogated: the borderlines between author's voice and character's voice are deliberately blurred.' *The Challenge of D. H. Lawrence*, eds Michael Squires and Keith Cushman, Madison: University of Wisconsin Press, 1990, 16. David Lodge, in 'Lawrence, Dostoevsky, Bakhtin: Lawrence and Dialogic Fiction', comments, on 'Things', that while the story is told in the characters' 'own kind of language . . . this discourse is *itself* a kind of doubly-oriented discourse, since it always seems to be anxiously aware of some other discourse – pragmatic, rational, sceptical – against which it is defending itself.' *Rethinking Lawrence*, ed. Keith Brown, Milton Keynes, Open University Press, 1990, 102. James C. Cowan talks of Lawrence's 'shifting narrative identification with first one character and then another, not so much with their technical point of view as with their subjective position.' *D. H. Lawrence and the Trembling Balance*, Pennsylvania and London: Pennsylvania State University Press, 1990, 85. G. M. Hyde describes the 'fascinating s/he that is half an 'I' . . . making a dialogue of the descriptive writing, turning it into a drama of consciousness (rather than an 'objective' fact) in a set of changing subject positions.' *D. H. Lawrence*, London: Macmillan, 1990, 84. In a more recent essay, Hyde offers another general description of Lawrence's characteristic method which seems particularly appropriate to this revised passage in 'In Love': 'The narrator is half inside the mind of his character, and half suspended in a neutral space which opens towards a hypothetical future.' 'Suave Loins, Venison Pasties, and Other Tasty Nonsense: The Unacceptable Face of Lawrence', *Kyoto Women's University Essays and Studies*, no. 47, 2001, 8.

4 *Sketches of Etruscan Places and other Italian Essays*, ed. Simonetta de Filippis, Cambridge: Cambridge University Press, 1992, 123–4.
5 Probably the clearest statement of Lawrence's touchiness on this point is in *Mr Noon*, when Joanna asks Gilbert 'Can I never laugh at you?' and he replies 'Not more than enough.' *Mr Noon*, ed. Lindeth Vasey, Cambridge: Cambridge University Press, 1984, 225.
6 Cowan discusses some comparable if rather less wittily flamboyant 'sexual double entendres' provoked by machinery, in the conversation when Clifford and Mellors are trying to restart the wheelchair in chapter 13 of *Lady Chatterley's Lover*: '"Have you looked at the rods underneath?" asked Clifford . . ."Sounds as if she'd come clear," said Mellors . . ."Do you mind pushing her home, Mellors!"' *Lady Chatterley's Lover*, ed. Michael Squires, Cambridge: Cambridge University Press, 1993, 188–90. James C. Cowan, *D. H. Lawrence and the Trembling Balance*, 224.
7 *Mazeppa*, line 697. *Byron: Poetical Works*, ed. Frederick Page, corrected edition by John Jump, Oxford: Oxford University Press, 1970, 347.
8 *The Letters of D. H. Lawrence*, vol. V., eds James T. Boulton and Lindeth Vasey, Cambridge: Cambridge University Press, 1989, 568. Elsa's sister Barbara wrote the following in her memoirs:

'When my sister Elsa was going to be married, Lawrence wrote to me, 'Don't let her marry a man unless she feels his physical presence warm to her.'
'I don't need Lawrence's advice,' Elsa told me.
In this letter he also said, I think, 'Passion has dignity; affection can be a very valuable thing, and one can make a life relationship with it.'

From the memoirs of Barbara Weekley Barr, included in *D. H. Lawrence: A Composite Biography*, vol. III., ed. Edward Nehls, Madison: University of Wisconsin Press, 1959, 189.
9 *Sea and Sardinia*, ed. Mara Kalnins, Cambridge: Cambridge University Press, 1997, 67.
10 Joe seems to have left it fairly late to make this move, since while large numbers of ex-servicemen had set up smallholdings soon after the war, many assisted by grants from the Land Settlement Association, more than a quarter of them had given it up by 1926 as hopelessly unprofitable. Joe, like Colonel Hale in 'Glad Ghosts', who also came home rather disturbed from the army and is last heard of 'farming in Wiltshire, raising pigs' (*The Woman Who Rode Away and Other Stories*, 210), presumably has private means to support him.
11 *The Virgin and the Gipsy*, in *The Short Novels of D. H. Lawrence*, vol. II., London: Heinemann, 1956, 16.
12 'The Good Man', in *Phoenix*, ed. Edward D. McDonald, London: Heinemann, 1936, 753; 'The Novel and the Feelings', in *Study of Thomas Hardy and Other Essays*, ed. Bruce Steele, Cambridge: Cambridge University Press, 1985, 205.

13 *The First and Second Lady Chatterley Novels*, 203. Kyle Crichton, an American writer who interviewed Lawrence in New Mexico in June 1925, recounted Lawrence's fondness for factually detailed adventure stories; *D. H. Lawrence: A Composite Biography*, vol. II., ed. Edward Nehls, Madison: University of Wisconsin Press, 1958, 416. In *Lorenzo in Taos*, Mabel Luhan quotes Lawrence as saying, during a contretemps with a car, 'You know I don't know anything about automobiles, Frieda! I *hate* them!' *Lorenzo in Taos*, New York, Knopf, 1932, 39. Lawrence's occasional attempts to sound informed about motoring are at least slightly more successful than his forays into sporting idiom; these range from Mrs Bolton's account of Parkin's father as 'a cricketer, who went off all summer professional cricketing' (*The First and Second Lady Chatterley Novels*, 403; it's hard to see any evidence that Mrs Bolton is being consciously satirised here), via the footballer in 'Strike Pay' who 'did some handsome work, putting the two goals through' (*Love Among the Haystacks and Other Stories*, ed. John Worthen, Cambridge: Cambridge University Press, 1987, 139), to the mysterious and mortifyingly inept attempt to describe a cricket match in chapter 8 of *The Boy in the Bush* (ed. Paul Eggert, Cambridge: Cambridge University Press, 1990, 112–14) – unless we see it all as an elaborately staged disdain for the accuracy so dear to sports-lovers.
14 Lawrence made a series of references to this incident in letters of 27 and 28 October 1926; *Letters*, vol. V, 563–6.
15 I am sure Lawrence would have concurred with the reaction of Rose Aubrey, the narrator of Rebecca West's novel *The Fountain Overflows*, to her first experience of a motor-car in the Edwardian period: 'The miracle of not being pulled by anything, of the nothingness in front of the driver, was more staggering than can now be believed'. *The Fountain Overflows*, London: Virago Press, 1984, 186.
16 Linda Ruth Williams, *Sex in the Head: Visions of Femininity and Film in D. H. Lawrence*, Hemel Hempstead: Harvester Wheatsheaf, 1993, 43.
17 Kinkead-Weekes recounts an episode in 1914 when Middleton Murry claimed to have acted as the reconciler: 'What is interesting ... is that (the quarrel between Lawrence and Frieda) was both a very serious crisis ... and yet played to an audience by both Lawrences too, heightening drama and emotion more than if they had been alone'. Mark Kinkead-Weekes, *D. H. Lawrence: Triumph to Exile, 1912–22*, Cambridge: Cambridge University Press, 1996, 157.
18 *Lady Chatterley's Lover*, 201.
19 *The First and Second Lady Chatterley Novels*, 184.
20 The character of Duncan Forbes appears to have been based in part on Duncan Grant, whose studio Lawrence had visited in 1915. Lawrence would almost certainly have known the not very well kept secret in Bloomsbury and Garsington circles, that Duncan Grant was the real father of Vanessa Bell's daughter Angelica, and that Vanessa's husband Clive Bell had agreed to let it be thought that he was himself the father.

21 'Sex versus Loveliness' (1928), in *Phoenix II*, eds Warren Roberts and Harry T. Moore, London: Heinemann, 1968, 529.
22 See, for example, the poem 'Film Passion':

> If all those females who so passionately loved
> the film face of Rudolf Valentino
> had had to take him for one night only, in the flesh,
> how they'd have hated him!

*The Complete Poems of D. H. Lawrence*, vol. I., eds Vivian de Sola Pinto and Warren Roberts, London: Heinemann, 1964, 538.

## 2 At Home, at Peace: 'Glad Ghosts'

1 'Glad Ghosts', in *The Woman Who Rode Away and Other Stories*, eds Dieter Mehl and Christa Jansohn, Cambridge: Cambridge University Press, 1995, 210. Subsequent references are to this edition. The textual apparatus shows the extent of Lawrence's alterations to his manuscripts.
2 'Accumulated Mail', in *Reflections on the Death of a Porcupine and Other Essays*, ed. Michael Herbert, Cambridge: Cambridge University Press, 1988, 239.
3 Lawrence first wrote 'The Colonel is a ruddy Bacchus', and then 'The Colonel is a ruddy and benevolent Circe' (353), still unsure which gender to give him, before crossing it all out. Colonel Hale seems a little to resemble Lawrence's old benefactor Ford Madox Ford, who, having come home weary from the war and in indifferent health, tried to settle down to raise pigs, with the Australian painter Stella Bowen.
4 'The Ladybird', in *The Fox, The Captain's Doll, The Ladybird*, ed. Dieter Mehl, Cambridge: Cambridge University Press, 1992, 219.
5 *Quetzalcoatl* (the first version, written in 1923, of *The Plumed Serpent*), ed. Louis L. Martz, Redding Ridge, CT: Black Swan Books, 1995, 164.
6 *The Dictionary of National Biography* (1894 edition), vol. 39, 51. Lawrence had a copy of Morier's sequel, *The Adventures of Hajji Baba in England*, in Spotorno. He may have found it there, but it seems more likely to have been part of the very small library he carried with him. He asked Martin Secker to send him Morier's first volume, but evidently failed to word his request clearly enough, and what arrived was another copy of the book he already had. *The Letters of D. H. Lawrence*, vol. V, eds James T. Boulton and Lindeth Vasey, Cambridge: Cambridge University Press, 1989, 386.
7 *Letters*, vol. V, 266.
8 *Letters*, vol. V, 292–3.
9 *Letters*, vol. V, 319.
10 David Ellis, *D. H. Lawrence: Dying Game*, Cambridge: Cambridge University Press, 1998, 270.
11 *Letters*, vol. V, 318.

12 *Letters*, vol. V, 319; Catherine Carswell, *The Savage Pilgrimage*, London: Chatto & Windus, 1932, 229.
13 *Letters*, vol. V, 313, 322, 293.
14 *Letters*, vol. V, 330; 'A Little Moonshine with Lemon', in *Mornings in Mexico and Etruscan Places*, Harmondsworth: Penguin Books, 1960, 92.
15 Adam Phillips, 'Coming to Grief', in *Promises, Promises*, London: Faber & Faber, 2000, 263.
16 John Worthen has written in detail about the later Lawrence's reinventions of his earlier life, in *D. H. Lawrence: The Early Years*, Cambridge: Cambridge University Press, 1991, 500–3.
17 In a letter to Arthur McLeod, of 5 December 1910. *The Letters of D. H. Lawrence*, vol. I., ed. James T. Boulton, Cambridge: Cambridge University Press, 1979, 192. The poem is considerably misquoted in 'Smile'; *The Woman Who Rode Away and Other Stories*, 72 and note on 393.
18 *The Woman Who Rode Away and Other Stories*, 75, 73.
19 In his 1924 essay 'On Being A Man', Lawrence had written of men who 'take off their hats to a lump of stone in Whitehall', which is where the Cenotaph stands, but when he refers a little later in the same essay to 'a great lump of stone to the Unknown Warrior', he seems to be confusing the Cenotaph with the tomb of the Unknown Warrior in Westminster Abbey. On the other hand, since at the end of the essay he claims that 'the tomb isn't empty', he was clearly aware that 'Cenotaph' was the name in general use. 'On Being A Man', in *Reflections on the Death of a Porcupine and Other Essays*, ed. Michael Herbert, Cambridge: Cambridge University Press, 1988, 220, 222.
20 Kathleen Woodward, *Aging and its Discontents*, Bloomington: Indiana University Press, 1991, 116.
21 *The Times*, 12 November 1925. The paper would have been available in the hotel in Spotorno owned by Rina Secker's father, where the Lawrences stayed on their arrival in mid-November.
22 There are interesting comments on the history of the Cenotaph in an article by Eric Homberger in *The Times Literary Supplement*, 12 November 1976, and on the enthusiasm of the post-war public both for war memorials and for spiritualism in Jay Winter, *Sites of Memory, Sites of Mourning: The Great War in European Cultural History*, Cambridge: Cambridge University Press, 1995, and David Cannadine, 'War and Death, Grief and Mourning in Modern Britain', in *Mirrors of Mortality*, ed. J. Whaley, London: Europa Publications, 1981, 187–242.
23 Raymond Asquith's memorial tablet was unveiled by Sir Edwin Lutyens, the architect of the Cenotaph.
24 A recurrent view transmitted by those who had passed on was that 'not only was . . . lingering sadness unnecessary, but it tended to "mar the happiness of our friends in the Beyond"'. Jay Winter, *Sites Of Memory, Sites of Mourning*, 67.
25 The manuscript had 'naked' for 'crude'. *The Woman Who Rode Away and Other Stories*, 470.

26 Linda Ruth Williams, in her essay on the borders and transgressions in 'Glad Ghosts', noticed the second of these quotations, commenting that '"she" can become "he" when the body turns uncanny'. '"We've been forgetting that we're flesh and blood, Mother": "Glad Ghosts" and Uncanny Bodies', *The D. H. Lawrence Review*, vol. 27, nos 2–3, 1997–98, 242.
27 Rita Felski, *The Gender of Modernity*, Cambridge, Mass. and London: Harvard University Press, 1995, 134.
28 Hale goes on to say 'And the minute I saw the Lizard light – it was evening when we got up out of the Bay – I realized that Lucy had been waiting for me. I could feel her there, at my side, more plainly than I feel you now' (190). This must have been strikingly close to Lawrence's own sensations when he came past the Lizard light in December 1923 on his journey from Mexico, knowing that it was Frieda, who had come to Europe without him some months earlier, who had drawn him reluctantly but inexorably back. He promptly wrote the essay 'On Coming Home', which evokes, firstly, the intense feelings aroused by the sight of the lighthouse, secondly, an England filled with 'queer, insane, half-female-seeming men, not quite men at all . . . not a man left inside all the millions of pairs of trousers', and thirdly, a punitive desire to break through the 'box after box of safeguards' inside which each such half-man encloses himself. *Reflections on the Death of a Porcupine and Other Essays*, 177, 182–3. The character of Major Eastwood is considered briefly in my Chapter 3.
29 'Hawthorne's *Blithedale Romance*', in *Studies in Classic American Literature*, Harmondsworth: Penguin Books, 1977, 116.
30 Fiona Becket, 'Being There: Nostalgia and the Masculine Maternal in D. H. Lawrence', *The D. H. Lawrence Review*, vol. 27, nos 2–3, 1997–98, 255–68.
31 Octavio Paz, *The Labyrinth of Solitude*, trans. Lysander Kemp, Yara Milos, and Rachel Phillips Belash, London: Penguin Books, 1990, especially 81–3, 336.
32 'Medlars and Sorb-Apples', in Lawrence's revised version; *The Complete Poems of D. H. Lawrence*, vol. I, eds Vivian de Sola Pinto and Warren Roberts, London: Heinemann, 1964, 280–1.
33 The theory of encryption and 'impossible' mourning is outlined in Nicolas Abraham and Maria Torok, *Cryptonymie: le verbier de l'Homme aux loups*, Paris, 1976, which includes as an appendix Jacques Derrida's commentary on the theory, *Fors*. *Fors* was published separately in *The Georgia Review*, vol. 31 no. 1, Spring 1977, 64–116.
34 Nicolas Joost and Alvin Sullivan, *D. H. Lawrence and The Dial*, Carbondale and Edwardsville: Southern Illinois University Press, 1970, 135.
35 Lathkill's effusions are strikingly similar in content and tone to Lawrence's own, more than twelve years earlier, towards the end of his review of *Georgian Poetry*; (*Phoenix*, 304–7).
36 Thomas Hardy, *Jude the Obscure*, ed. Norman Page, New York and London: W. W. Norton, 1999, 285.
37 *Jude the Obscure*, 285.
38 Linda Ruth Williams argued, *à propos* of *The Plumed Serpent*, that '"renewal" is simply for the male – women act as mediators of male desire, the junctions through which it passes on its way back to the self'.

*Sex in the Head: Visions of Femininity and Film in D. H. Lawrence*, Hemel Hempstead: Harvester Wheatsheaf, 1993, 38.
39 'Spirits Summoned West', in *The Complete Poems of D. H. Lawrence*, vol. I, 410–12.
40 Fiona Becket, 'Being There: Nostalgia and the Masculine Maternal in D. H. Lawrence', 256.
41 The first version of Lathkill's letter also recycled Morier's phrase 'the heart of the world' (353, 208) – which might suggest that the idea of suffusing the letter with recyclings was present from an early stage in the story's composition.
42 Stanley Cavell discusses this problem in his essay 'Recounting Gains, Showing Losses: Reading *The Winter's Tale*', in *Disowning Knowledge in Six Plays of Shakespeare*, Cambridge: Cambridge University Press, 1987, 193–221.
43 'The Rocking-Horse Winner', in *The Woman Who Rode Away and Other Stories*, 243. Cynthia Asquith did not think 'Glad Ghosts' was suitable for her anthology (see ibid., xxxiii–iv), but Lawrence does not appear to have been as upset by this as she had feared.
44 'Making Love to Music', in *Phoenix*, 160.
45 '[Autobiographical Fragment]', in *Phoenix*, 821.
46 *Phoenix*, 819–20.
47 Fray Bernardo de Sahagún's *Historia general de las cosas de la Nueva España* (1569–82), also known as the Florentine Codex, describes the birth of Huitzilopochtli as the result of the earth-goddess Coatlicue's having been mysteriously impregnated by a ball of feathers; her 400 children, enraged by the pregnancy, were preparing to attack her, when the infant god sprang from her womb, fully armed and dressed for war, and proceeded to destroy all his siblings.
48 Shortly before starting work on 'Glad Ghosts', Lawrence had been reading Oliver Onions' new (1925) novel, *Whom God Hath Sundered*, which featured a pugilist and a longstanding semi-clandestine love-relationship. Lawrence had asked Secker to send him a copy with a view to reviewing it, but no evidence that he actually wrote a review has yet (2002) come to light.

## 3  'Sun' and *The Virgin and the Gipsy*

1 *The Woman Who Rode Away and Other Stories*, eds Dieter Mehl and Christa Jansohn, with additional editing by N. H. Reeve, London: Penguin Books, 1996, 287, 34. This volume in the Penguin Lawrence Edition uses the texts from the Cambridge edition, but for ease of reference prints the texts of both versions of 'Sun' in full, the 1928 version on pages 19–38, and the 1925 version on pages 275–91. Subsequent references appear in this form: (1925: 287), etc.
2 *The Woman Who Rode Away and Other Stories*, 34. The 1925 text has 'gathered' for 'took' (287).

3   Letter to Cynthia Asquith of 3 June 1918, in *The Letters of D. H. Lawrence*, vol. III, eds James T. Boulton and Andrew Robertson, Cambridge: Cambridge University Press, 1984, 247.
4   1925 has 'interested in' for 'consumed about'.
5   Judith Ruderman, *D. H. Lawrence and the Devouring Mother*, Durham, North Carolina: Duke University Press, 1984, 178–9.
6   Johnny's situation is close to the one described in Žižek's elucidation of Lacan's argument in *The Plague of Fantasies*: 'A small child is embedded in a complex network of relations; he serves as a kind of catalyst and battlefield for the desires of those around him. . . . While he is well aware of this role, the child cannot fathom what object, precisely, he is to others, what the exact nature of the games they are playing with him is'. Slavoj Žižek, *The Plague of Fantasies* (London and New York: Verso, 1997), 9.
7   From the memoirs of Barbara Weekley Barr, included in *D. H. Lawrence: A Composite Biography*, vol. III, ed. Edward Nehls, Madison: University of Wisconsin Press, 1959, 9.
8   *The Virgin and the Gipsy*, in *The Short Novels of D. H. Lawrence*, vol. II, London: Heinemann, 1956, 3. Subsequent references are to this edition.
9   In the new 'Introduction' to his translation of Verga's *Mastro-don Gesualdo*, which was reissued by Jonathan Cape in 1928, Lawrence wrote of the 'heroic effort . . . that instinctive fighting for more life to come into being, which is a basic impulse in more men than we like to admit; women too. Or it used to be. The discrediting of the heroic effort has almost extinguished that effort in the young, hence the appalling "flatness" of their lives. It is the parents' fault.' *Phoenix II*, eds Warren Roberts and Harry T. Moore, London: Heinemann, 1968, 282.
10  *D. H. Lawrence: A Composite Biography*, vol. III, 9.
11  Ibid., 7.
12  Even at such a high-pitched moment, Lawrence has Arthur make a pedantically correct distinction between 'will' and 'shall'. Ernest Weekley was of course a leading authority on language-use.
13  M. M. Lally, '*The Virgin and the Gipsy*: Rewriting the Pain', in *Aging and Gender in Literature*, eds A. Wyatt-Brown and J. Rossen, Charlottesville and London: University of Virginia Press, 1993, 121–37.
14  'The Flying-Fish', in *St Mawr and Other Stories*, ed. Brian Finney, Cambridge: Cambridge University Press, 1983, 216.
15  Julian Moynahan, *The Deed of Life*, New Jersey: Princeton University Press, 1963, 210–11.
16  Carol Siegel, *Lawrence Among the Women*, Charlottesville and London: University Press of Virginia, 1991, 176.
17  M. Elizabeth Sargent, 'The Wives, The Virgins, and Isis: Lawrence's Explorations of Female Will in Four Late Novellas of Spiritual Quest', *The D. H. Lawrence Review*, vol. 26, nos 1–3, 1995–96, 240.
18  David Ellis, *D. H. Lawrence: Dying Game*, Cambridge: Cambridge University Press, 1998, 286.
19  John Worthen, *D. H. Lawrence*, London: Edward Arnold, 1991, 101.

20 'Frieda doesn't like the title of "The Virgin and the Gipsy": she prefers something with Granny: like "Granny Gone" or "Granny on the Throne". What do you think?' Letter to Martin Secker, 1 February 1926, in *The Letters of D. H. Lawrence*, vol. V, eds James T. Boulton and Lindeth Vasey, Cambridge: Cambridge University Press, 1989, 388.
21 Julian Moynahan, *The Deed of Life*, 214.
22 Judith Ruderman, *D. H. Lawrence and the Devouring Mother*, 157.
23 *Twilight In Italy and Other Essays*, ed. Paul Eggert, Cambridge: Cambridge University Press, 1994, 124.
24 David Ayers, *English Literature of the 1920s*, Edinburgh: Edinburgh University Press, 1999, 185.
25 Sheila MacLeod presents this idea in her commentary on *St Mawr* in *Lawrence's Men and Women*, London: Heinemann, 1985, 140–53.
26 *The Letters of D. H. Lawrence*, vol. VI, eds James T. Boulton and Margaret H. Boulton, with Gerald M. Lacy, Cambridge: Cambridge University Press, 1991, 388.
27 The story is told in detail in David Ellis, *D. H. Lawrence: Dying Game*, 405–8.
28 *Letters*, vol. VI, 505.
29 'Only slightly different', in separate letters to David Lederhandler and Laurence Pollinger; 'only very slightly different', in a letter to Maurice Speiser. *The Letters of D.H. Lawrence*, vol. VII, eds. Keith Sagar and James T. Boulton, Cambridge: Cambridge University Press, 1993, 240, 243, 308. The 1928 collection, *The Woman Who Rode Away and Other Stories*, was published simultaneously by Secker in the UK and Knopf in America.
30 Linda Ruth Williams, *Sex in the Head: Visions of Femininity and Film in D. H. Lawrence*, Hemel Hempstead: Harvester Wheatsheaf, 1993, 99. Williams restricts her interpretation to Lawrence's male figures, thinking specifically of scenes in which 'the male body is primary spectacle which invites the fetishistic gaze', but 'Sun' appears to invite a comparable voyeurism towards both sexes.
31 Julia Kristeva, *Black Sun: Depression and Melancholia*, trans. Leon Roudiez, New York and Oxford: Columbia University Press, 1989, 78.
32 The arguments are set out with great clarity in Stephen Frosh's review of *Essential Papers on Narcissism*, ed. Andrew P. Morrison, New York and London: New York University Press, 1986, in *Free Associations* 18, 1989, 22–48; the quotation here is from page 33.
33 Frosh, 45–6.
34 'Europe versus America', in *Sketches of Etruscan Places and Other Italian Essays*, ed. Simonetta de Filippis, Cambridge: Cambridge University Press, 1992, 200.
35 *Letters*, vol. V, 341.
36 Frieda Lawrence, *Not I, But The Wind . . .*, Santa Fé: Rydal Press, 1934, 167.
37 *Letters*, vol. V, 223.
38 *Lady Chatterley's Lover*, ed. Michael Squires, Cambridge: Cambridge University Press, 1993, 118.
39 The 1925 text does not have 'between the lights'.

40  The *Letters of D. H. Lawrence*, vol. IV, eds Warren Roberts, James T. Boulton and Elizabeth Mansfield, Cambridge: Cambridge University Press, 1987, 481.
41  The landscape in which the story is set draws on Lawrence's memories of the gardens of the Fontana Vecchia, in Taormina, Sicily, where the Lawrences lived between 1920 and 1922 – and where Lawrence was himself occasionally in the habit of walking naked.
42  The 1925 text does not have 'half mockery'.
43  *Women in Love*, eds David Farmer, Lindeth Vasey and John Worthen, Cambridge: Cambridge University Press, 1987, 246.

## 4  Parkin's Wedding Photograph

1  *The First and Second Lady Chatterley Novels*, eds Dieter Mehl and Christa Jansohn, Cambridge: Cambridge University Press, 1999, 97. Subsequent page references in the text are to this edition.
2  In *A Propos of Lady Chatterley's Lover*, Lawrence claimed, rather cagily, that Clifford's paralysis was 'symbolic of ... the deeper emotional or passional paralysis, of most men of his sort and class, today', but that this only became clear to the author after he had written the first version. In fact, Constance's view, that the injury has not fundamentally altered Clifford but merely brought out what was already there, was introduced about halfway through the first novel, when she read his letters to her in France. *A Propos of Lady Chatterley's Lover*, in *Lady Chatterley's Lover*, ed. Michael Squires, Cambridge: Cambridge University Press, 1993, 333.
3  See in particular, John Worthen, *D. H. Lawrence and the Idea of the Novel*, London: Macmillan, 1979; Derek Britton, *Lady Chatterley: The Making of the Novel*, London: Unwin Hyman, 1988, 56; Lydia Blanchard, 'Women Look at Lady Chatterley', *The D. H. Lawrence Review*, vol. 11, no. 3, 1978, 255–6.
4  Tony Pinkney, *D. H. Lawrence*, Brighton: Harvester Press, 1990, 140.
5  'Morality and the Novel', in *Study of Thomas Hardy and Other Essays*, ed. Bruce Steele, Cambridge: Cambridge University Press, 1985, 172; see also 175.
6  'The Crucifix Across the Mountains', in *Twilight in Italy and Other Essays*, ed. Paul Eggert, Cambridge: Cambridge University Press, 1994, 94.
7  'No wonder the soldiers were terrified. No wonder they thrilled in horror when, deep in the woods, they found the skulls and trophies of their dead comrades upon the trees. ... The true German ... is a tree-soul. ... His instinct still is to nail skulls and trophies to the sacred tree.' *Fantasia of the Unconscious*, London: Heinemann, 1961, 40.
8  Bachelard gave the name 'Empedocles complex' to the reverie in which 'fire suggests the desire to change, to speed up the passage of time, to bring all of life to its conclusion, to its hereafter. ... The fascinated individual hears *the call of the funeral pyre*. For him destruction is more than a change, it is a renewal ...'. Gaston Bachelard, *The Psychoanalysis of Fire*, trans. Alan C. Ross, London: Quartet Books, 1987, 16.

9 David Leon Higden delineated the extensive resemblances between Bertha Coutts and Bertha Mason; Carol Siegel suggested that Connie herself also has something of Bertha Mason in her. David Leon Higden, 'Bertha Coutts and Bertha Mason: A Speculative Note', *The D. H. Lawrence Review*, vol. 11, no. 3, 1978, 294–6; Carol Siegel, *Lawrence Among The Women*, Charlottesville and London: University Press of Virginia, 1991, 85–6.
10 Philip Larkin, 'MCMXIV', from *The Whitsun Weddings*, London: Faber & Faber, 1964, 28, ll. 30–1.
11 'He paid the shilling, took the photograph away with him, and burnt it, frame and all, when he reached his lodging.' Thomas Hardy, *Jude the Obscure*, ed. Norman Page, New York and London: W. W. Norton and Company, 1978, 61.
12 Pierre Bourdieu commented on the historic link between photography and the solemnization of family life, in *Photography: A Middle-brow Art*, trans. Shaun Whiteside, Cambridge: Polity Press, 1990, especially pp.19–24.
13 In the course of his memoir of Maurice Magnus, Lawrence wrote 'It is terrible to be agreed with. . . . All that one says, and means, turns to nothing' (*Phoenix II*, eds Warren Roberts and Harry T. Moore, London: Heinemann, 1968, 323). A striking instance of what I have in mind is the scene in *Aaron's Rod* where, in their discussion of the burdensome effects of women and children, Lilly and Aaron encourage each other to increasingly vehement complaints, to the point where they seem so much in accord as to become suspicious of each other. *Aaron's Rod*, ed. Mara Kalnins, Cambridge: Cambridge University Press, 1988, 99–101. Parkin's photograph is presumably as dusty as it is because his mother, who comes once a week to clean for him, refuses to go near it.
14 T. J. Clark, *Farewell to an Idea: Episodes from a History of Modernism*, New Haven and London: Yale University Press, 1999, 2.
15 Michael Squires, 'Introduction' to his edition of *Lady Chatterley's Lover*, London: Penguin Books, 1994, xxii.
16 'Pictures on the Walls', *Phoenix II*, 608.
17 Susan Sontag, *On Photography*, London: Allen Lane, 1977, 155, 161.
18 Witter Bynner, *Journey with Genius*, London: Peter Nevill, 1953, 151.
19 Marcel Proust, *À la recherche du temps perdu*, ed. Jean-Yves Tadié, Paris: Editions Gallimard, 1987, vol. I, 157–63. There is of course no direct evidence to link this scene with Lawrence's – indeed, it is impossible to gauge, from Lawrence's scattered and almost wholly disparaging remarks about him, how much Proust he had actually read. But he was certainly reading him around the time of writing *Lady Chatterley*, and it would not be unreasonable to suppose that he might have got this far.
20 Carol Siegel, comparing the equivalent scene in the final version of the novel to the scenes in *Wuthering Heights* where Heathcliff attacks the affectations of the younger Cathy, implies that Mellors' behaviour is intended to help the elder Connie to deconstruct her own 'lady' self. I find it difficult to read the scene as dispassionately as this. But most of

its original intricacy has been lost or jettisoned in the final version anyway. Carol Siegel, *Lawrence Among The Women*, 58.
21 Frank Harris regularly drew on the sexual meaning of 'pussy' in *My Life and Loves* (1923), which Lawrence read in Orioli's bookshop in Florence in 1926 and which very probably had some influence on the composition of the *Lady Chatterley* novels. See Ellis, *Dying Game*, 689; Britton, *Lady Chatterley: The Making of the Novel*, 98–9.
22 *Sons and Lovers*, eds Helen Baron and Carl Baron, Cambridge: Cambridge University Press, 1992, 88. In one of the last pieces of writing Lawrence ever completed, his review of Eric Gill's *Art-Nonsense and Other Essays*, he argued that 'happy, intense absorption in any work . . . is a state of being with God, and the men who have not known it have missed life itself'. *Phoenix*, ed. Edward D. McDonald, London: Heinemann, 1936, 396.
23 In *Lady Chatterley's Lover*, Clifford calls Mellors by tooting the horn on his wheelchair: 'In the silence a wood-pigeon began to coo, roo-hoohoo! roo-hoohoo! Clifford shut her up with a blast on the horn' (*Lady Chatterley's Lover*, 187). As a result of this change, virtually all the subtlety and intensity of the earlier version of the scene is thrown away. How many exasperating times does one find oneself thinking that? The chopping-signal is, of course, dropped altogether from the final version of the novel.
24 Lawrence may have been remembering his own strictures, in the essay 'Art and Morality' (1925), against photography and the mode of seeing the world which it imposes. 'Art and Morality', in *Study of Thomas Hardy and Other Essays*, 163–8.
25 Elizabeth Fox, '*Lady Chatterley's Lover*: A Departure from Pastoral into Delusion', in *Études Lawrenciennes*, no. 16, 1997, 18.
26 In Lawrence's 1925 play *David*, the hero says of Saul's daughter Michal, 'Her eyes are like stars shining through a tree at midnight', to which she pertly replies, 'Why through a tree?' *The Plays*, eds Hans-Wilhelm Schwarze and John Worthen, Cambridge: Cambridge University Press, 1999, 456.

## 5 Strange Women with White Hair: 'The Lovely Lady','Mother and Daughter', 'The Blue Moccasins'

1 'Glad Ghosts', in *The Woman Who Rode Away and Other Stories*, eds Dieter Mehl and Christa Jansohn, Cambridge: Cambridge University Press, 1995, 210.
2 Lawrence used this phrase in a letter to Katherine Mansfield, of 5 December 1918: 'In a way, Frieda is the devouring mother'. *The Letters of D. H. Lawrence*, vol. III, eds James T. Boulton and Andrew Robertson, Cambridge: Cambridge University Press, 1984, 302.
3 Lawrence wrote to Earl Brewster on 13 May, 1927, 'I feel I never want to see an unattached woman any more while I live: specially an elderly one'; *The Letters of D. H. Lawrence*, vol. VI, eds James T. Boulton and Margaret

H. Boulton, with Gerald M. Lacy, Cambridge: Cambridge University Press, 1991, 56. See also poems such as 'Elderly Discontented Women' and 'The Grudge of the Old', in *The Complete Poems of D. H. Lawrence*, vol. I, eds Vivian de Sola Pinto and Warren Roberts, London: Heinemann, 1964, 502–3.

4  Linda Ruth Williams seems to have missed this, when claiming in her article on 'Glad Ghosts' that 'Luke's own father is never mentioned'. Linda Ruth Williams, '"We've been forgetting that we're flesh and blood, Mother": "Glad Ghosts" and Uncanny Bodies', *The D. H. Lawrence Review*, vol. 27, nos 2–3, 1997–98, 245.

5  Lawrence sent his revised version to Nancy Pearn, at his agent's (Curtis Brown), on 12 May 1927, complaining about Cynthia Asquith's 'absurd' objection to the rain-pipe incident. By the 28 May, he tells Cynthia that he 'can't in the least remember the differences between the two' versions. *Letters*, vol. VI, 54, 71.

6  'The Lovely Lady', in *The Woman Who Rode Away and Other Stories*, 252. Subsequent page references are to this edition, which includes both versions of the story.

7  'It is evidently the thing, in these parts, to deny that the malaria has ever touched you.' *Sketches of Etruscan Places and other Italian Essays*, ed. Simonetta de Filippis, Cambridge: Cambridge University Press, 1992, 147.

8  Joan Rivière, 'Womanliness as a Masquerade', originally published in *The International Journal of Psychoanalysis*, 10, 1929, reprinted in *Formations of Fantasy*, eds Victor Burgin, James Donald and Cora Kaplan, London: Methuen, 1986, 35–44.

9  Lawrence seems to have in mind here the kinds of document assembled by the bibliographer Joaquin Icazbalceta in the archives in Mexico City. Many of these were translated and published in various forms by the ethnologist Adolph Bandelier and his wife Fanny; for example the series of *Historical Documents Relating to New Mexico, Nueva Viscaya, and Approaches Thereto*, the first volume of which was published in Washington in 1923.

10  There is a curious pre-echo of Pauline's remark in Lawrence's letter to Thomas Seltzer, dated 3 June 1921: 'Orchestra concert in Kurhaus last night – Siegfried Wagner conducted – Great men should *never* have sons.' *Letters*, vol. III, 733.

11  *Aaron's Rod*, ed. Mara Kalnins, Cambridge: Cambridge University Press, 1988, 30.

12  Frank's absence from his son Cyril's life creates a space which Cyril tries to use both George and Annabel to fill. A further gap is created by Cyril's inability to form any coherent reaction to his father's death, in the strange, half-comic scene with the deaf old woman in the room with the body, and the doctor tacitly playing along with Cyril's mother's pretence that she was not the dead man's wife; a scene in which certain possibilities of emotional settlement for the son seem to have been deliberately taken away. *The White Peacock*, ed. Andrew Robertson, Cambridge: Cambridge University Press, 1983, 35–43.

13 Walter Morel's 'wife was casting him off, half regretfully, but relentlessly; casting him off and turning now for love and life to the children. . . . And he half acquiesced, as so many men do, yielding their place to their children'. *Sons and Lovers*, eds Helen Baron and Carl Baron, Cambridge: Cambridge University Press, 1992, 62.
14 In order to tell Louie Burrows of this dream, Lawrence broke into French halfway through his letter to her of 26 May 1911 (presumably so that no one else in her household would understand it if they found it lying around): 'C'étais moi qui devait disparaître de la scène et il y avait une ombre noire à ma place' (*sic*). *The Letters of D. H. Lawrence*, vol. I, ed. James T. Boulton, Cambridge: Cambridge University Press, 1979, 272.
15 'For true it is that the one bright male germ which went to your begetting was drawn from the blood of the father. . . . And furthermore true is it that this unquenched father-spark within you sends forth vibrations and dark currents of vital activity all the time; connecting direct with your father. You will never be able to get away from it while you live'. *Fantasia of the Unconscious*, London: Heinemann, 1961, 23–4.
16 'Introduction to *Memoirs of the Foreign Legion*', in *Phoenix II*, eds Warren Roberts and Harry T. Moore, London: Heinemann, 1968, 317. Mauro was the real name of the monk referred to as Don Bernardo in Lawrence's text.
17 *Phoenix II*, 354. Some of Lawrence's biographers take the view that the phrase 'half my money' was rather self-exoneratingly economical with the truth. Brenda Maddox claims that Lawrence's sense of guilt led him to falsify the real state both of his resources at the time and of Magnus's debts. Mark Kinkead-Weekes is more circumspect, but he does accept the possibility that Lawrence did conceal certain facts about his financial position when writing his introduction to Magnus's book. See Brenda Maddox, *The Married Man: A Life of D. H. Lawrence*, London: Sinclair-Stevenson, 1994, 299; Mark Kinkead-Weekes, *D. H. Lawrence: Triumph to Exile*, Cambridge: Cambridge University Press, 1996, 583.
18 *Phoenix II*, 358.
19 Ibid., 359.
20 Ibid., 358.
21 Ibid., 325.
22 Ibid., 328.
23 David Ellis, *D. H. Lawrence: Dying Game*, Cambridge: Cambridge University Press, 1998, 345.
24 This feeling was of course already beginning to emerge in the stories written at Spotorno in 1925–26, even where their outcomes appeared more optimistic than this. Linda Ruth Williams, in '"Glad Ghosts" and Uncanny Bodies', cited above, mentions W. S. Marks' comment that 'The Rocking-Horse Winner' was 'intended to make us feel . . . a greater respect for the traditional view of a family unified under the vital authority of the father'. W. S. Marks, 'The Psychology of the Uncanny in Lawrence's "The Rocking-Horse Winner"', *Modern Fiction Studies*, 11, Winter 1965–66, 391.

25  *Phoenix II*, 359.
26  'Mother and Daughter', in *The Princess and Other Stories*, ed. Keith Sagar, Harmondsworth: Penguin Books, 1971, 235, 239. Subsequent page references to the story are to this edition.
27  Janice Hubbard Harris, *The Short Fiction of D. H. Lawrence*, New Jersey: Rutgers University Press, 1984, 214.
28  Geoffrey Strickland argued that 'Mother and Daughter' was one of the stories in which 'we are . . . shown . . . the best conceivable choice that an individual can make for himself, given the *circumstances* of his life, in the far from ideally satisfactory conditions of the world as it is' – a comment that could cover both the options which seem to me equivocally poised at the end of the story. Geoffrey Strickland, 'The First "Lady Chatterley's Lover"', in *Encounter*, vol. xxxvi, no. 1, January 1971, 47–8.
29  *Sketches of Etruscan Places and other Italian Essays*, 16.
30  'If only one had some warm and comforting thought somewhere! – It's so awful to grow old! . . . if I'd had the arms of a man like that round me when I was young, perhaps I shouldn't feel so stiff and stark now I'm getting old.' *The First and Second Lady Chatterley Novels*, eds Dieter Mehl and Christa Jansohn, Cambridge: Cambridge University Press, 1999, 288.
31  'Sun', in *The Woman Who Rode Away and Other Stories*, 24.
32  'Sun', 24.
33  'The Blue Moccasins', in *The Princess and Other Stories*, 192. Subsequent references to the story are to this edition.
34  'Shagput', in the Penguin edition; 'Shagpat' in the manuscript.
35  Manuscript of early version of 'The Blue Moccasins': Roberts E50a, Austin: University of Texas, 2, 3. Lawrence presumably came to feel that he could not seriously give the name 'Barclay' to a character who worked in a bank. In the 1928 version of 'Sun', written a few months before 'The Blue Moccasins', Juliet believes that the peasant's dissatisfaction with his wife is caused not by her childlessness, as was implied in the 1925 story, but by the fact that she is older than he: 'that great difference that lies between a rather overbearing, superior woman over forty, and her more irresponsible husband of thirty-five or so. It seemed like the difference of a whole generation. "He is my generation," thought Juliet, "and she is Maurice's generation."' 'Sun', 36.
36  Achsah Brewster recalled the occasion, though not the details of the dispute, in her reminiscences of Lawrence, reproduced in *D. H. Lawrence: A Composite Biography*, ed. Edward Nehls, Madison: University of Wisconsin Press, 1959, 228.
37  *The Plays*, eds Hans-Wilhelm Schwarze and John Worthen, Cambridge: Cambridge University Press, 1999, 472.
38  'Mother and Daughter', 236; *Phoenix*, ed. Edward D. McDonald, London: Heinemann, 1936, 239.
39  This detail did not appear in *The First Lady Chatterley*.
40  *Sons and Lovers*, 106, 171.
41  'The Man Who Died', in *Love Among The Haystacks and Other Stories*, Harmondsworth: Penguin Books, 1979, 136–7. Simon Jarvis, in an essay

called 'Tombeau', drew attention to the symbolic relationship between Death and Father Christmas, as a motif in various writings by Claude Lévi-Strauss. Simon Jarvis, 'Tombeau', *Parataxis*, 8/9, 1996, 144–52.
42  *Sons and Lovers*, 46.
43  *Sketches of Etruscan Places and other Italian Essays*, 49.
44  *Sons and Lovers*, 37–8.
45  'Insouciance', in *Phoenix II*, 534, 532. In this extraordinary line Lawrence almost seems to be envying Death for being able to breathe more freely than he can. Only a few days earlier his party had been asked to leave a hotel at Saint-Nizier, near Grenoble, because he was coughing so much in the night. See Ellis, *Dying Game*, 422.
46  *Phoenix II*, 534.
47  *The Complete Poems of D. H. Lawrence*, vol. II, eds Vivian de Sola Pinto and Warren Roberts, London: Heinemann, 1964, 628.
48  Catherine Carswell recalled Lawrence performing Carpenter's piece with her husband during a visit to the Carswells' temporary home in Lydbrook, in the summer of 1918: 'a great success given as a duet by Lawrence and Donald, with Lawrence in the male part'. Catherine Carswell, *The Savage Pilgrimage: A Narrative of D. H. Lawrence*, London: Martin Secker, 1932, 107.

# Bibliography of Lawrence's Works

The following are all published in Cambridge by Cambridge University Press, unless otherwise stated.

*Aaron's Rod*, ed. Mara Kalnins, 1988.
'The Blue Moccasins', manuscript of early unfinished version: Roberts E50a, Austin: University of Texas.
*The Boy in the Bush*, ed. Paul Eggert, 1990.
*The Complete Poems of D. H. Lawrence*, 2 vols, eds Vivian de Sola Pinto and Warren Roberts, London: Heinemann, 1964.
*England, My England*, ed. Bruce Steele, 1990.
*Fantasia of the Unconscious and Psychoanalysis of the Unconscious*, London: Heinemann, 1961.
*The First and Second Lady Chatterley Novels*, eds Dieter Mehl and Christa Jansohn, 1999.
*The Fox, The Captain's Doll, The Ladybird*, ed. Dieter Mehl, 1992.
*Kangaroo*, ed. Bruce Steele, 1994.
*Lady Chatterley's Lover and A Propos of Lady Chatterley's Lover*, ed. Michael Squires, 1993.
*Lady Chatterley's Lover and A Propos of Lady Chatterley's Lover*, ed. Michael Squires, London: Penguin Books, 1994.
*The Letters of D. H. Lawrence*, vol. I, ed. James T. Boulton, 1979.
*Letters*, vol. II, eds George J. Zytaruk and James T. Boulton, 1981.
*Letters*, vol. III, eds James T. Boulton and Andrew Robertson, 1984.
*Letters*, vol. IV, eds Warren Roberts, James T. Boulton and Elizabeth Mansfield, 1987.
*Letters*, vol. V, eds James T. Boulton and Lindeth Vasey, 1989.
*Letters*, vol. VI, eds James T. Boulton and Margaret H. Boulton, with Gerald M. Lacy, 1991.
*Letters*, vol. VII, eds Keith Sagar and James T. Boulton, 1993.
*Love Among the Haystacks and Other Stories*, ed. John Worthen, 1987.
*Love Among the Haystacks and Other Stories*, Harmondsworth: Penguin Books, 1979.
*The Lost Girl*, ed. John Worthen, 1981.
*Mornings in Mexico* and *Etruscan Places*, Harmondsworth: Penguin Books, 1960.
*Mr Noon*, ed. Lindeth Vasey, 1984.
*Phoenix: The Posthumous Papers of D. H. Lawrence*, ed. Edward D. McDonald, London: Heinemann, 1936.
*Phoenix II: Uncollected, Unpublished, and Other Prose Works by D. H. Lawrence*, eds Warren Roberts and Harry T. Moore, London: Heinemann, 1968.
*The Plays*, eds Hans-Wilhelm Schwarze and John Worthen, 1999.

*The Plumed Serpent*, ed. L. D. Clark, 1987.
*The Princess and Other Stories*, ed. Keith Sagar, Harmondsworth: Penguin Books, 1971.
*The Prussian Officer and Other Stories*, ed. John Worthen, 1983.
*Quetzalcoatl*, ed. Louis L. Martz, Redding Ridge, CT: Black Swan Books, 1995.
*The Rainbow*, ed. Mark Kinkead-Weekes, 1989.
*Reflections on the Death of a Porcupine and Other Essays*, ed. Michael Herbert, 1988.
*Sea and Sardinia*, ed. Mara Kalnins, 1997.
*The Short Novels of D. H. Lawrence*, London: Heinemann, 1956.
*Sketches of Etruscan Places and other Italian Essays*, ed. Simonetta de Filippis, 1992.
*Sons and Lovers*, eds Helen Baron and Carl Baron, 1992.
*St Mawr and Other Stories*, ed. Brian Finney, 1983.
*Studies in Classic American Literature*, Harmondsworth: Penguin Books, 1977.
*Study of Thomas Hardy and Other Essays*, ed. Bruce Steele, 1985.
*The Trespasser*, ed. Elizabeth Mansfield, 1981.
*Twilight in Italy and Other Essays*, ed. Paul Eggert, 1994.
*The White Peacock*, ed. Andrew Robertson, 1983.
*The Woman Who Rode Away and Other Stories*, eds Dieter Mehl and Christa Jansohn, 1995.
*The Woman Who Rode Away and Other Stories*, eds Dieter Mehl and Christa Jansohn, with additional editing by N. H. Reeve, London: Penguin Books, 1996.
*Women in Love*, eds David Farmer, Lindeth Vasey and John Worthen, 1987.

# Bibliography

Nicolas Abraham and Maria Torok, *Cryptonymie: le verbier de l'Homme aux loups, précédé de Fors, par Jacques Derrida*, Paris: Aubier Flammarion, 1976.
David Ayers, *English Literature in the 1920s*, Edinburgh: Edinburgh University Press, 1999.
Gaston Bachelard, *The Psychoanalysis of Fire*, trans. Alan C. Ross, London: Quartet Books, 1987.
Peter Balbert and Phillip L. Marcus, eds, *D. H. Lawrence: A Centenary Consideration*, Ithaca and London: Cornell University Press, 1985.
Fiona Becket, 'Being There: Nostalgia and the Masculine Maternal in D. H. Lawrence', *The D. H. Lawrence Review*, vol. 27, nos 2–3, 1997–98.
Fiona Becket, *D. H. Lawrence: The Thinker as Poet*, London and New York: Macmillan, 1997.
Lydia Blanchard, 'Women Look at Lady Chatterley', *The D. H. Lawrence Review*, vol. 11, no. 3, 1978.
Diane S. Bonds, *Language and the Self in D. H. Lawrence*, Ann Arbor: UMI Research Press, 1987.
Wayne C. Booth, 'Confessions of a Lukewarm Lawrentian', in *The Challenge of D. H. Lawrence*, eds Michael Squires and Keith Cushman, Madison: University of Wisconsin Press, 1990.
Pierre Bourdieu, *Photography: A Middle-Brow Art*, trans. Shaun Whiteside, Cambridge: Polity Press, 1990.
Derek Britton, *Lady Chatterley: The Making of the Novel*, London: Unwin Hyman, 1988.
Keith Brown, ed., *Rethinking Lawrence*, Milton Keynes: Open University Press, 1990.
Victor Burgin, James Donald, and Cora Kaplan, eds, *Formations of Fantasy*, London: Methuen, 1986.
Witter Bynner, *Journey with Genius*, London: Peter Nevill, 1953.
*Lord Byron: Poetical Works*, ed. Frederick Page, corrected edition by John D. Jump, Oxford: Oxford University Press, 1970.
David Cannadine, 'War and Death, Grief and Mourning in Modern Britain', in *Mirrors of Mortality*, ed. J. Whaley, London: Europa Publications, 1981.
Catherine Carswell, *The Savage Pilgrimage: A Narrative of D.H. Lawrence*, London: Martin Secker, 1932.
Stanley Cavell, *Disowning Knowledge in Six Plays of Shakespeare*, Cambridge: Cambridge University Press, 1987.
T. J. Clark, *Farewell to an Idea: Episodes from a History of Modernism*, New Haven and London: Yale University Press, 1999.
James C. Cowan, *D. H. Lawrence and the Trembling Balance*, Pennsylvania and London: Pennsylvania State University Press, 1990.
Jacques Derrida, 'Fors', *The Georgia Review*, vol. 31 no. 1, 1977.

*The Dictionary of National Biography*, London, 1894.
Geoff Dyer, *Out Of Sheer Rage*, London: Little, Brown, 1997.
Paul Eggert and John Worthen, eds, *Lawrence and Comedy*, Cambridge: Cambridge University Press, 1996.
David Ellis, *D. H. Lawrence: Dying Game*, Cambridge: Cambridge University Press, 1998.
Rita Felski, *The Gender of Modernity*, Cambridge and London: Harvard University Press, 1995.
Anne Fernihough, *D. H. Lawrence: Aesthetics and Ideology*, Oxford: Oxford University Press, 1993.
Brian Finney, 'A Newly-Discovered Text of D. H. Lawrence's "The Lovely Lady"', *Yale University Library Gazette*, xlix, 1975.
Elizabeth Fox, '*Lady Chatterley's Lover*: A Departure from Pastoral into Delusion', *Études Lawrenciennes*, no. 16, 1997.
Stephen Frosh, 'On Narcissism', *Free Associations*, 18, 1989.
David Gervais, *Literary Englands*, Cambridge: Cambridge University Press, 1993.
Sandra M. Gilbert, *Acts of Attention: The Poems of D. H. Lawrence*, Ithaca and London: Cornell University Press, 1972.
Thomas Hardy, *Jude the Obscure*, ed. Norman Page, New York and London: W.W. Norton, 1978.
Janice Hubbard Harris, *The Short Fiction of D.H. Lawrence*, New Jersey: Rutgers University Press, 1984.
David Leon Higden, 'Bertha Coutts and Bertha Mason: A Speculative Note', *The D. H. Lawrence Review*, vol. 11, no. 3, 1978.
Eric Homberger, 'The Story of the Cenotaph', *The Times Literary Supplement*, 12 November, 1976, 1429–30.
G. M. Hyde, *D. H. Lawrence*, London: Macmillan, 1990.
G. M. Hyde, 'Suave Loins, Venison Pasties, and Other Tasty Nonsense: The Unacceptable Face of Lawrence', *Kyoto Women's University Essays and Studies*, 47, 2001.
Simon Jarvis, 'Tombeau', *Parataxis*, 8/9, 1996.
Nicholas Joost and Alvin Sullivan, *D. H. Lawrence and The Dial*, Carbondale and Edwardsville: Southern Illinois University Press, 1970.
Mara Kalnins, ed., *D. H. Lawrence: Centenary Essays*, Bristol: Bristol Classical Press, 1986.
Mark Kinkead-Weekes, *D. H. Lawrence: Triumph to Exile*, Cambridge: Cambridge University Press, 1996.
Julia Kristeva, *Black Sun: Depression and Melancholia*, trans. Leon Roudiez, New York and Oxford: Columbia University Press, 1989.
M. M. Lally, '*The Virgin and the Gipsy*: Rewriting the Pain', in *Aging and Gender in Literature*, eds A. Wyatt-Brown and J. Rossen, Charlottesville and London: University of Virginia Press, 1993.
Philip Larkin, *The Whitsun Weddings*, London: Faber and Faber, 1964.
Frieda Lawrence, *Not I, But the Wind . . .* , Santa Fé: Rydal Press, 1934.
David Lodge, 'Lawrence, Dostoevsky, Bakhtin: Lawrence and Dialogic Fiction', in Keith Brown, ed., *Rethinking Lawrence*, Milton Keynes: Open University Press, 1990.

Sheila MacLeod, *Lawrence's Men and Women*, London: Heinemann, 1985.
Brenda Maddox, *The Married Man: A Life of D. H. Lawrence*, London: Sinclair Stevenson, 1994.
W. S. Marks, 'The Psychology of the Uncanny in Lawrence's "The Rocking-Horse Winner"', *Modern Fiction Studies*, 11, Winter 1965–66.
Peter Middleton, *The Inward Gaze*, London: Routledge, 1992.
James Justinian Morier, *The Adventures of Hajji Baba of Ispahan*, London, 1824, reprinted, with an introduction by Richard Jennings, London: The Cresset Press, 1949.
Julian Moynahan, *The Deed of Life*, New Jersey: Princeton University Press, 1963.
Andrew P. Morrison, ed., *Essential Papers on Narcissism*, New York and London: New York University Press, 1986.
Edward Nehls, ed., *D. H. Lawrence: A Composite Biography*, 3 vols, Madison: University of Wisconsin Press, 1959.
Oliver Onions, *Whom God Hath Sundered*, London: Martin Secker, 1925.
Octavio Paz, *The Labyrinth of Solitude*, trans. Lysander Kemp, Yara Milos, and Rachel Phillips Belash, London: Penguin Books, 1990.
Adam Phillips, *Promises, Promises*, London: Faber and Faber, 2000.
Tony Pinkney, *D. H. Lawrence*, Brighton: Harvester Press, 1990.
Marcel Proust, *À la recherche du temps perdu*, ed. Jean-Yves Tadié, Paris: Editions Gallimard, 1987.
Joan Rivière, 'Womanliness as a Masquerade', *The International Journal of Psychoanalysis*, 10, 1929, reprinted in *Formations of Fantasy*, eds Victor Burgin, James Donald, and Cora Kaplan, London: Methuen, 1986.
Judith Ruderman, *D. H. Lawrence and the Devouring Mother*, Durham, NC: Duke University Press, 1984.
M. Elizabeth Sargent, 'The Wives, The Virgins, and Isis: Lawrence's Explorations of Female Will in Four Late Novellas of Spiritual Quest', *The D. H. Lawrence Review*, vol. 26, nos 1–3, 1995–96.
Carol Siegel, *Lawrence Among the Women*, Charlottesville and London: University Press of Virginia, 1991.
Carol Sklenicka, *D. H. Lawrence and the Child*, Columbia: University of Missouri Press, 1991.
Susan Sontag, *On Photography*, London: Allen Lane, 1977.
Michael Squires and Keith Cushman, eds, *The Challenge of D. H. Lawrence*, Madison: University of Wisconsin Press, 1990.
Michael Squires and Dennis Jackson, eds, *D. H. Lawrence's 'Lady'*, Athens: University of Georgia Press, 1985.
Geoffrey Strickland, 'The First *Lady Chatterley's Lover*', *Encounter*, vol. xxxvi, no. 1, January 1971.
Tony Tanner, review of David Ellis, *D. H. Lawrence: Dying Game*, in *The Times Literary Supplement*, 9 January 1998, 3–4.
Giovanni Verga, *Little Novels of Sicily*, trans. D. H. Lawrence, London: Martin Secker, 1925.
Rebecca West, *D. H. Lawrence*, London: Martin Secker, 1930.
Rebecca West, *The Fountain Overflows*, London: Virago Press, 1984.

Linda Ruth Williams, *Sex in the Head: Visions of Femininity and Film in D. H. Lawrence*, Hemel Hempstead: Harvester Wheatsheaf, 1993.

Linda Ruth Williams, '"We've been forgetting that we're flesh and blood, Mother": 'Glad Ghosts' and Uncanny Bodies', *The D. H. Lawrence Review*, vol. 27, nos 2–3, 1997–98.

Jay Winter, *Sites of Memory, Sites of Mourning: The Great War in European Cultural History*, Cambridge: Cambridge University Press, 1995.

Kathleen Woodward, *Aging and its Discontents*, Bloomington: Indiana University Press, 1991.

John Worthen, *D. H. Lawrence and the Idea of the Novel*, London: Macmillan, 1979.

John Worthen, *D. H. Lawrence: The Early Years*, Cambridge: Cambridge University Press, 1991.

John Worthen, *D. H. Lawrence*, London: Edward Arnold, 1991.

A. Wyatt-Brown and J. Rossen, eds, *Aging and Gender in Literature*, Charlottesville and London: University Press of Virginia, 1993.

Slavoj Žižek, *The Plague of Fantasies*, London and New York: Verso, 1997.

# General Index

Abraham, Nicholas  37
Andromeda  67
Asquith, Lady Cynthia  viii, 18, 159, 164; *The Ghost Book*  21, 46, 122–3; *The Black Cap*  122–3
Asquith, Herbert  29
Asquith, Raymond  29, 156
Ayers, David  66

Bachelard, Gaston, *The Psychoanalysis of Fire*  93, 161
Baden-Baden  21
Bakhtin, Mikhail  ix
Bandelier, Adolph  164
Bandelier, Fanny  164
Becket, Fiona  35, 42
Bell, Angelica  154
Bell, Clive  154
Bell, Vanessa  154
Black Sun Press  70
Blanchard, Lydia  161
Boccaccio, Giovanni  80
Booth, Wayne C.  152
Bourdieu, Pierre  162
Bowen, Stella  155
Brett, Dorothy  15
Brewster, Achsah  147, 166
Brewster, Earl  147, 163
Britton, Derek  161
Brontë, Charlotte, *Jane Eyre*  93
Brontë, Emily, *Wuthering Heights*  162
Brown, Curtis  69, 164
Brown, Keith  152
Burrows, Louie  130, 165
Bynner, Witter  99
Byron, George Gordon, Lord  4

Cannadine, David  156
Carnivalesque  ix, 23, 46
Carpenter, Joseph Edwards  149

Carswell, Catherine  21, 167
Cavell, Stanley  46, 158
Cenotaph, The  27–8, 31, 39
Chatsworth  53
Clark, T. J.  97
Conrad, Joseph  17
Cooper, James Fenimore  108
Cowan, James C.  152–3
Crichton, Kyle  154
Crosby, Harry  69–70
Cushman, Keith  152

Danaë  67
Derrida, Jacques  157
Dickens, Charles, x; *Dombey and Son*  149
Dyer, Geoff  151

Eggert, Paul  vii, ix–x, 2, 151
Eliot, George, *The Mill on the Floss*  41
Eliot, T. S., *The Waste Land*  23, 144–5
Ellis, David  21, 63, 134, 152
*Eve: The Lady's Pictorial*  141

Felski, Rita  32
Florence  8, 12, 145
Ford, Ford Madox  155
Fox, Elizabeth  114
Freud, Sigmund  27
Frosh, Stephen  160

Gallipoli  145
Gertler, Mark  19
Goethe, Johann Wolfgang  123
Grant, Duncan  154

Haggard, H. Rider  125
Hardy, Thomas, *Jude the Obscure*  39, 94, 162

Harris, Frank  163
Harris, Janice Hubbard  137
Hemingway, Ernest, *Fiesta*  23
Higden, David Leon  93, 162
Homberger, Eric  156
Hood, Thomas  25
Huitzilopochtli  25, 48
Huxley, Aldous  8
Hyde, G. M.  152

Ibsen, Henrik, *Ghosts*  125
Icazbalceta, Joaquin  164
Italy  xi

James, Henry  20, 48, 126
Jansohn, Christa  xii
Jarvis, Simon  166–7
Johnson, Dr Samuel  25, 30, 47
Joost, Nicholas  38, 157

Keats, John  134
Kernberg, Otto  76
Kinkead-Weekes, Mark  10, 154, 165
Knopf, Blanche  77
Kohut, Heinz  75
Kristeva, Julia  44; *Black Sun*, 75

Lacan, Jacques  51, 159
Lally, M. M.  59
Land Settlement Association, The  153
Larkin, Philip  94
Lawrence, Ada  20–1, 52–3, 150
Lawrence, Arthur  22, 31–2, 42–4, 47, 130, 135, 150
Lawrence, Emily  21, 150
Lawrence, Frieda  5, 10, 39, 52–3, 56, 59, 63, 77–9, 105, 163
Lawrence, Lydia  22, 31–2, 42–3, 47–8, 134, 150
Lévi-Strauss, Claude  167
Lodge, David  152
Luhan, Mabel Dodge  154

Maddox, Brenda  165
Magnus, Maurice  130–3, 135, 165

Mackenzie, Compton  123
MacLeod, Sheila  66, 160
Mahler, Margaret  50
Mansfield, Katherine  25, 163
Marks, W. S.  165
McDonald, Edward  153
Mehl, Dieter  xii
Morier, James Justinian  19, 155
Moynahan, Julian  61, 64
Murry, John Middleton  25–6, 78–9, 154

Narcissism  75–6
Nehls, Edward  153–4
*New Coterie*  69–70
New Mexico  x, 20

Onions, Oliver  158
Orpheus  37, 44

Pascal, Blaise  25
Paz, Octavio  36, 46
Pearn, Nancy  69, 164
Perseus  17, 67
Phillips, Adam  22
Pinkney, Tony  90
Poe, Edgar Allan, 'Ligeia'  83, 111
Pound, Ezra  131
Proust, Marcel  x, 99, 162
Pushkin, Alexander  4

Rivière, Joan  126
*Rosenkavalier, Der*  147
Ruderman, Judith  50, 64
Ruskin, John  138

Sagar, Keith  xii, 46
Sahagún, Fray Bernardo de  158
Sargent, M. Elizabeth  63
Seaman, Teddy  5
Secker, Martin  ix, 21, 70, 160
Secker, Rina  156
Seltzer, Thomas  164
Shakespeare, William, *The Winter's Tale*  46
Siegel, Carol  63, 162–3
Skinner, Jack  20, 22

Skinner, Mollie   20, 22
Slade School of Art   19
Sontag, Susan   99
Spooning   5–6, 10–11
Spotorno   ix, 21, 28, 39, 52, 77, 82, 165
Squires, Michael   xii, 98, 152
Steele, Bruce   153
Strickland, Geoffrey   166
Sullivan, Alvin   38, 157

Tanner, Tony   152
Tchaikovsky, Peter Ilyich   4
*Times, The*   28, 30
Torok, Maria   37

Valentino, Rudolf   13–14, 141
Vasey, Lindeth   153
Verga, Giovanni   79
Virgil   37

Weekley, Barbara   39, 52–3, 56, 60, 105, 153
Weekley, Elsa   5, 39, 52, 105, 153
Weekley, Ernest   52, 58–9, 159
West, Rebecca, *The Fountain Overflows*   154
Williams, Linda Ruth   9, 26, 42, 71, 157–8, 160, 164–5
Winter, Jay   156
Woodward, Kathleen   27
Wordsworth, William   41
Worthen, John   63, 151–2, 156, 161

Yeats, William Butler, 'Leda and the Swan'   23

Žižek, Slavoj   159

# Index of Lawrence's Works

*Aaron's Rod* 129, 148, 162
'Accumulated Mail' 17
'Art and Morality' 163
'Art-Nonsense and Other Essays', review of 163

'Blue Moccasins, The' vii–viii, xii, 121, 140–9
'Border Line, The' ix, 23
*Boy in the Bush, The* 154

'Captain's Doll, The' 9
'Crucifix Across the Mountains, The' 90

*David* 23, 147, 163
'Dream of Life, A' 46–8

'Elderly Discontented Women' 164
'England, My England' viii, 151
'Enslaved by Civilisation' 22
'Escaped Cock, The' xii, 148
*Etruscan Places* 3, 82, 125, 139, 149, 164
'Europe vs. America' 76

*Fantasia of the Unconscious* 161, 165
'Film Passion' 155
*The First Lady Chatterley* (1944) xii
*The First and Second Lady Chatterley Novels* xii, 2–3, 8–9, 12–13, 16, 19, 29, 31, 41, 83–118, 129, 139, 145, 154, 166
'Flowery Tuscany' x
'Flying-Fish, The' 23, 33, 60
'Fox, The' viii–ix, 148, 151

'Georgian Poetry', review of 157
'Glad Ghosts' vii–viii, x, xii, 15–49, 52, 63–4, 94, 106, 119–22, 129, 133, 135, 138, 144, 153
'Grudge of the Old, The' 164

'Hawthorne's *Blithedale Romance*' 34

'In Love' viii, xii, 1–14, 55, 103
'Insouciance' 149, 167
'Introduction to *Mastro-don Gesualdo*' 159
'Introduction to *Max Havelaar*' 147–8
'Introduction to *Memoirs of the Foreign Legion*' 130–3, 135, 162, 165
'Introduction to *The Memoirs of the Duc de Lauzun* ('The Good Man')' 7

*John Thomas and Lady Jane* xii

*Kangaroo* 6, 15

'Ladybird, The' viii, 18, 123
*Lady Chatterley's Lover* vii, 4, 12, 23, 29, 41, 66, 71, 78, 86–7, 90, 97, 99, 113–18, 148, 153, 163
*Lost Girl, The* 123
*Love Among the Haystacks and Other Stories* xii, 154
'Lovely Lady, The' vii, xii, 29, 76, 122–36, 138, 140–1, 145

'Making Love to Music' 46
'Medlars and Sorb-Apples' 37, 45

'Morality and the Novel'   90
'More Modern Love'   1–14
'Mother and Daughter'   xii,
   122, 136–41, 147
*Mr. Noon*   6, 153

'Nathaniel Hawthorne and
   *The Scarlet Letter*'   130
'New Mexico'   9
'Nottingham and the Mining
   Countryside'   22
'Novel and the Feelings, The'
   7, 153

'On Being a Man'   156
'On Coming Home'   157

'Paul Morel'   109
'Pictures on the Walls'   98
*Plumed Serpent, The*   21, 39, 71
*Princess and Other Stories, The*   xii

*Quetzalcoatl*   19

*Rainbow, The*   5
'Return to Bestwood'   9, 22
'Rocking-Horse Winner, The'   xii,
   46, 74, 165

*Sea and Sardinia*   6
'Sex versus Loveliness'   13, 155

'Smile'   xii, 15, 25–7
*Sons and Lovers*   31, 109, 128,
   130, 144, 148, 165
'Spirits Summoned West'   23,
   42, 48
*St. Mawr*   12, 66
'Sun'   vii–viii, xii, 15, 49–52,
   60, 65–82, 123, 140, 142,
   166

'Thimble, The'   viii
'Tickets Please'   11
*Trespasser, The*   88
*Twilight in Italy*   65

*Virgin and the Gipsy, The*   xii, 7,
   12, 15, 29, 33, 41, 52–65, 69,
   109, 122, 126, 142–3

'What are the Wild Waves Saying'
   149–50
*White Peacock, The*   20, 130, 164
'Wintry Peacock'   20
*Woman Who Rode Away and
   Other Stories, The* (Mehl and
   Jansohn)   xii
*Woman Who Rode Away and
   Other Stories, The* (Secker)
   ix, 70
*Women In Love*   9, 80, 97
'Work of Creation, The'   viii